The Antelope Wife

Also by Louise Erdrich

NOVELS

Love Medicine
The Beet Queen
Tracks
The Crown of Columbus (with Michael Dorris)
The Bingo Palace
Tales of Burning Love
The Last Report on the Miracles at Little No Horse
Four Souls
The Master Butchers Singing Club
The Painted Drum
The Plague of Doves
Shadow Tag
The Round House

SHORT STORIES

The Red Convertible

POETRY

Jacklight
Baptism of Desire
Original Fire

FOR CHILDREN

Grandmother's Pigeon
The Range Eternal
The Birchbark House
The Game of Silence
The Porcupine Year
Chickadee

NONFICTION

The Blue Jay's Dance
Books and Islands in Ojibwe Country

The Antelope Wife

A Novel

New and Revised Edition

Louise Erdrich

HARPER PERENNIAL

NEW YORK • LONDON • TORONTO • SYDNEY • NEW DELHI • AUCKLAND

HARPER PERENNIAL

"The Ojibwe Week" was first published in *Granta* 115,
published in Summer 2011.

HarperCollins books may be purchased for educational, business, or sales promotional use. For information please write: Special Markets Department, HarperCollins Publishers, 10 East 53rd Street, New York, NY 10022.

FIRST EDITION

Designed by Katy Riegel

Library of Congress Cataloging-in-Publication Data is available upon request.

ISBN 978-0-06-176796-8

12 13 14 15 16 OV/RRD 10 9 8 7 6 5 4 3

To Aza

Contents

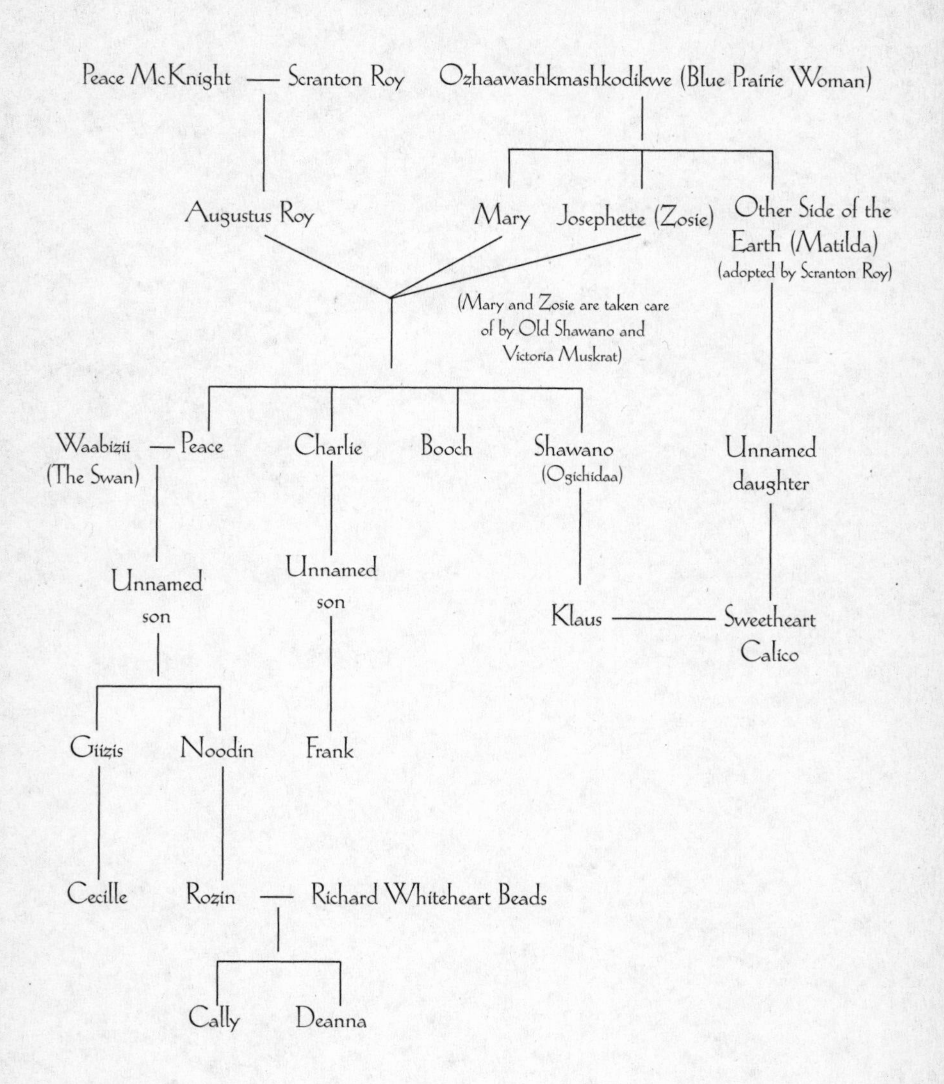

Peace McKnight — Scranton Roy
Ozhaawashkmashkodikwe (Blue Prairie Woman)
Augustus Roy
Mary
Josephette (Zosie)
Other Side of the Earth (Matilda)
(adopted by Scranton Roy)
(Mary and Zosie are taken care of by Old Shawano and Victoria Muskrat)
Waabizii (The Swan) — Peace
Charlie
Booch
Shawano (Ogichidaa)
Unnamed daughter
Unnamed son
Unnamed son
Klaus — Sweetheart Calico
Giizis
Noodin
Frank
Cecille
Rozin — Richard Whiteheart Beads
Cally
Deanna

Part One

Bezhig

The niizhoodenhyag are very old when they decide to sew this world into being. One twin uses light and the other dark. The first twin's beads are cut-glass whites and pales, and the other twin's beads are glittering deep red and blue-black indigo. One twin uses an awl made of an otter's sharpened penis bone, the other uses that of a bear. They sew with a single sinew thread, in, out, fast and furious, each woman trying to set one more bead into the pattern than her sister, each trying to upset the balance of the world.

1

Father's Milk

Scranton Roy

Deep in the past during a spectacular cruel raid upon an isolated Ojibwe village mistaken for hostile during the scare over the starving Dakota, a dog bearing upon its back a frame-board dikinaagan enclosing a child in moss, velvet, embroideries of beads, was frightened into the vast carcass of the world west of the Otter Tail River. A cavalry soldier, spurred to human response by the sight of the dog, the strapped-on child, vanishing into the distance, followed and did not return.

What happened to him lives on, though fading in the larger memory, and I relate it here in order that it not be lost.

Private Scranton Teodorus Roy was the youngest son of a Quaker father and a reclusive poet mother who established a small Pennsylvania community based on intelligent conversation. One day into his view a member of a traveling drama troupe appeared. Unmasked, the woman's stage glance broke across Roy like fire. She was tall, fatefully slender, pale, and paler haired, resolute in her character, and simple in her amused scorn of Roy—so young, bright faced, obedient. To prove himself, he made a rendezvous promise and then took his way west following her glare. An icicle, it drove into his heart and melted there, leaving a trail of cold water and blood. The way was long. She glided like a snake beneath his footsteps in fevered dreams. When he finally got to the place they had agreed upon, she was not there, of course. Angry and at odds, he went against the radiant ways of his father. He enlisted in the army and was sent to join the cavalry at Fort Snelling on the banks of the Mississippi in St. Paul, Minnesota.

There, he was trained to the rifle, learned to darn his socks using a wooden egg, ate many an ill-cooked bean, and polished his officers' harness leather until one day, in a state of uneasy resignation, he put on the dark blue uniform, fixed his bayonet, set off marching due west.

The village his company encountered was peaceful, then not.

In chaos of groaning horses, dogs screaming, rifle and pistol reports, and the smoke of errant cooking fires, Scranton Roy was most disturbed not by the death yells of old men and the few warriors shocked naked from their robes, but by the feral quiet of the children. And the sudden contempt he felt for them all. Unexpected, the frigid hate. The pleasure in raising, aiming. They ran fleet as their mothers, heading for a brush-thick gully and a slough of grass beyond. Two fell. Roy whirled, not knowing whom to shoot next. Eager, he bayoneted an old woman who set upon him with no other weapon but a stone picked from the ground.

She was built like the broken sacks of hay he'd used for practice, but her body closed fast around the instrument. He braced himself against her to pull free, set his boot between her legs to tug the blade from her stomach, and as he did so tried to avoid her eyes but did not manage. His glare was drawn into hers and he sank with it into the dark unaccompanied moment before his birth. She broke his gaze. In a groan of heat and blood she cried a word that would reverberate in his mind until the last moment of his life. He yanked the bayonet out with a huge cry, and began to run.

That was when he saw the dog, a loping dirt-brown cur, circle the camp twice with the child on its back and set off into open space. As much to escape the evil confusion of this village and his own dark act as out of any sympathy for the baby, though he glimpsed its face—mystified and calm—Scranton Roy started running after the two. Within moments, the ruckus of death was behind him. The farther away the village got, the farther behind he wanted it. He kept on, running, walking, managing to keep the dog in view only because it was spring and the new grass, after a burn of lightning, was just beginning its thrust, which would take it to well over a full-grown man's height.

From time to time, as the day went on, the dog paused to rest, stretched patient beneath its burden. Grinning and panting, it allowed Roy to approach, just so far. A necklace of blue beads hung from the brow guard of the cradle board.

It swayed, clattered lightly. The child's hands were bound in the wrappings. She could not reach for the beads but stared at them, mesmerized. The sun grew razor-hot. Tiny blackflies settled at the corners of her eyes. Sipped moisture from along her lids until, toward late afternoon, the heat died. A cold wind boomed against Scranton Roy in a steady rush. Still, into the emptiness, the three infinitesimally pushed.

The world darkened. Afraid of losing the trail, Roy gave his utmost. As night fixed upon them, man and dog were close enough to hear each other breathing and so, in that rhythm, both slept. Next morning, the dog stayed near, grinning for scraps. Afraid to frighten it with a rifle shot, Roy hadn't brought down game although he'd seen plenty. He managed to snare a rabbit. Then, with his tinderbox and steel, he started a fire and began to roast it, at which smell the dog dragged itself belly-down through the dirt, edging close. The baby made its first sound, a murmuring whimper. Accepting tidbits and bones, the dog was alert, suspicious. Roy could not touch it until he thought to wash himself all over and approach naked to diminish his whiteman's scent.

So he was able at last to remove the child from its wrappings and bathe it, a girl, and to hold her. He'd never done such a thing before. First he tried to feed her a tiny piece of the rabbit. She was too young to manage. He dripped water into her mouth, made sure it trickled down, but was perplexed at what to feed her, then alarmed when, after a night of deprivation, her tiny face crumpled in need. She peered at him in expectation and, at last, violently squalled. Her cries filled a vastness that nothing else could. They resounded, took over everything, and brought his heart clean to the surface. Scranton Roy cradled the baby, sang lewd camp tunes, then stalwart hymns, and at last remembered his own mother's lullabies. Nothing helped. It seemed, when he held her close upon his heart as women did, that the child grew angry with longing and desperately clung, rooted with her mouth, roared in frustration, until at last, moved to near insanity, Roy opened his shirt and put her to his nipple.

She seized him. Inhaled him. Her suck was fierce. His whole body was astonished, most of all the inoffensive nipple he'd never appreciated until, in spite of the pain, it served to gain him peace. As he sat there, the child holding part of him in her mouth, he looked around just in case there should be any witness to this act which seemed to him strange as anything that had happened in this sky-filled land. Of course, there was only the dog. Contented, freed, it lolled appreciatively near. So the evening passed and then the night. Scranton Roy was obliged to change nipples, the first one hurt so, and he fell asleep with the baby tucked beside him on his useless teat.

She was still there in the morning, stuck, though he pulled her off to slingshot a partridge, roasted that too, and smeared its grease on his two sore spots. That made her wild for him. He couldn't remove her then and commenced to walk, holding her, attached, toward a stand of cottonwood that wavered in the distance. A river. A place to camp. He'd settle there for a day or two, he thought, and try to teach the baby to eat something, for he feared she'd starve to death—although she seemed, except for the times he removed her from his chest, surprisingly contented.

He slung the blue beads around the baby's neck. Tied

the cradle board onto his own back. Then the man, the child, and the dog struck farther into the wilderness. They reached hills of sand, oak covered, shelter. Nearby, sod he cut painstakingly with the length of his bayonet and piled into a square, lightless but secure, and warm. Hoarding his shots, he managed to bring down a buffalo bull fat-loaded with the new grass. He fleshed the hide, dried the meat, seared the brains, stored the pounded fat and berries in the gut, made use of every bone and scrap of flesh even to the horns, carved into spoons, and the eyeballs, tossed to the dog. The tongue, cooked tender and mashed in his own mouth, he coaxed the baby to accept. She still much preferred him. As he was now past civilized judgment, her loyalty filled him with a foolish, tender joy.

He bathed each morning at the river. Once, he killed a beaver and greased himself all over against mosquitoes with its fat. The baby continued to nurse and he made a sling for her from his shirt. He lounged in the doorway of his sod hut, dreaming and exhausted, fearing that a fever was coming upon him. The situation was confusing. He did not know what course to take, how to start back, wondered if there'd be a party sent to search for him and then realized if they did find him he'd be court-martialed, if not hanged for desertion. The baby kept nursing and refused to stop. His nipples toughened. Pity scorched him, she sucked so blindly, so forcefully, and with such immense faith. It occurred to him one slow dusk as he looked down at her, upon his breast, that she was teaching him something.

This notion seemed absurd when he first considered it, and then, as insights do when we have the solitude to absorb them, he eventually grew used to the idea and paid attention to the lesson. The word *faith* hooked him. She had it in such pure supply. She nursed with utter simplicity and trust, as though the act itself would produce her wish. Half asleep one early morning, her beside him, he felt a slight warmth, then a rush in one side of his chest, a pleasurable burning. He thought it was an odd dream and fell asleep again only to wake to a huge burp from the baby, whose lips curled back from her dark gums in bliss, whose tiny fists were unclenched in sleep for the first time, who looked, impossibly, well fed.

Ask and ye shall receive. Ask and ye shall receive. The words ran through him like a clear stream. He put his hand to his chest and then tasted a thin blue drop of his own watery, appalling, God-given milk.

Miss Peace McKnight

Family duty was deeply planted in Miss Peace McKnight, also the knowledge that if she did not nobody else would—do the duty, that is, of seeing to the future of the McKnights. Her father's Aberdeen button-cart business failed after he ran out of dead sheep—his own, whose bones he cleverly thought to use after a spring disaster. He sawed buttons with an instrument devised of soldered steel, ground them to a luster with a polisher of fine sand glued to cloth, made holes with a bore and punch that he had self-invented. It was the absence, then, of sheep carcasses in Scotland that forced his daughter to do battle with the spirit of ignorance.

Peace McKnight. She was sturdily made as a captain's chair, yet drew water with graceful wrists and ran dancing across the rutted road on curved white ankles. Hale, Scots, full-breasted as a pouter pigeon, and dusted all over like an egg with freckles, wavy light brown hair secured with her father's gift—three pins of carved bone—she came to the Great Plains with enough education to apply for and win a teaching certificate.

Her class was piddling at first, all near grown, too. Three consumptive Swedish sisters not long for life, one boy abrupt and full of anger. A German. Even though she spoke plainly and as slow as humanly possible, her students fixed her with stares of tongueless suspicion and were incapable of following a single direction. She had to start from the beginning, teach the alphabet, the numbers, and had just reached the letter *v*, the word *cat*, subtraction, which they were naturally better at than addition, when she noticed someone standing at the back of her classroom. Quietly alert, observant, she had been there for some time. The girl stepped forward from the darkness.

She had roan coppery skin and wore a necklace of bright indigo beads. She was slender, with a pliable long waist, a graceful neck, and she was about six years old.

Miss McKnight blushed pink-gold with interest. She was charmed, first by the confidence of the child's smile and next by her immediate assumption of a place to sit, study, organize herself, and at last by her listening intelligence. The girl, though silent, had a hungry, curious quality. Miss McKnight had a teaching gift to match it. Although they were fourteen years apart, they became, inevitably, friends.

Then sisters. Until fall, Miss McKnight slept in the school cloakroom and bathed in the river nearby. Once the river iced over at the edges, an argument developed among the few and far-between homesteads as to which had enough room and who could afford her. No one. Matilda Roy stepped in and pestered her father, known as a strange and reclusive fellow, until he gave in and agreed that the new teacher could share the small trunk bed he had made for his daughter, so long as she helped with the poultry.

Mainly, they raised guinea fowl from keets that Scranton Roy had bought from a Polish widow. The speckled purple-black vulturine birds were half wild, clever. Matilda's task was to spy on, hunt down, and follow the hens to their hidden nests. The girls, for Peace McKnight was half girl around Matilda, laughed at the birds' tricks and hid to catch them. Fat, speckled, furious with shrill guinea pride, they acted as house watchdogs and scolded in the oak trees. Then from the pole shed where they wintered. In lard from a neighbor's pig, Scranton Roy fried strips of late squash, dried sand-dune morels, inky caps, field and oyster mushrooms, crushed twice-boiled acorns, the guinea eggs. He baked sweet bannock, dribbled on it wild aster honey aged in the bole of an oak, dark and pungent as mead.

The small sod and plank house was whitewashed inside and the deep sills of small bold windows held geraniums and started seeds. At night, the kerosene lamplight in trembling rings and halos, Miss Peace McKnight felt the eyes of Scranton Roy carve her in space. His gaze was a heat running up and down her throat, pausing elsewhere with the effect of a soft blow.

Scranton Roy

He is peculiar the way his mother was peculiar—writing poetry on the margins of bits of newspaper, tatters of cloth. His mother burned her life work and died a few years after the black-bordered message from the President arrived. She was comforted by the ashes of her words yet still in mourning for her son, who never did make his survival known but named his daughter for her. Matilda. One poem survived. A fragment. It goes like this: *Come to me, thou dark inviolate.* Scranton Roy prays to an unparticular god, communes with the spirit headlong each morning in a rush of ardor that carries him through each difficult day. He is lithe, nearly brown as his daughter, bearded, driven. He owns more than one dozen books and subscribes to periodicals that he lends to Miss McKnight.

He wants to be delivered of the burden of his solitude. A wife would help.

Peace tosses her sandy hair, feels the eyes of Scranton Roy upon her, appreciates their fire, and smiles into the eyes of his daughter. Technically, Miss McKnight soon becomes a stepmother. Whatever the term, the two women behave as though they've always known this closeness. Holding hands, they walk to school, kick dust, and tickle each other's necks with long stems of grama grass. They cook for Scranton Roy but also roll their eyes from time to time at him and break into fits of suppressed and impolite laughter.

Matilda Roy

Emotions unreel in her like spools of cotton.

When he rocks her, Matilda remembers the taste of his milk—hot and bitter as dandelion juice. Once, he holds her foot in the cradle of his palm and with the adept point of his hunting knife painlessly delivers a splinter, long and pale and bloody. Teaches her to round her *c*'s and put tiny teakettle handles on her *a*'s. Crooks stray hairs behind her ears. Washes her face with the rough palm of his hand, but gently, scrubbing at her smooth chin.

He is a man, though he nourished her. Sometimes across the room, at night, in his sleep, her father gasps as though stabbed, dies into himself. She is jolted awake, frightened, and thinks to check his breath with her hand, but then his ragged snore lulls her. In the fresh daylight, staring up at the patches of mildew on the ceiling, Matilda watches him proudly from the corners of her eyes as he cracks the ice in the washing pail, feeds a spurt of hidden stove flame, talks to himself. She loves him like nothing else. He is her father, her human. Still, sometimes, afflicted by an anxious sorrow, she holds her breath to see what will happen, if he will save her. Heat flows up the sides of her face and she opens her lips but before her mouth can form a word she sees yellow, passes out, and is flooded by blueness, sheer blueness, intimate and cool, the color of her necklace of beads.

Kiss

Have you ever fallen from a severe height and had your wind knocked forth so that, in the strict jolt's sway, you did experience stopped time? Matilda Roy did when she saw her father kiss the teacher. The world halted. There sounded a great gong made of sky. A gasp. Silence. Then the leaves ticked again, the guineas scornfully gossiped, the burly black hound that had whelped of the Indian dog pawed a cool ditch in the sand for itself. Sliding back from the window to the bench behind the house where she sat afternoons to shell peas, shuck corn, peel dinner's potatoes, pluck guinea hens, and dream, Matilda Roy looked at the gold-brown skin on her arms, turned her arms over, turned them back, flexed her pretty, agile hands.

The kiss had been long, slow, and of growing interest and intensity, more educational than any lesson yet given her by Miss Peace McKnight. Matilda shut her eyes. Within herself at all times a silent darkness sifted up and down. A pure emptiness fizzing and gliding. Now, along with the puzzling development between her friend and her father, something else. It took a long concentration on her stillness to grasp the elusive new sensation of freedom, of relief.

Ozhaawashkmashkodikwe / Blue Prairie Woman

The child lost in the raid was still nameless, still a half spirit, yet her mother mourned her for a solid year's time and nearly died of the sorrow. A haunting uncertainty dragged the time out. Ozhaawashkmashkodiwe might be picking blueberries and she feared she would come across her daughter's bones. In the wind at night, she heard her baby wailing, a black twig skeleton. As she stirred the fire, a cleft of flame recalled the evil day itself, the massed piles of meat put to the torch, their robes and blankets smoldering, the stinking singe of hair, and the hot iron of the rifle barrels. At night, for the first month after that day, her breasts grew pale and hard and her milk impacted, spoiling in her, leaking out under her burnt clothes so that she smelled of sour milk and fire. An old midwife gave her a new puppy and she put it to her breasts. Holding to her nipple the tiny wet muzzle, cradling the needy bit of fur, she cried. All that night the tiny dog mercifully drew off the shooting pains in her breasts and at dawn, drowsy and comfortable, she finally cuddled the sweet-fleshed puppy to her, breathed its salty odor, and slept.

Wet ash when the puppy weaned itself. Blood. Her moons began and nothing she pressed between her legs could stop the rush of life. Her body wanting to get rid of itself. She ate white clay, scratched herself with bull thorns for relief, cut her hair, grew it long, cut it short again, scored her arms to the bone, tied the bundle of a pretend baby to her chest, and for six moons ate nothing but dirt and leaves. It must have been a rich dirt, said her grandmother, for although she slept little and looked tired, Blue Prairie Woman was healthy as a buffalo cow. When Shawano the younger returned from his family's wild rice beds, she gave her husband such a night of sexual pleasure that his eyes followed her constantly after that, narrow and hot. He grew molten when she passed near other men, and at night they made their own shaking tent. They got teased too much and moved farther off, into the brush, into the nesting ground of shy and holy loons. There, no one could hear them. In solitude they made love until they became gaunt and hungry, pale wiindigoog with aching eyes, tongues of flame.

Twins are born of such immoderation.

By the time her husband left again with his sled of traps, she was pregnant and calm. During that winter, life turned more brutal. The tribe's stores had been burned by order, and many times in starving sleep Blue Prairie Woman dreamed the memory of buffalo fat running in rivulets across the ground, soaking into the earth, fat gold from piles of burning meat. She still dreamed, too, with wide-eyed clarity of the young, fleet brown dog, the cradle board bound to its body. Even carrying two, she dreamed of her first baby bewildered, then howling, then at last riding black as leather, mouth stretched wide underneath a waterless sky. She dreamed its bones rattled in the careful stitching of black velvet, clacked in the moss padding, grown thin. She heard their rhythm and saw the dog, the small skeleton flying. She howled and scratched herself half blind and at last so viciously took leave of her mind that the old ones got together and decided to change her name.

On a cool day in spring in the maple-sap-running moon the elders held a pitiful feast—only nothing seems pitiful to survivors. In weak sunlight they chewed spring-risen mud-turtle meat, roasted waabooz, the remaining sweet grains of manoomin, acorns, puckoons from a squirrel's cache, and the fresh spears of dandelion. Blue Prairie Woman's name was covered with blood, singed with fire. Her name was old and exquisite and had belonged to many powerful mothers. Yet the woman who had fit inside of it had walked off. She couldn't stop following the child and the dog. Someone else had taken her place. Who, as yet, was unclear. But the old ones agreed that the wrong name would kill what was in there and it had to go—like a husk dried off and scattered. Like a shell to a nut. Hair grown long and sacrificed to sorrow. They had to give her another name if they wanted her to return to the living.

The name they gave her had to be unused. New. Oshki. They asked the strongest of the namers, the one who dreamed original names. This namer was nameless and was neither a man nor a woman, and so took power from the in-between. This namer had long, thick braids and a sweet shy smile, charming ways but arms tough with roped muscle. The namer walked like a woman, spoke in a man's deep voice. Hid coy behind a fan and yet agreed to dream a name to fit the new thing inside Blue Prairie Woman. But what name would help a woman who could be calmed only by gazing into the arrowing distance? The namer went away, starved and sang and dreamed, until it was clear that the only name that made any sense at all was the name of the place where the old Blue Prairie Woman had gone to fetch back her child.

Other Side of the Earth

Once she was named for the place toward which she traveled, the young mother was able to be in both places at once—she was following her child into the sun and also pounding the wiiyaas between rocks to dried scruffs of pemmican. She was searching the thick underbrush of her own mind. She was punching holes to sew tough new soles on old makizinan and also sew new ones, tiny, the soles pierced before she beaded the tops. She starved and wandered, tracking the faint marks the dog left as she passed into the blue distance. At the same time, she knocked rice. She parched and stored the grains. Killed birds. Tamed horses. Her mind was present because she was always gone. Her hands were filled because they grasped the meaning of empty. Life was simple. Her husband returned and she served him with indifferent patience this time. When he asked what had happened to her heat for him, she gestured to the west.

The sun was setting. The sky was a body of fire.

In the deep quiet of her blood the two babies were forming, creating themselves just as the first twin gods did at the beginning. As yet, no one had asked what might happen next. What would happen to the woman called Other Side of the Earth when Blue Prairie Woman found Matilda Roy?

A Dog Named Sorrow

The dog nursed on human milk grew up coyote gray and clever, a light-boned, loping bitch who followed Blue Prairie

Woman everywhere. Became her second thought, lay outside the door when she slept, just within the outer flap when it rained, though not in. Not ever actually inside a human dwelling. Huge with pups or thin from feeding them, teats dragging, the dog still followed. Close and quiet as her shadow, it lived within touch of her, although they never did touch after the dog drew from Blue Prairie Woman's soaked and swollen nipples the heat, the night milk, the overpowering sorrow.

Always there, jumping up at the approach of a stranger, guarding her in the dusk, alert for a handout, living patiently on bits of hide, guts, offal, the dog waited. And was ready when Blue Prairie Woman set down her babies with their grandmother and started walking west, following at long last the endless invisible trail of her daughter's flight.

She walked for hours, she walked for years. She walked until she heard about them. The man. The young girl and the blue beads she wore. Where they were living. She heard the story. The twins, two girls, she left behind to the chances of baptism. They were named Mary, of course, for the good blue-robed woman, and Josephette, for the good husband. Only the Ojibwe tongue made Zosie of the latter name. Zosie. Mary. Their relatives, who had survived the bluecoat massacre, would raise them as their own.

When she reached the place, Blue Prairie Woman settled on a nearby rise, the dog near. From that distance, the two watched the house—small, immaculate, scent of a hearth fire made of crackling oak twigs. Illness. There was sickness in the house, she could sense it—the silence, then the flurries of motion. Rags hung out. Water to haul. One shrill cry. Silence again. All day in thin grass, the dog, the woman, sunlight moving across them, breathed each other's air, slept by turns, waited.

Matilda Roy

She heard the gentle approach that night, the scrawl of leaves, the sighing resonance of discovery. She sat up in her crazy quilt, knowing. Next to her, held in the hot vise of fever, Peace muttered endlessly of buttons and sheep bones. Sounds—a slight tap. The clatter of her beads. In the morning, there was no Matilda Roy in the trunk bed. There was only a note, folded twice, penned in the same exquisite, though feminized, handwriting of her father.

She came for me. I went with her.

Scranton Roy

Peace McKnight was never devout, so there was no intimacy of prayer between the newlyweds. Their physical passion suffered, as well, because of the shortness of his bed. There was, after all, very little space inside the sod house. Scranton Roy had slept in a tiny berth on one side of the room, his daughter on the other. Both slept curled like snails, like babies in the wombs of their mothers. More difficult with an extra person in the bedding. It wasn't long before, in order to get any rest at all, Peace slipped outside to sleep with the guineas, took up nightly residence apart from her husband.

Still, there were evenings when Scranton was inflicted with ardor and arranged them both, before she could leave, in the cramped and absurd postures of love. If only he had imagined how to use the armless rocking chair before the fire! Peace's mind flashed on the possibility, but she was too stubborn to mention it. Even the floor, packed dirt covered with skins, would have been preferable. Again, she didn't care to introduce that possibility into his mind. Anyway, as it happened she had every right to turn her back when the tiny knock of new life began in the cradle of her hip bones. As he retreated, missed the rasp of her breath, wondered about Matilda, and imagined the new life to come all at once, Scranton Roy prayed. Wrote poems in his head. *Come to me, thou dark inviolate.*

After her deliverance from the mottled-skin sickness, the gasping and fever that made her bones ache, Peace was in her weakness even warier of her new husband. For the rest of her pregnancy, she made him sleep alone. Her labor began on a snowy morning. Scranton Roy set out for the Swedish housewife's in a swallowing blizzard that would have cost him his life but for his good sense in turning back. He reached the door. Smote, rattled, fell into the heat of a bloody scene in which Peace McKnight implored her neglected God in begging futility. For two days, then three, her labor shook her in its jaws. Her howls were louder than the wind. Hoarser. Then her voice was lost, a scrape of bone. A whisper. Her face bloated, dark red, then white, then gray. Her eyes rolled back to the whites, so she stared mystified with agony into her own thoughts when at last the child tore its way from her. A boy, plump and dead blue. Marked with cloudy spots like her earlier disease. There was no pulse in the birth cord but Scranton Roy thought to puff his own air into the baby's lungs. It answered with a startled bawl.

Augustus. She had already named her baby. Known that it would be a boy.

Scranton wrapped the baby in a rabbit fur blanket and kissed the smoothed, ravaged temples of Peace with tender horror at her pains, at the pains of his own mother, and of all mothers, and of the unfair limitations of our bodies, of the hopeless settlement of our life tasks, and finally, of the boundless iniquity of the God to whom she had so uselessly shrieked. *Look at her*, he called the unseen witness. And perhaps God did or Peace McKnight's mind, pitilessly wracked, finally came out of hiding and told her heart to beat twice more. A stab of fainting gold heeled through a scrap of window. Peace saw the wanton gleam, breathed out, gazed out. And then, as she stepped from her ripped body into the utter calm of her new soul, Peace McKnight saw her husband put his son to his breast.

Blue Prairie Woman

All that's in a name is a puff of sound, a lungful of wind, and yet it is an airy enclosure. How is it that the gist, the spirit, the complicated web of bone, hair, brain, gets stuffed into a syllable or two? How do you shrink the genie of human complexity? How the personality? Unless, that is, your mother gives you her name, Other Side of the Earth.

Who came from nowhere and from lucky chance.

Whose mother bore her in shit and fire. She is huge as half the sky. In the milk from her rescuer's breasts she has tasted his disconcerting hatred of her kind and also protection, so that when she falls into the fever, she doesn't suffer of it the way Peace did. Although they stop, make camp, and Blue Prairie Woman speaks to her in worried susurrations, the child is in no real danger.

The two camp on the trail of a river cart. The sky opens brilliantly and the grass is hemmed, rife with berries. Blue Prairie Woman picks with swift grace and fills a new-made makak. She dries the berries on sheaves of bark, in the sun, so they'll be easy to carry. Lying with her head on her mother's lap, before the fire, Matilda asks what her name was as a little baby. The two talk on and on, mainly by signs.

Does the older woman understand the question? Her face burns. As she sinks dizzily onto the earth beside her daughter, she feels compelled to give her the name that brought her back. Other Side of the Earth, she says, teeth tapping. Hotter, hotter, first confused and then dreadfully clear when she sees, opening before her, the western door.

She must act at once if her daughter is to survive her.

The clouds are pure stratus. The sky is a raft of milk. The coyote gray dog sits patiently near.

Blue Prairie Woman, sick to death and knowing it, reaches swiftly to her left and sets her grip without looking on the nape of the dog's neck. First time she has touched the dog since it drank from her the milk of sorrow. She drags the dog to her. Soft bones, soft muzzle then. Tough old thing now. Blue Prairie Woman holds the dog close underneath one arm and then, knife in hand, draws her clever blade across the beating throat. Slices its stiff moan in half and collects in the berry-filled makak its gurgle of dark blood. Blue Prairie Woman then stretches the dog out, skins and guts it, cuts off her head, and lowers the chopped carcass into a deep birch-bark container. She heats stones red-hot, lowers them into the water with a pair of antlers. Tending the fire carefully, weakening, she boils the dog.

When it is done, the meat softened, shredding off the bones, she tips the gray meat, brown meat, onto a birch tray. Steam rises, the fragrance of the meat is faintly sweet. Quietly, she gestures to her daughter. Prods the cracked oval pads off the cooked paws. Offers them to her.

IT TAKES SIXTEEN hours for Blue Prairie Woman to contract the fever and only eight more to die of it. All that time, as she is dying, she sings. Her song is wistful, peculiar, soft, questing. It doesn't sound like a death song; rather, there is in it the tenderness and intimacy of seduction addressed to the blue distance.

Never exposed, healthy, defenseless, her body is an eager receptacle for the virus. She seizes, her skin goes purple, she vomits a brilliant flash of blood. Passionate, surprised, she dies when her chest fills, kicking and drumming her heels on the hollow earth. At last she is still, gazing west. That is the direction her daughter sits facing all the next day and the next. She sings her mother's song, holding her mother's hand in one hand and seriously, absently, eating the dog with the other hand—until in that spinning cloud light and across rich level earth, pale reddish curious creatures, slashed with white on the chest and face, deep-eyed, curious, pause in passing.

The antelope emerge from the band of the light at the world's edge.

A small herd of sixteen or twenty flickers into view. Fascinated, they poise to watch the girl's hand in its white sleeve dip. Feed herself. Dip. They step closer. Hooves of polished metal. Ears like tuning forks. Black prongs and velvet. They watch Matilda. Blue Prairie Woman's daughter. Other Side of the Earth. Nameless.

She is ten years old, tough from chasing poultry and lean from the fever. She doesn't know what they are, the beings, dreamlike, summoned by her mother's song, her dipping hand. They come closer, closer, grazing near, folding their legs under them to warily rest. The young nurse from their mothers on the run or stare at the girl in fascinated hilarity, springing off if she catches their wheeling flirtation. In the morning when she wakens, still holding her mother's hand, they are standing all around. They bend to her, huff in excitement when she rises and stands among them quiet and wondering. Easy with their dainty precision, she wanders along in their company. Always on the move. At night she makes herself a nest of willow. Sleeps there. Moves on. Eats bird's eggs. A snared rabbit. Roots. She remembers fire and cooks a handful of grouse chicks. The herd flows in steps and spurting gallops deeper into the west. When they walk, she walks, following, dried berries in a sack made of her dress. When they run, she runs with them. Naked, graceful, the blue beads around her neck.

2

Wiindigoo Story

The Cracker Tin

Scranton Roy touched the dirty brown hair of his beautiful son, Augustus, and said, "I am tired of my numb heart."

Augustus looked down at his feet, knowing he would hear more.

"I thought when I loved your mother my heart had come to life, but then her death killed my heart again. Even watching you grow hasn't brought it back. I have been reading the ancients."

Augustus looked at the pile of books. He was twenty-three years old and had read most of them with his father, who admired the Greek philosophers. Anaximander viewed time as a judge, and Scranton Roy had meditated on this concept until its truth came clear. Time had judged and sentenced him in the form of an unforgettable word.

"As a young man I committed a crime in the fever of

war. Although I have tried to absolve myself repeatedly—I even took up self-scourging for a year—I still see the old woman's face and hear her say that word. The word wakes me up at night. It is written in my brain. As you know, it is carved into my arm."

Augustus looked at his father's arm, the white scars, the letters carefully blocked and scored. The word was a long word. The word reached up past his elbow.

"I still see the children who fell," his father continued. "Especially them. I still taste on my tongue the smoke, powder, blood, and burning fat."

Augustus had grown up in the shadow of his father's ever more complex grief, and although he had few other adults to compare him with, he did think his father was lost. His father wandered in the dark. But Augustus himself grew up in wind and sun. He loved perpetual change and was glad it was the law of the universe. Heracleitus had also declared there to be a balance of opposites, and so Augustus was the balance of his wracked father, a happy child who ran boundless, hunting prairie chickens, stealing the blue eggs of robins, caring for descendants of the agile guinea hens his mother had laughed at. He walked overland to attend the same school, set in the center of the township, where his mother had taught.

At home, he read with his father, and both agreed with Pythagoras that the essence of things was to be found in numbers. At school, Augustus's best subject was math. He collected numbers until they made him dizzy. He counted everything around him and totaled it up with other countings and subtracted or divided those countings just to have the numbers in his head. Each number had a color and some had a sound or taste.

"We are going to search out the people I wronged and give them the cracker tin," said Scranton Roy.

Augustus knew the tin well. Once very light, it had contained Christmas crackers sealed against moisture. Now the cracker tin was very heavy and contained gold and silver money. Exactly $438.13. A bright purple number. A noble number, scraped of sacrifice. When Scranton Roy felt the sad heat come on him, he put a bit of money in the tin and it helped to ease his burden. When Augustus Roy felt slightly morose, he took some money from the tin and it helped to ease his burden. It was hard caring for a father who raved of smoke and blood and carved into his arm the letters of a word he did not understand.

I hope I don't have to carry the cracker tin, thought Augustus. But of course he did, and it made his back sore, or his arms when he hefted it before him. Sometimes he made a pillow of his shirt and carried the tin on his head. As they walked on and on, Augustus was increasingly grateful that he had lightened the tin and he smiled to think how he'd spent the money—on home-brew fire. As he walked toward the place where his father had killed the woman and perhaps the children, too, Augustus counted the clouds until they blended together and there was just one gloomy sky. He counted trees until they turned into a crowded woodland. Where were they going? They were going backward, out of the good simple world he'd lived in so far and into complex rolling prairie. Every so often the land dipped and the trees stood thick. Sometimes they towered in lightless stands.

The sloughs turned to shallow lakes and then the lakes deepened. Abruptly there began vast lumbered areas of rotting pine stumps surrounded by springy popple. He feared his father didn't know where he was going and had forgotten where he'd murdered the harmless old woman.

"Here is the place," said his father at last. He put down the cracker tin. "Here is where I betrayed the silent light in which I was raised. Here is what desire made of me, and foolishness, and an irresistible and bloody impulse."

Scranton lay down in some poison ivy.

"Cut my throat, please," he said to Augustus, and handed his son the whetted knife he kept in his belt.

Augustus kept the knife and spoke gently to his father. "Let time do its work," he said. "Perhaps you will be pardoned." Eventually he convinced Scranton that they must travel to the place where the Indians had fled.

"Where did they go?" he asked.

His father pointed in all directions. Augustus chose north, and again picked up the cracker tin.

The Ones

Inevitably, they crossed paths with Indians.

"Are these the ones?" asked Augustus.

His father looked carefully at the people, but shook his head and said no, that the people he'd killed were beautifully dressed in calico, buckskins, beads and strips of velvet. They'd been strong and well fed. These two people were skinny and ragged and they walked with a discouraged air.

The man frowned and the woman glared suspiciously at the two white men.

"I think these are the ones," said Augustus, who longed to put down the cracker tin. "I think these are the children who survived, all grown up. Look what you did to them, father!"

"My Lord," said Scranton Roy.

He took the tin of money from his son. As the people edged away from the two, he held it out with an awful smile and pressed it forward.

"That's all right," said the woman. "We don't need crackers."

Scranton's sleeve was rolled up and she looked at his arm, then nudged her husband, who craned his head sideways and carefully mouthed the letters of the word.

"All right," said the Indian man, startled. "You can follow us. We don't have much to eat, but we'll shoot something. We live over there."

He pointed at a place that seemed empty. Augustus, sensing that he'd soon be relieved of the tin, followed eagerly so that his father was forced to stumble along behind.

Old Shawano

The man who read the word scored into Scranton Roy's arm was named for the southern wind, just like his father and grandfather. Shawano. His wife was Victoria Muskrat. They knew about the old woman who was slaughtered and they knew about the woman's great-nieces. Shawano had taken them after their mother disappeared. They were pretty girls but something was not right about them. Victoria thought they were coldhearted liars. Shawano said he pitied them, but did not trust them. The two white men and the Indians now ached to be delivered of different burdens. Both of the old people hurried along, sensing that they soon might be relieved of the girls' disquieting presence.

The Number Blue

When the number two in any of its permutations entered Augustus Roy's thoughts a limpid blue atmosphere surrounded it. The color darkened, tinged with indigo, as it climbed into the solid sky of twoness. Entering the tar-paper and scrap-board house of the people to whom he was determined to give the cracker tin, he saw the spectrum of blue that went with the number when he saw the twins. Zosie and Mary were identical. They dressed alike in flour-sacking frocks, gray with white piping, and they both wore their hair pulled back in long braids. Their eyes were cool and watchful. Their hands moved constantly at endless tasks that they took up and put down without seeming to notice. Augustus was too shy to look at them straight on, but he was moved by their uncanny harmony.

His father seemed dazzled, struck dumb. His clothes had grown huge around him and he sat in a puddle of cloth, itching already from the leaves he'd lain in, and smiling. Idiotically, Augustus thought, with weary concern. He brought the cracker tin to a wooden table, the only piece of furniture besides the one chair Augustus occupied. He set the tin down with a solid metallic clunking jingle that could only be the sound of money. The heads of the twins turned with a jerk and their eyes fixed on the tin.

"It is money," said Augustus Roy. "It is for you. Many years ago my father killed an old lady of your tribe and he wants forgiveness. He has been saving up."

The old people and the girls were absolutely silent for some time. Then one or another of the twins spoke.

"You've come to the right place."

AFTER THE OJIBWE PEOPLE accepted the money and told Scranton Roy that he was forgiven, his eyes shed water. He was not exactly weeping because his teeth showed in a broad and grateful smile. He was scratching madly now. Water trickled down the angular creases at either side of his mouth and collected against the curb of his collarbone.

"My father wants to sleep," said Augustus.

Victoria Muskrat pointed to a heap of blankets on the floor, in the corner, and said that he could lie down there and sleep as long as he wanted. Scranton thanked her, lay down in the corner, and pulled a blanket over himself. Old Shawano indicated a place on another blanket and Augustus sat. His eyes itched drowsily but he did not sleep. He read the walls, which were covered with catalog, magazine, and newspaper pages neatly pasted around the window frames. Land! the pages shouted. Rich, cheap, fertile, easy title! Indian Land for Sale! The wood slats were from broken-up cracker crates, probably salvaged from lumber camps. The slats were stamped with accidental word puzzles based on the word *cracker*. No wonder they didn't want more crackers, Augustus thought. The family busied themselves, went in and went out. After a while Augustus roused himself. He noticed that his foot was getting wet, looked down, and saw that a trickle of blood was flowing from beneath his father's blanket. Augustus reached for the knife his father had offered him, knowing it was gone. All four of the Ojibwe people entered. They studied the flow of blood and bowed their heads. For a long while, nobody spoke. The unmistakable still form in the corner dominated the room. At last one or the other of the twins turned to Augustus and said, "We will bury him in our own way. We will wrap him in that blanket and make him a fire. We will stand watch and help his spirit onto the road to the next life. We will feed his spirit and sing for him."

"Thank you," said Augustus.

He continued to sit on the floor. When everyone moved outdoors, he followed and sat down. Other people came with water drums, pipes, feathers, food, whiskey, more blankets. His father's body was removed from the house through a window. The fire was lit for his spirit to follow. Sometimes Augustus lay on the ground near the fire. Sometimes he ate. The days came and went and in the flow of singing and drumming he seemed to pass into another life along with his father. At last, they told him that his father was safe on the other side. They showed him the small grave house, which was carefully made of boards, roofed, painted red, and placed over the spot where his father was buried. They waited for him to leave.

Niizhoodenhyag

Augustus Roy did not leave. The family spoke English with him, wrote in a finer script than he did, and used better grammar. They had been whipped into shape by the government. They'd been to boarding school. He got a job. Every day he walked to a bank in the nearest town, four miles each way. The work involved the essence of things as defined by number, and counting, his favorite pastime. His days were filled with color because of the pleasurable flow in numbers. He also enjoyed walking back and forth, especially after one or the other of the twins began to meet him on the way home. They walked along silently at first, not even holding hands. He was thrilled by each young woman's singularity and by the game of trying to figure out whether she was Zosie or Mary. Sometimes both women came to meet him. Then the twoness, the blueness, flowed over him. He was lost in its choreography. Their voices and their movements were mirrors within mirrors. He decided they defined eternity although they lied and mocked him. They grew sly and bold. Spied on him, poked him, threw twigs at him. Kissed him. He was never certain. He would not be sure which one he married the Indian way. He would not be sure which one he slept with on whatever was their wedding night. Which one he got pregnant.

Love and the Dawes Act

Augustus built a cabin of thin logs and clay. He bought real shingles for the roof. The twins lived next door with the old people who had sheltered them. The twins also lived with him. He had tossed a coin and asked Mary to be his wife, but sometimes he was sure that Zosie took her place. Augustus put in a bedstead with a saggy mattress, and the twins curtained off another room. He built a kitchen table where the women sat at night. They made moccasins from the deerskin they'd tanned with the deer's own brains. They sat in the lamplight, talking softly in their own language. In the cracker tin, empty now of money, they kept their quills and beads. At all times, as they talked or laughed, their needles moved in and out of the soft deerhide, complicating the design.

Because of the Dawes Act, reservation land was parceled out to individuals instead of remaining in tribal trust possession. Land was the only thing that hungry people owned, and it started to disappear with astounding haste. At the bank, Augustus assisted every day with transferring money from white hands into Ojibwe hands. He then witnessed the signing of a land deed by Ojibwe hands and saw it transferred into white hands, which then placed the land deed in a safe-deposit box. Invariably, he begged the person with the money to open a savings account. That rarely happened. The money usually flung itself around the town.

Augustus knew an Ojibwe man and woman named Whiteheart Beads who were persuaded to buy a grand piano with their land payment, and now their whole family slept beneath it just beside the road. Fancy clothing, rifles, liquor, pink and yellow and aqua shawls, and shiny buttoned boots appeared. Barrels of salted doves and sacks of white flour, dairy butter and tinned peaches, went out into the bush. People still lived on the margins of the land they had owned. But the land was gone, gone, gone and subject to the plow and No Trespassing. People milled about their old houses like ghosts and were driven off, bewildered. Augustus railed and threatened. He beat a speculator, nearly lost his job. Shrieked when his calm advice was ignored. He sprinted home every night and told his family not to sell their land.

The twins answered that Old Shawano and Victoria and the two of them were not stupid like the others. They drank very little whiskey, not like the others. They were in addition apt to think in the old ways, not like the others. They had Augustus, too, not like the others. Augustus, who brought home provisions when the hunting failed and the garden was resting. They had no reason to sell their land, even though, and here one twin paused and looked down at her belly, there was going to be a baby.

The other twin sucked in her breath ferociously and said, "Yes, it is I who will have the baby."

Augustus looked from one to the other, terrified.

After that announcement he got no sleep. One twin and then the other crawled into his bed. Or was it twice and the same woman? Their ways devoured him. Mornings, they glared at each other and then at him, and did not speak. He thought of running away before they wore him out, but could not because he was helpless before the nights, cold nights, northern and slow. And although he knew he'd be called to superhuman effort later on, he loved to watch them, just rest his eyes on them at their work every evening.

The lamp shone a peach golden circle at the table where Mary and Zosie arranged their saucers of beads—white for the background, Hungarian cut glass, delicate size 13, tiny loops of old greasy yellows and blues, a hank of mauves, a collection of glossy whiteheart reds. Mary worked on moccasins already bought and half paid for by a missionary chimookomaan lady who would get them in the mail. Zosie worked on tiny slippers for the baby who was growing in one, the other, or perhaps both of them. As they worked, the two grew calmer. Augustus did not move. They were spooky as cats, but he could tell that his presence soothed them.

They breathed in the tobacco scent of Augustus's once-a-week cigar, and the very slight undertone of whiskey. Augustus had begun to take a shot with Shawano, who liked him and decided to adopt him. He was glad to have a son with a quick smile and a friendly outlook—these things seemed surprising in a whiteman. Augustus was glad to have as a father a man who quietly went about the business of life, and taught him how to dream the whereabouts of animals and to follow their tracks and use the wind to catch them. Old Shawano taught Augustus how to pick wild rice, weave nets, tap maples, and ignore the doings of women. Augustus became adept at all but the last thing. As the twins worked, they breathed the smoked hide and touched the rabbit fur and tasted the duck grease of the birds the two men shot together. They breathed Augustus's clean sweat, for he bathed in the lake each morning, even breaking the ice sheaves once November came around. He had learned from Shawano an old-time Indian's habits. But also like Shawano, he wore suspenders and read aloud from the newspapers. Augustus acted like an akiwenzii although he was very young. This confused the twins' rivalry and dulled their glares. Protected by his books and pens and envelopes and bills, Augustus tried to remain oblivious. But their feelings for him were a long thread. The two sisters had licked, threaded, and waxed either end. They began to sew with it, adding to their own peculiar pattern bead by bead until, one night, the thread pulled taut, the space shortened, Zosie's and Mary's needles halted, and they looked each other in the eye.

Fried Robins

Although the twins enjoyed flummoxing people, especially Augustus, with their sameness, they were in truth very different. Zosie liked sweet things and Mary preferred sour and salty. Mary hated to eat birds, eggs, and any roots that came out of the ground. Zosie liked those foods but rejected green cabbage and complained that if any maple sugar was added to her meat she was likely to get the runs. Mary was good at small things and Zosie was good at large. For instance, Mary could mend a sock to perfection while Zosie could help Augustus split new shingles for the roof. Zosie could also cook for many people at once while Mary was better at more intricate food tasks, although she cried while plucking birds. Zosie liked to snare birds although Mary called her heartless. Zosie was frying up six robins one day when she decided that she was tired of sharing her sister with Augustus. A husband was all right to have, as long as he could be controlled. But you couldn't get along without your twin. If he ever learned their differences, he might tell one from the other and choose. So that night, as they looked at each other over their beadwork, Zosie put her hand on her head and twirled the crown of her hair. Mary put down her needle and did the same. "The robins are sacred," said Mary. "If you ever eat one again, you will choke on its tiny breastbone." "I will give them up," said Zosie. Then they both laughed so hard, blowing and snorting with relief, that they didn't stop until they felt drunk.

The Hidden Knot

A woman used to deception knows how to hide her stitches. The twins' beadwork was tight and true. No visible beginning or end to the design. Impossible to find the starting knot, the final tie. Unseeable the place where the needle went in or out. Their maple leaf or prairie rose or vines twisting skeletal on black velvet were done with invisible thread. They used those threads on Augustus. He never saw the stitch work that kept him sewed to their side. He never saw the fabric upon which their passion was marked out in chalk. Or the inlay, one bead to the next, the remarkable interpenetration of colors.

There was one secret way to tell the twins apart. Victoria

had pity on Augustus one day and told him to check the whirlwinds at the crown of their heads. One swirled to the left, the other swirled to the right.

Augustus had fallen in love with the enigma of duplication, and the hold had deepened. The confusion of sameness between the twins made him tremble like an animal caught in a field of tension. Sitting at the table, he'd feel the current of their likeness. Things even they did not notice. Mary pricked herself. Zosie muttered *owey*! Zosie started a legging and Mary, without even trying to copy, constructed another of an identical design. They got hungry at exactly the same time. Started humming one tune suddenly, no sign having passed between them.

When making love, there was barely anything one did differently from the other. He could tell them apart only with the greatest difficulty, even in their nakedness beneath his hands, but this exploration, rather than daunting, excited him. He could always make certain which was which by touching the whirlwinds at the crowns of their heads—that is, until suddenly it seemed they started combing their hair in new ways. This way, that. Messing with his one sure proof.

After they messed up the hair on their whirlwinds, he searched and searched for another way to identify them. Soon one of them would show her pregnancy. He had to know which one or he would be lost. For a time, as they beaded, he surreptitiously examined their fingers. Curled around the needles, each nail was just that slightest bit different from the next. He marked out the degree of growth, fixed in his mind a nick or a tatter.

He was driven to noticing the tiniest things. Became a

devotee of pricks and scratches. Sometimes, in his desperation, he tried placing a mark on one of them himself.

You could say he started what happened next.

The accident occurred as a stroke of luck. Augustus knocked a hot fry pan over and grease splattered Zosie's wrist. Mary was so upset that she gasped out Zosie's name. For several weeks Augustus had a certain sign of Zosie's identity and this quieted him. He even gained a few pounds, for anxiety had thinned him terribly. But Zosie's scar was fading. Just before it disappeared, he tipped the hot fry pan over once again, this time onto Mary, whose painfully burned foot had to be bandaged and unbandaged twice a day. Yet she, too, recovered and her skin stayed unmarred.

How to leave a more permanent mark? He took a knife one day. Cutting a rope, he sliced through the air and nearly took off the tip of Mary's right ear. She ducked in time, but it gave him an idea and that night when Zosie came to him he worked himself into a heat and climaxed with the lobe of her ear between his teeth.

FOR THE REST of the pregnancy, he slept alone. The twins both feared he had gone wiindigoo. The child was born, but even Victoria was confused. The baby had two whorls of hair, clockwise, counterclockwise, on the crown of its head.

"An unusual situation," said Augustus, holding his little daughter, who clutched his finger and stared up at him in focused intensity. "I am your father, but we may never know the exact identity of your mother. Even if one tells us, she may be lying. I give up."

Augustus accepted that he was lost. That his predicament was insoluble now. Time was marked both ways on the crown of his daughter's head. Time was moving forward with the clock, time was moving backward, against the clock. Time had judged his father. But perhaps time does not recognize the particulars of human identity, thought Augustus, and keeps track only of the magnitude of crime. If there were those yet living affected by his father's murder of the old woman, then it stood to reason that punishment would also be carried out upon his father's descendant.

I am the one, Augustus concluded. The one who will answer.

3

Answers

When Scranton Roy had explained his cracker tin dilemma so long ago, one of the twins had answered, *You've come to the right place.* Augustus thought the answer was a typically quick-witted response to the jingle of money. But he was wrong. That answer was the truth. Over time, he discovered that the women he loved were great-nieces of the old woman eagerly slaughtered by his father. The old woman who died had been high-spirited, a tease, always ready to laugh. She had suffered three days before she died of the wound. Raving, she had cried out exactly what was carved into Scranton's arm. Augustus covered his face and breathed deeply when he learned what it meant. He also learned the name Blue Prairie Woman and understood that she was the mother of the women he loved.

Zosie and Mary were the twins created of immoderation in the nesting ground of shy and holy loons. Perhaps, as they owed their origins to that haunting and ironic laughter, they tended to take their jokes too far. Augustus thought so. But just as he finally accepted that he would never tell one from the other, his child, their child, a daughter he named Peace, began to speak. She spoke Ojibwe, but eventually Augustus came to the exciting conclusion that she consistently called Zosie Nimaamaa, and Mary Inninoshenh. My mother and my auntie.

The spell was broken. Augustus was astonished he'd ever thought them so exactly alike. One had a slightly crooked nose! The other's eyes were wider apart. Mary even had a tiny permanent dimple in her chin. This entire realization presented a new problem.

Knowing that Zosie was the mother of his child, he felt he should marry her correctly in the eyes of the law and the state of Minnesota. And if he married Zosie, then he could not, of course, sleep with Mary. He watched them with grief in his heart. They had sewn themselves new wash dresses out of the lengths of green flowered fabric he'd given them. They were combing out their long, wet, dark masses of hair. Sometimes they wore simple braids; other times pinned up their hair in charmingly untidy arrangements. He loved their smooth skin, handsome faces, their fine thin noses, and even their lips, cruel but perfectly formed. Their teeth were very white and sharp. Both were vain about their smiles and showed them off broadly when he bought them fancy boar-bristle toothbrushes and whitening tooth powder. He had softened them with his attention, he thought. For they treated Peace with utmost tenderness. He didn't want to give either one of them up. Not only that, but it would cause such unthinkable discord.

So Augustus spent the rest of his life pretending that he

could not distinguish between them, even though as they grew older they also grew even more unlike. When Mary bore him a son, Augustus rejoiced and named him Charles. When Zosie bore him another son he rejoiced and tried to name the baby Arthur, but nobody would call the willful, cheerful ball of boy Arthur. They called him Booch. The last son came along the same year Old Shawano passed over to the spirit world, so that baby was named Shawano and the family was complete.

The Train Station

Peace, Charlie, Booch, and Shawano were all as fine-looking as their mothers, tall with clear features and thoughtful eyes. They were each a year or two apart in age and played together in isolation. The allotment land fiercely protected by Shawano, Victoria, the twins, and Augustus was prime lakeshore property. By the time Peace was five years old, all the land around them was lumbered to stumps. By the time Charlie was five, the lakeshore was filled with white people's cabins. By the time Booch and young Shawano were five, the Indian agent came while Augustus was at work and their mothers out picking medicines. Only old Victoria was there.

The agent, Hiram Talp, believed that he was doing the best for all concerned except the children. He had received a letter from a government boarding-school superintendent informing him that in order to meet a certain quota at his school, he was willing to pay Talp good money for his assistance in persuading students from his reservation to attend.

Talp collected the children by assuring Victoria that he was going to show them the newly built train station. It was the talk of the town.

At the train station, the agent showed Victoria the fancy ladies' restroom. He encouraged her to step inside. When she did, he locked the door. Then he tried to herd the children onto the train. When Peace saw that he'd locked their grandmother in the bathroom she took Charlie's hand and they backed slowly away from the agent. Booch and Shawano slipped behind their sister and brother. This was the way they had been taught to treat a bear. They backed toward the ladies' restroom door, which had a frosted glass window. A blurred version of their grandmother jumped up and down behind the window, screaming in an eerie tremolo. People gathered. Sound of the commotion reached the bank. Augustus walked across the street toward the familiar tone of distress. The children were silent. Victoria tore a piece of framing from a mirror and began to beat at the window. Still, Hiram Talp persisted, talking soothingly to the children and explaining the situation to the people who surrounded the scene. He tried to take Peace's hand and she bit him. He tried to take Charlie's hand and she kicked him hard enough to make him double over. When Talp staggered up she put a finger in his eye. She was not her mothers' daughter for nothing.

Augustus waded into the shocked little crowd surrounding Talp, who had doubled over in pain again. The people murmured warily at Peace, who did not look fierce at all in her neat blue dress, trimmed with a yellow collar, cuffs, and even a yellow ruffle. It was made by the screaming grandma in the frosted window, and lent to all of the children an air of respectability even though, well, they were clearly Indians.

Augustus registered the crowd's comments without surprise. Once they saw that the children belonged to him, the people hushed.

"Give me the key," said Augustus to the stationmaster, who pointed mutely at the agent. Augustus said to Hiram, again, "The key." A woman looked at Hiram's eye and declared he deserved to be blinded. Everyone was now on the children's side. Hiram pointed at his shirt pocket. Augustus removed the key and released Victoria.

As the children and their grandmother walked away with Augustus, the Indian agent called out, warning everyone that the children would now grow up to be illiterate and violent drunks. Augustus stopped in the door of the train station.

"Hiram Talp," he called, "what is six plus its additive inverse?"

Hiram glowered out of one eye. His hand was still clapped over the other.

"Zero," said Peace.

"What is the sum of 20,862, 39, 459, 66, and 7,088?" asked Augustus. He saw the answer spiral from soft yellow to a scorched orange, but Peace saw the sum as violently green. As she answered, they kept walking, adding and subtracting numbers as they went along. It was a game they played. Augustus looked at his daughter and noticed that the freckles just beneath her skin stood out like flecks of iron.

The Storyteller

After what Old Shawano and Victoria had told him about their days in boarding school, Augustus was determined to educate his children at home. He understood that the loneliness the elders had suffered in those schools remained forever within them unsolved. In the evenings, by kerosene lantern light, the children worked regularly at their lessons. During the days, their mothers educated their children in all that was Ojibwe, all that they needed to survive. In this way, the family escaped many of the harms around them. They kept to themselves, rarely walked into town. They spent their time together and made themselves mute around others so as not to draw unnecessary attention. Augustus was anxious also to preserve his privacy from any who might guess that he was not legally married to either one of the women he lived with. He feared that his standing at the bank would suffer. But since no white people ever visited, nobody really understood that Mary and Zosie were different people. The two of them never appeared in the town together.

Occasionally, people did try to visit them. Old Shawano had placed his tar-paper house with a view to the small winding road that led up to it. Augustus had added a small white frame house to the same site, and so the family often had time to vanish before a visitor arrived to stand before their silent door. For a few people, though, the family stayed put. One visitor was a bachelor named Asin, Stone, and another was Bagakaapi, Sees Clear. They came originally to visit Old Shawano, but continued even after he entered the spirit world. They came for the remarkable bannocks and jellies that Victoria set before them, and they came because the children were curious and asked them questions, which they were only too happy to answer.

Questions

"What were we?" asked Charles. "Before this?"

He looked down at his overalls and bare feet. Asin knew just what the boy was asking. It was summer. They sat behind the house, which did not face the lake the way white people's houses did, but sat sideways to catch the calmer breeze and protection of the woods. There was a low bluff at the side of the lake and a path that led through it to a broad velvety beach, which today was hot and windy. The women had cut leafy poles to make a cooling arbor and an outdoor kitchen. Augustus had pegged together a plank table. The children could hear the waves from where they sat, and the searching cries of gulls.

Zosie paddled out to an island and gathered two baskets of gull eggs. Now the eggs were boiling gently in a black iron kettle hung from a tripod on an iron hook. Zosie kept the fire low and even. Mary told her that the gulls would peck her eyes out when she was dead. Zosie shrugged and poured cups of tea.

Asin repeated the question, with a nod significant of its complexity. Then he cried out.

"What were we? We were warriors! The women too!"

Zosie smiled. Asin went on. "We hunted and trapped for the fur companies. However, we understood they were trapping us the way we trapped the animals. They were using their goods as bait. They used their rum too. Rum cut with pepper, water, tobacco. One swig would make you crazy. We knew most of those traders were against us at heart, but of course we needed more territory to hunt animals. We fought our way out here from the east and encountered the powerful Bwaanag. We fought them hard and never would have beat them except the whites attacked them, too, from all sides. They had good warriors, those Bwaanag. We made a mistake not to band up with them to extinct the whiteman. Now like us they are forced to hide their eagle feathers. And it is no use to make any war parties against the Bwaanag for land, because the now the whiteman has our land and their land too."

Asin slapped at the cloth of his frayed pants. He looked down at his knees. "You know what we call these trousers? Giboodiyegwaazonag. Sewed up the butt. Sewed up the butt! We had freedom once!"

"Freedom of the butt?" asked Booch, and the children rolled with laughter, the women too. Asin and Bagakaapi laughed, repeated Booch's question, then variations of the question, and laughed again until they laughed all afternoon and it was time to go.

Sugar Point

Asin showed his ten fingers twice and told the boys only that long ago their people, the Anishinaabe, had turned back a horde of soldiers. Nobody intended for the fight to get so out of hand. But it had! It had! Asin twisted his fingers together. How he wished he were a Pillager!

Those warriors of the Pillager hid among the trees when the soldiers marched in to take their leaders prisoner.

Nobody intended it to start, they say. A boy stacked their rifles. One went off!

Asin made an explosive sound and raised an imaginary Winchester. He shot and shot, pulling back at each recoil.

One soldier down, another two. A wound to their head man and then another. He is killed. We don't attack them—just kill the ones who stick their heads up. We could have killed them all! Asin's face worked. We could have killed them all. But because we showed our power, they brought us food and blankets. They made us more promises. We were not punished because they knew we were in the right. On that day, the only day we shot the whiteman, we won. We should do it again.

Warriors

The boys did every chore after that as warriors. If they were sent out to net fish, they worked as army scouts. The fish were the enemy. They netted and killed as many of the warrior fish as they could. The boys carried on their victory celebration far out on the lake, then came to shore and gutted all their enemies and put them up on drying racks.

They snared rabbits, hunted muskrats, gophers, any animal, with ferocity of purpose. They pestered Asin and Bagakaapi about warrior ways, learned that a war party was signaled to assemble by a deadly symbolic red glove. They carefully sewed one of tanned deerhide, dyed it with mashed cranberries, stuffed it with sage and stolen pipe tobacco. They kept it hidden in their blankets. Each brother kept the red glove until he wanted to declare a war party, then it was sent to the others in turn and the time was set for them to convene. Sometimes they attacked fallen timber, reduced their enemy to stove lengths and kindling. Surprised, their mothers praised them. They gloated proudly. Peace, the only one of the children who had ever actually waged war on a whiteman, thought her brothers were ridiculous.

Peace Roy

She had authority, though she was shy. Her eyes quickened with understanding, and she moved with deliberation. She was meticulous. Her smile flashed ironically, her eyebrows lifted in amusement, but she rarely spoke. She was guarded because, like her father, she was emotional. She was precious because she was the only daughter. Her hands liked to stack, smooth, fold, and slice. Her brain counted everything her hands touched. Again, like her father. Her grandmother and namesake had given Peace a few of her freckles. A shade darker than her skin, they dusted her nose and cheekbones. They were truly visible only when she was angry or upset. When she laughed, as she often did at the absurd things her brothers did, her laugh was soft and breathy. Her brothers felt like they were being tickled with a brushy wand of grass.

Peace was the first Indian to work in a bank. She cleaned the floors.

Later, much later, she became a teller and then a manager. Indian people came to the bank just to look at her and see for themselves that one of them knew how to handle the whiteman's white metal, zhooniyaa. It was this stuff, this material of no possible use, that their parents and grandparents had been forced to admit into their lives. Americans seemed glad to perish over pitiless coin and paper, which now controlled their destinies but seemed, still, in its essence a symptom of madness.

Peace began cleaning floors at the bank when she was twelve. She got out the mop and bucket after everyone but her father had left the building. When she was done, Augustus taught her how the bank worked. When they went home, she was supposed to pass this knowledge on to her brothers. But although money and all that it represented in the world—territory, goods, religion—was the basis of war, they had no feel for it. They could write and calculate, those boys, but it was war stories that they fed upon.

Despairing of their attention, Augustus read *The Iliad* out loud every night after they were finished with mathematics. That the translation was ornate and repetitive was so much the better—the boys sank into the drama and made their father read it many times. It became the only book that mattered. They chased one another around the house brandishing long sticks for spears; as either Hector or Achilles, they destroyed and mutilated each other over and over. Shawano, the youngest, got the hardest treatment. They pretended to burn him on a funeral pyre or even chopped him up with their hands to feed him, raw, to the dogs. He had to lie still and not laugh while he was gorged upon by vultures. Although Augustus had been careful to teach them the realities of carnage—even to the point of telling them about their own family tragedy—the boys gloried in Asin's narratives, and in the glamour of the Trojan War, and they lamented that these conflicts were long finished. So it was with tremendous excitement that they learned, through reading their father's newspaper, that a fresh, new war was being waged in France, against Germany. Real bloodshed, real valor, real killing, real heroes. Moreover, they were thrilled to find out they could join this war. There was also a recruitment notice in the newspaper.

One day, without telling anybody but Asin, whose clouded eyes lit with supreme joy, the brothers went to the town hall, where the recruiter sat waiting in a corner, at a wooden desk. They signed up to become soldiers and were delighted to learn they would be given uniforms with round hats and pants with legs that puffed at the hips. They would also have tailored jackets, but only after they'd passed certain tests. Once they were trained, they would also be given new guns. After that they would be transported to the war.

"How soon can we get there?" asked Charlie.

ZOSIE AND MARY could not bear for their sons to leave. Both mothers threatened to cut their hair and slash their arms, but in the end they seethingly wept and packed lunches for their boys to eat on the train. They said good-bye in the road and

told Augustus that their hearts were too full to go along. Actually their hearts were full of rage. Once their sons were out of sight, they took the path to old Asin's house, where they drew their razor-keen fish knives and assured him that

if any harm came to their sons they would carve him up and dry him on a rack.

They had said nothing to Augustus the night before, however, for it was obvious that he was stricken when he threw the Oxford World's Classics edition of *The Iliad* into the outdoor cooking fire. He intended to stamp the ashes of the book into the earth, but to his surprise Zosie plucked the book out before the cover was more than scorched.

"I listen too," she said. "We're just like those people, never knowing what the gods or the government is going to do to us next."

AUGUSTUS AND PEACE walked into the train station with the young men. The freckles appeared on Peace's face, dark points of distress. It appeared to Augustus that he had spent his life in error. He had protected his sons from the train station by educating them as best he could—still they chose the same inscrutably violent path as Scranton Roy. The boys already had their tickets, so Augustus and Peace sat down with them on a long bench. Silently, they waited. The floor of the train station was polished terrazzo based on a singular slate-green crushed marble. The walls were paneled with ancient oak worked into scenes of progress. There were wagons, valiant pioneers, oxen, plows, trains of course. As the Americans advanced counterclockwise around the great waiting room, Indians melted away before them, looking sadly back over their shoulders or turning their backs entirely as if to walk straight into the wood, which was carved into a simulacra of its origin as an unrepeatable forest. It is unnerving, thought Peace, to see my ancestors swallowed into the exact same wood that was stolen from us. She tried to divert her thoughts from her brothers living and breathing beside her not in fear but silent exaltation. She had to try and think of something other than the monstrous crack she sensed was developing in her father's heart.

The train arrived. The boys left. Peace and her father watched the train disappear and then watched the place into which it had disappeared. Augustus gestured with his open hands and dropped them to his sides. Time, he thought, has most certainly been a ruthless judge. He turned with Peace and they walked through the town, greeting and shaking hands with people, gravely, as they passed. People had found out that the three brothers had joined the war. When they got onto the road and began their walk home, Augustus felt the feeling that was too large for him. He dropped to his knees as though a great hand had struck him down. Peace helped him up and when he rose he held her arm, tottered forward, suddenly feeble. They began to sob. The road became a path and the surrounding half-grown scrub, rotting stumps, vigorous new popple and maple kindly closed over the two of them. They walked slowly, weeping. From time to time they held each other, or braced themselves against small saplings. Each had a handkerchief. They wiped their faces. But still their fears flowed down their throats and wet their collars and dampened their shoulders.

"Please take care of them," Augustus prayed to ruthless Time.

"Bring them home, please protect them," prayed Peace to the spirits of her ancestors who had peered over their shoulders at her in the train station.

4

The Blitzkuchen

1918. END OF THE WAR. So many spirits out, wandering, including Augustus Roy, who looked down into the sum of money he was counting one day and saw a shade of blue he had never seen before roar open marvelously into another life. And so he died. His wives mourned him, but not as deeply as Peace, who really did cut most of her hair off and slash her arms before she felt any better. It helped when she found out all three of her brothers would return.

When the youngest, Shawano, came home from the land of the frog people he was half spirit, too. But that is often how warriors are when they return. Booch had served in the supply lines and come down with the Spanish flu. Charlie had spent the war in an army kitchen. Only young Shawano got decorated with a medal and a ribbon. Only he felt crazy. Ogichidaa, they called him, now, warrior. Ogichidaa had lost his best buddy, who in the warrior's blood relation was more like another self and could not be adequately revenged.

"Sa tayaa," he cried suddenly. They were sitting at Asin's

house. "I tried. I made his mark on every German soldier that I killed!"

"Was it a deep mark?" hissed wrinkled-up Asin. The old man had become so violent in his thoughts he seemed unhinged to most people. For instance his opinion was that the Americans should make all the Germans into slaves. Ship the whole country full of people here and teach them to be humble. That's how they would have done it in the old days. He couldn't get over how he had heard our government gave back most of their territory. Bagakaabi, whose name implied that he saw clearly, was more reasonable and said everyone was humbled by this war. He had heard it took a wheelbarrow full of money there to buy a loaf of bread.

"They get to eat bread?" cried Asin. "While the Indians must eat bannock?"

Bagakaabi shrugged. He loved bannock.

Ogichidaa was a slim and handsome boy when he left, but his look when he returned was reeling and deathly. His face was puffed up and his eyes were like pits in his face. He had a thousand-year-old stare.

"My buddy, he took a stomach wound," said Ogichidaa. "I had to stuff his guts in loops back into his body, and all the time he kept his eyes on me. He couldn't look down. When I had them back in, his teeth were clicking together and he got these words out. 'You sure you got them back in the right order?' I said I did my best. 'Because I don't wanna be pissing out my ears,' he said. His voice was real serious and I answered, 'I checked. Your pisser made it. No damage, brother.' He seemed real happy with that statement. The ground shook around us. Close one landed. I lost my hold and they all poured out of him again."

Ogichidaa was exhausted and his brothers urged him to sleep. Before he slept, though, he gave Asin a funny look and repeated himself, "Old man, I did what you told me. I sent as many as I could with him after that to be his slaves in the land of spirits. It didn't help."

Old Asin looked at him long, deeply, watching.

"Maybe," said Asin at last, "you need to do the next thing."

"Which is what?"

Asin hunched into his gnarled body and then tapped a leathery bone finger on the pocket of his shirt just over his heart.

"Replace your war brother with a slave brother."

The Capture

Ogichidaa mulled the idea over, took it in slowly. It was not a bad idea, he thought, a way to kill the rage that soured his heart and woke him in the night. A way to erase the picture of those guts. But he could hardly go all the way back to Germany, and the idea of taking revenge on a German immigrant who'd been turned into an American citizen seemed an act of weakness. In the morning he asked Asin where he could get a German.

"Oh, they're all over the place here," Asin said, sweeping at the air side to side with the flat of his hand. "All over here like frogs. Perhaps they are called Omakakii-wininiwag because they popped out of nowhere," said the old man. "In the beginning, there were whole village tribes of them, we heard, shipped over here to tear up our land. They took it over. They killed it. Most of the land is now half dead. Plowed up.

"There is also a whole bunch of defeated soldiers who shipped over because of that money problem. They want to stay in this country now. They moved up north and work the timber, two on a cross-end saw. Ditch timber roads. Learn only swear English. Walk along piercing the earth with pointed iron bars, tamping in seedlings with their shoes."

Asin smiled. "You could take one of those."

On a moonless night then, Ogichidaa sneaked into the lumber camp.

The men were summoned the next morning to his house.

"I stole the German at night," said Ogichidaa. "I crept right up to the barracks without detection."

"Without detection." Asin gloated. He was excited by this ancient working out of the old-way vengeance, pleased young Ogichidaa had taken his advice. He nodded at Booch and Charlie, grinning. The old man's teeth were little black stubs—all except for a gold one. That tooth glinted with a mad sheen.

"I dropped the gunnysack over the Kraut's head when he came outside to take a leak," Ogichidaa went on. "Bound his arms behind him. Got him right back through the fence and from there, here."

Silent, they looked at the figure sitting bound in the corner. Barefooted. Wearing a baggy shirt and pants of no particular color. The man, his head covered by the gunnysack, was quiet with a peculiar stillness that was not exactly fear. Nor was it sleep. He was awake in there. The men could feel him straining to see through the loose weave over his face.

Bagakaabi got spooked by the way the German composed himself, and suddenly he couldn't stand it. He went over and ripped away the gunnysack hood. Maybe some expected to see a crazy eagle—how they stare mad into the air from their warrior hearts of ice—but they did not see an eagle. Instead, blinking out at them from spike tufts of hair, a chubby boy face, round-cheeked, warm and sparkling brown eyes. The men all reared back at the unexpected sense of warmth and goodwill from the German's pleasant smile.

"Hay'," they exclaimed. Expectation was something more impressive than a porcupine man! His hands were chubby, his skin almost as brown as theirs. Around his circle eyes his stubby hair poked out like a quill headdress. His smell—that came off him too now—was a raw and fearful odor like the ripe armpit stink of porcupine. He moved slowly like that creature, his deep eyes shining with tears. He took them all in one by one and then cast his eyes down, bashful, as though he would rather be under the porch or inside his own burrow.

"Babagiwayaaneshkimod atoon imaa oshtigwaaning jigaajigaadenig omaji-dengway," said Asin hurriedly.

"No," said Ogichidaa, hurt and surprised at the meekness of his catch.

"Grüsse!" The prisoner bowed. His voice was pie sweet and calm as toast. *"Was ist los? Wo sind wir?"*

Nobody answered his words even though he next made known by signs—an imaginary scoop to his mouth, a washing motion on his rounded stomach—his meaning.

"Haben Sie Hunger?" he asked hopefully. *"Ich bin ein sehr guter Küchenchef."*

"Gego bizindawaaken waa-miigaanik!" Asin's attitude was close to panic. The kitchen window shed frail light on an old wooden table, the stove in the background of the room, the prisoner blinking.

Shawano picked up the gunnysack uncertainly, ready to lower it back onto the porcupine man's head.

"Nishi! Aapijinazh! Nishwanaaji' a'aw maji-ayi'aawish ji-minonawe'angwaa gigichi-Anishinaabeminaanig gaa-onjigiyang." Asin now spoke in a low and threatful tone. At his command, everyone fell silent. The old man was behaving in a way that did not befit an elder. Yet the younger men had been taught to respect him.

"Why should we do that?" asked Bagakaabi. "He can't be a slave if he is dead."

"It is the only way to satisfy the ghosts," Asin answered.

"Haben Sie alle Hunger, bitte? Wenn Sie Hunger haben, werde ich für Sie einen Kuchen machen. Versuches mal, bitte." The prisoner offered to bake for them. He spoke modestly and pleasantly, though he seemed now in his wary poise to have understood the gravity of Asin's behavior. He seemed, in fact, to know that his life might hang in the balance. Although Asin had spoken his cruel command in the old

language, his ferocity was easily translated. With a burst of enormous energy, the German tried to make good on his offer using peppy eating motions and rubbing his middle with more vigor.

Booch, always eager for food, finally nodded. He knew the word *Kuchen*. "Why not let him prepare his offering? We will test it and see if his sweet cake can save his life."

He said this jokingly, but Asin's gleam and nod told that he took the baking test seriously and looked forward to the German's failure.

The First Metaphorical Cake

The porcupine man drew a tiny diagram or symbol for each thing he needed. Little oval eggs, flour in a flour sack, nuts of a rumpled shape, strawberries, sugar, and so on. By now, even though the men had no money extra, they had to go along and so they all dug deep into their hands, socks, the liners of their shoes, and the rabbit fur inside their moccasins. They sent Charlie to the traders' for these things and he returned with his lower lip stuck out and fire in his eyes. He thought this whole plan was wrong and yet he was curious about the cooking aspect, the baking, which would in time become his passion.

The stove. The German seemed to have a problem with that. He fiddled and poked it and tried to figure out its quirks. The brothers picked red berries for him, though, ode'iminan, heart berries, from the clearings. So fresh and dewy and tender. The sweet red melted in your mouth. Charlie gave the prisoner a makak full of the berries, and was surprised by the emotional way he accepted the offering. The German lifted the container in his hand, inhaled the fragrance of the berries. His dark round eyes filled again and this time spilled over with tears.

"*Erdbeeren,*" he said, softly, with mistaken and genuine sincerity. "I fuck you thank you. Klaus. Klaus." He pointed at his chest.

The men stood there in the kitchen before the stove and looked down at their feet, at the floor. Charlie reached out and shook the German's hand, or paw, which he saw with a certain fear had fur on the back.

"Gaawiin niminwendanziinan omaamiishininjiin misawaago minode'ed," he said.

Charlie's kindness was tinder to Asin's low fury. Asin flared up, insisted that Klaus had just delivered a most clever insult veiled in ignorance, fixed Klaus with a crushing stare. Asin bared his black teeth and gave a startling snarl. Booch and Shawano stepped out the door. Klaus waved Asin and Bagakaapi away from the smoking woodstove abruptly and began his efforts. Charlie stayed.

From inside the kitchen, then, where Charlie had stubbornly placed himself, the others got as much of the story as they could, or maybe as anyone was ever supposed to know.

First, the prisoner pounded almonds to a fine paste between two lake rocks. Took the eggs, just the yellows in a little tin cup. He found a long piece of wire and cleverly twisted it into a beater of some sort. He began to work things over, the ingredients. Using the bottom of an iron skillet, he ground pods and beans and spices into the nuts. He added the sugar spoon by spoon.

When he was finished, he took the thick syrupy batter and poured it as though it contained, as it did for him, the very secret of life. He made dark pools in four round baking pans. He bore them ceremonially toward the oven, which yawned, perfectly stoked beneath with coals glowing in the firebox. Bending with maternal care, he placed the pans within the dark aperture. Closed with a toweled hand the oven door. For a moment Charlie, mesmerized by the calm music of the German's efforts, regarded the words set in raised letters upon the oven door. The Range Eternal. He backed slowly away from the stove and sat down. He offered Klaus a cigarette.

Outside, the other men sat smoking and thinking. They paid respect to the east. In their thoughts, in their prayers. They respected the manito who guards the south. They regarded with humble pleading the direction of our dead, the west. North was last.

After a while Charlie went out and sat near them. He sat alone. He sat in a fugue trying to remember each action, each movement, each ingredient. Mary, Zosie, and Peace came into the yard.

"Don't go in there," said Asin.

"We are waiting for something to bake," said Charlie.

The women did not wait, of course. What woman sits waiting for something to cook in the oven? Disgusted by the male mystery and presence in the kitchen, they bustled ostentatiously. Made a lot of noise coming, going. Banged washing boards and banged pots. Banged anything they could, including the chairs of the men, who jumped. Once, but just once, Zosie banged the stove. At which point Klaus leaped high and with a scream that unnerved them all, grabbed her by the apron strings and swung her toward the door. She flew as though shot from a bow. Limber as a wildcat, Klaus poised, light on the balls of his feet, and motioned one and all to hush.

Everyone crept near, caught in the grip of what the prisoner sensed happening behind the blue enamel of the oven door.

Light in the window turned subtly more golden. Klaus set pans of water in the oven like offerings. A breeze sprang up. Leaves tapped. Nobody said a thing. Asin's eyes grew bloody. His hands trembled and the air whistled between his teeth. They sat until finally Klaus rose. Like a groom pacing tranced toward his bride, he approached the oven. At the lip of the door he closed his eyes, cocked his head to the side, listening. Slowly and pliantly Klaus bent, hands wrapped in two thick rags. With firm control he pulled the handle on the door until it opened. Then, just for a moment, the waiting men lost their bearings as the scent of the toasted nuts, honey, vanilla, wild strawberries, sugar, and subtly united oils and flours escaped the oven box. The scent trembled in the air.

More than delicious. Impossible. Perhaps an Anishinaabe vision-word comes close. Perhaps there is no way to describe what they all experienced as Klaus tenderly drew the pan along the rack until it rested secure between his thick, furry, rag-protected paws.

More sitting while the brown cake cooled. Eyes of Asin sunk, blackening. He made everyone uneasy now with his scratchy breathing. As the creation cooled, the watchers remembered things they'd rather have forgotten: how Asin had suffered from time to time with nameless rages, pointless furies. These angers had assumed a name and form in the person of the porcupine man, Klaus.

Air poured in the screen door, cooling and healing. Dusk air. Pure air. Moved onto Ogichidaa. Bagakaabi took his fan, the wing of an eagle, and with immense care he swept the air toward Asin, whose face now worked in and out like a poisoned mud puppy's, and who said, fixing everyone with eyes crossed:

"Let us deliver him to the west. We are Ojibwe men—the name has a warrior's meaning. We roast our enemies until they pucker! Once, we were feared. Our men brought sorrow. Mii-go iw keyaa gaa-izhi-mashkawigaabawiyang mewinzha. What have we here? Chimookomaanag? Women? Our enemy is in our hands and we do not make him suffer to console the spirits of our brothers. We let him cook our food. It is this . . . Klaus"—he scoured the name off his tongue—"whom we should burn to death!"

In the space of quiet that followed on his words, then, everyone realized the old man's bitter ghost was talking.

"Oooo, ishte, niiji," Bagakaabi said, drawing the wing of the eagle through the air in a soothing and powerful fashion. "Good thing you've told us this." Looking at the rest of the men meaningfully, he said to Asin in a calm tone, "We respect your wishes, brother. However"—and now Bagakaabi held the wing of the eagle stiffly pointed toward the cake—

"would we be honorable men if we did not keep our promise even to our enemy? Before we roast the prisoner, let us try his offering."

Klaus, whose intuition of their meaning just barely kept him horrified, then took from his pile of ingredients a tiny packet of white sweet powder and, with a gravity equal to Bagakaabi's, coated the top of the cake with the magical dust. Klaus then motioned to everyone to cup their hands, Asin, too. He cut the cake into pieces and served them out. When they all had the cake in hand, they looked at it hungrily and waited for the elder to taste. Asin, however, was too slow and Charlie the future baker too tempted. Charlie bit into the cake. Before he chewed, he gave a startled and extraordinary squeak and his eyes went wide. It was too much for the rest. They all bit. Or nibbled. Tasted. And everyone emitted some particular and undiluted sound of pleasure. There was not a one who'd ever tasted the taste of this cake. It was a quiet and complex sensation on the tongue.

We are people of simple food straight from the earth, thought Charlie. Food from the lakes and from the woods. Manoomin. Wiiyaas. Baloney. A little maple sugar now and then. Suddenly this: a powerful sweetness that opened the ear to sound. Embrace of roasted nut-meats. A tickling sensation of grief. A berry tartness. Joy. Klaus had inserted jam in thin-spread layers. And pockets of spices that have no origin in our language. So, too, there was no explanation for what happened next.

Together, they sat, swallowed the last crumbs, pressed up the powdery sweetness with their fingers. When they had licked every grain into themselves, they sat numb with pleasant feelings. Then, over the group, there stole a tender poignance. Some saw in the lowering light the shadows of loved ones, whose spirits they had fed, as well as they could, food of the dead. Curious, they doubled back. Others heard the sharp violin string played in the woods, the song of the white-throated sparrow. Mary and Zosie spoke lovingly to each other. Booch saw the face of his favorite nurse in the hospital. Bagakaapi tasted on his face the hot sun. He breathed warm thick berry odor and the low heat of the dancing white grass that grows along the road to the other world.

They breathed together. They thought like one person. They had for a long unbending moment the same heartbeat, the same blood in their veins, the same taste in their mouth. How, when they were all one being, kill the German? How, in sharing this sweet intensity of life, deny its substance in even their enemies?

When there is an end of things, and when we fade into the random scheme and design, thought Charlie, I believe we will taste the same taste, mercy on the tongue. And we will laugh the way we are laughing now in surprise and at the same sweet joke, even old Asin.

Ogichidaa rose with his hand out, then embraced Klaus like a brother. It was the first of many times he would imagine his pain was solved.

More and more often, as the years went on, Ogichidaa saw his pain vanish at the golden bottom of a whiskey bottle. He would find his way down to the Cities and there, late in age, still gripped by shell shock before there was PTSD, he would father a son. He would name the baby Klaus, remembering the taste of mercy. His brother Charlie would bake a cake for the occasion and feed it also to his own little grandson, Frank, then watch the toddler's face for a reaction. Booch would eat two pieces of the cake to make sure, but then he would place his fork on the plate with a sigh.

Ogichidaa would shake his head.

Hope would sink down Charlie's face and add a few molecules to his baker's belly.

It was a good cake, there was even poignance and sweet intensity. But always, always, there was something missing.

Part Two

Niizh

The pattern glitters with cruelty. The blue beads are colored with fish blood, the reds with powdered heart. The beads collect in borders of mercy. The yellows are dyed with the ocher of silence. There is no telling which twin will fall asleep first, allowing the other's colors to dominate, for how long. The design grows, the overlay deepens. The beaders have no other order at the heart of their existence. Do you know that the beads are sewn onto the fabric of the earth with endless strands of human muscle, human sinew, human hair? We are as crucial to this making as other animals. No more and no less important than the deer.

5

Wiindigoo Dog

Almost Soup

So now you have got the story of how the Roys and Shawanos got tangled up. A dog's-eye view of history, includes certain details that human people might rather skip. I have no illusions. Humans are capable of anything. For instance, you could end up puppy soup if you're born a pure white dog on the reservation, unless you're one who is extra clever, like me. I survived into my old age through dog magic. That's right. You see me, you see the result of dog wit. Dog skill. Medicine ways I learned from my elders, and want to pass on now to my relatives. You. So listen up, animoshag. You're only going to get this knowledge from the real dog's mouth once.

There is a little of a coyote in me, just a touch here in my paws, bigger than a dog's paws. My jaw, too, strong to snap rabbit bones. Prairie-dog bones as well. That's right. Prairie. I don't mind saying to you that I'm not a full-blood Ojibwe reservation dog. I'm part Dakota, born out in Bwaanakiing, transported here just after I opened my eyes. I still remember all that sky, all that pure space, all that blowing dirt of land where I got my name, which has since become legendary.

Here's how it happened.

I was underneath the house one hot slow day panting in the dirt. I was a young thing. Just chubby, too, and like I said white all over. That worried my mother. Every morning she scratched dirt on me, threw me in the mud, rolled me in garbage to disguise my purity. Her words to me were this—My son, you won't survive if you lick your paws. Don't be respectable. Us Indian dogs have got to look as unappetizing as we can! Slink a little, won't you? Stick your ears out. Grow ticks. Fleas. Bite your fur here and there. Strive for a disreputable appearance, my boy. Above all, don't be clean!

Like I say, born pure white you usually don't stand a chance, but me, I took my mama's advice. After all, I was the son of a blend of dogs stretching back to the beginning of time on this continent. We sprang up here. We had no need to cross on any land bridge. We know who we are. Us, we are descended of Original Dog.

I think about her lots, and also about my ancestor, from way way back, the dog named Sorrow who drank a human's milk. I think about her because I know it was the first dog's mercy and the hand-me-down wit of the second that saved my life that time they were boiling the sacred soup.

I hear these words—Get under the house, Melvin, fetch that white puppy now. Bam! My mama throws me in the farthest house corner and sits down on me. I cover up with her but once Melvin is in play distance I can't help it. I've got that curious streak of all the Indian dogs. I peek right around my mother's tail and whoops, he's got me. He drags me out and gives me to a grandma, who stuffs me in a gunnysack and slings me down beside the fire.

I fight the bag there for a while but it's warm and cozy and I go to sleep. I don't think much of it. Just another human habit I'll get used to, this stuffing dogs in sacks. Then I hear them talking.

Sharpen up the knife. Grandma's voice.

That's a nice fat white puppy. Someone else.

He'll make a good soup for the ceremony, but do you think enough to go around? Should we kill another one?

Then, right above me, they start arguing about whether or not I'll feed twenty. Me, just a little chunk of a guy, Gawiin! No! I bark. No! No! I'm not enough for even five of your big strong warrior sons. Not me. What am I saying? I'm not enough for any of you! Anybody! No! I'm sour meat. I don't want to be eaten! In response, I get this tap from a grandma shoe, just a tap, but all us dogs know feet language. Be quiet or you'll get a solid one, it means. I shut up. Once I stop barking all I can do is think and I think fast. I think furious. I think desperate puppy thoughts until I know what I'll do the moment they let me out.

A puppy has just one weapon, and there really is no word for it but puppyness. Stuck in that bag, I muster all my puppyness. I call my tail wags and love licks up from deep way back, from the dogs going back to dogs unto the beginning of our association with these predictable and exasperating beings. I hear them stroking the steel on steel. I hear them tapping the boiling water pot. I hear them deciding I'll be enough, just barely. Then daylight. The bag loosens and a grandma draws me forth and just quick, because I'm smart, desperate, and connected with my ancestors, I look for the nearest girl child in the bunch around me. I spot her. I pick her out.

She's a visitor, sitting right there with a cousin, playing, not noting me at all. I give a friendly little whine, a yap, and then, as the grandma hauls me toward the table, a sharp loud bark of fear. That starts out of me. I can't help it. But good thing, because the girl hears it and responds.

"Grandma," she says, "what you going to do with the puppy?"

"Gabaashimgabaashimgabaashim," mumbles Grandma, the way they do when trying to hide their actions.

"What?" That gets her little-girl curiosity up, a trait us dogs and children share in equal parts, what makes us love each other so.

"Don't you know, you dummy," shouts that boy cousin in boy knowledge, "Grandma's going to boil it up, make it into soup!"

"Aaay," my girl says, shy and laughing. "Grandma wouldn't do that." And she holds out her hands for me. Which is when I use my age-old Original Dog puppyness. I throw puppy love right at her in loopy yo-yos, puppy drool, joy, and big-pawed puppy clabber, ear perks, eye contact, most of all the potent weapon of all puppies, the head cock and puppy grin.

"Gimme him, gimme!"

"Noooo," says Grandma, holding me tight and pursing

her lips in that terrible way of grandmas, when they cannot be swayed. But she's dealing with her own descendant in its purest form—pure girl. Puppy-loving girl.

"*Grandmagrandmagrandma!*" she shrieks.

"Eeeeh!"

"GIMMEDAPUPPY!GIMMEDAPUPPY!"

Now it's time for me to wiggle, all over, to give the high-quotient adorability wiggle all puppies know. This is life or death. I do it double time, triple time, full of puppy determination, desperate to live.

"Ooooh," says another grandma, sharp-eyed, "quick, trow him in the pot!"

"Noooo," says yet another, "she wants that puppy bad, her."

"Give her that little dog," says a grandpa now, his grandpa heart swelling up. "She wants that dog. So give her that little dog."

That is how it goes pretty much all the time, now, these-adays. In fact I've heard even grandmas have softened their hearts for us and we Indian dogs are safe as anywhere on earth, which isn't saying much.

My girl's doll-playing fingers are brushing my fur. She's jumping for me. Spinning like a sweet maple seed. Straining up toward her grandma, who at this point can't hold on to me without looking almost supernaturally mean. And so it is, I feel those ancient dog-cooking fingers give me up before her disappointed voice does.

"Here."

And just like that I'm in the most heavenly of places. Soft, strong girl arms. I'm carried off to be petted and played with, fed scraps, dragged around in a baby carriage made of an old shoe box, dressed in the clothing of tiny brothers and sisters. Yes. I'll do anything. Anything. This is when my naming happens. As we go off I hear the grandpa calling from behind us in amusement, asking the name of the puppy. Me. And my girl calls back, without hesitation, the name I will bear from then on into my age, the name that has given so many of our breedless breed hope, the name that will live on in dogness down through the generations. You've heard it. You know it. Almost Soup.

Up to the Present

Having introduced myself, I believe that it is now appropriate to bring time and place back into the picture. Time the judge has released Augustus Roy to easy death. Zosie and Mary have also trudged with their brothers toward the spirit world. Peace lived quietly, like her name. She was a shy old woman married to a shy old man named Waabizii, The Swan. She bore one son and feared to have more children lest they turn out twins. Her mothers always made her enough trouble. But her son grew up safely in her care and then fathered twin girls at too young an age. Their mother disappeared and Peace raised them. Until Zosie and Mary died, Peace was caught between two sets of yoked wills. At least she had the numbers, the bank, her father's desk, and a changing array of colors that flowed beneath her pencil. Her father had taught her to love the sun on her shoulders and wind in every mood. She named the twins for these pleasures, Giizis and Noodin, hoping for happy spirits. But they turned out shrewd, sour, and sometimes ferocious, like their great-grandmothers. In the end, Peace just gave up.

There was a wave of giving up, and then there was a new government policy designed in the kindest way to make things worse. It was called Relocation and helped Indians move to cities all over the country. Helped them move away from family. Helped them move away from their land. Helped them move away from their dogs. But don't worry. We followed them down to Gakaabikaang, Minneapolis, Place of the Falls. I will return. But I am sorry to say that I must leave you now.

I must give the story over to one particular descendant, Klaus, a man whom we dogs have failed to shape. Though named for the German, an industrious man, Klaus was a sorry piece of work from the get-go. Even though his elderly father counseled him with care, Klaus was lazy, needy, skilled from a tender age at self-deceptions, according to impartial dogs. He was always pining for something over the horizon. I am only letting him speak because he is, unfortunately, and to his own shame, best qualified to tell what happened next. Though sky and space divided the oldest daughter of Blue Prairie Woman from her sisters, her tribe, her family, and the descendants of her rescuers who walk this earth, it only took one drunken idiot to reconnect.

6

The Antelope Woman

Klaus

I used to make the circuit as a trader at the western pow-wows, though I am an urban Indian myself, a sanitation engineer. I'd hit Arlee, Montana. Elmo, Missoula, swing over Rocky Boy's, and then head on down to the Crow Fair. I liked it out there in all that dry space; at first that is, and up until last year. It was restful, a comfort to let my brain wander across the mystery where sky meets earth.

Now, that line disturbs me with its lie.

Earth and sky touch everywhere and nowhere, like sex between two strangers. There is no definition and no union for sure. If you chase that line, it will retreat from you at the same pace you set. Heart pounding, air burning in your chest, you'll pursue. Only humans see that line as an actual place. But like love, you'll never get there. You'll never catch it. You'll never know.

Open space plays such tricks on the brain. There and

gone. I suppose it is no surprise that it was on the plains that I met my wife, my sweetheart rose, Niinimoshenh, kissing cousin, lover girl, the only one I'll ever call my own. I take no credit for what happened, nor blame, nor do I care what people presently think of me—avoiding my eyes, trying not to step in the tracks I've left.

I only want to be with her, or be dead.

You wouldn't think a man as ordinary as myself could win a woman who turns the heads of others in the streets. Yet there are circumstances and daughters that do prevail and certain ways. And, too, maybe I have some talents.

I WAS SITTING underneath my striped awning there in Elmo—selling carved turtles. You never know what will be the ticket or the score. Sometimes they're buying baby moccasins, little beaded ones the size of your big toe. Or the fad is cheap neckerchiefs, bolo slides, jingles. I can sell out before noon if I misjudge my stock, while someone else set up next to me who took on a truckload is raking the money in with both hands. At those times, all I can do is watch. But that day, I had the turtles. And those people were crazy for turtles. One lady bought three—a jade, a malachite, a turquoise. One went for seven—small. Another bought the turtle ring. It was the women who bought turtles—the women who bought anything.

I had traded for macaw feathers also, and I got a good price on those. I had a case of beautiful old Navajo pawn which I got blessed, because the people who wore that turquoise seem to haunt the jewelry, so I believe. A piece gets sold on a sad drunk for gas money, or it's outright stolen—what I mean is that it comes into the hands of traders in bad ways and should be watched close. I have a rare piece I never did sell, an old cast-silver bracelet with a glacier-green turquoise the shape of a wing. I have to tell you, I can hold that piece only a moment, for when I polish the pattern on some days it seems to start in my hands with a secret life, a secret pain.

I am just putting that old piece away when they pass. Four women eating snow cones as they stroll the powwow grounds.

Who wouldn't notice them? They float above everyone else on springy, tireless legs. It's hard to tell what tribe people are anymore, we're so mixed—I've got a buffalo soldier in my own blood, I'm sure, and on the other side I am all Ojibwe. Though my name is Klaus, a story in itself. These ladies are definitely not from anywhere that I can place. Their dance clothes are simple—tanned hide dresses, bone jewelry, white doeskin down the front and two white doeskin panels behind. Classy, elegant, they set a new standard of simplicity. They make everyone else around them look gaudy or bold, a little foolish in their attempts to catch the eyes of the judges.

I watch these women put their mouths on ice. They tip their faces down and delicately kiss the frozen grains. As they sip the sweet lime and blueberry juice, their black, melting eyes never leave the crowd, and still they move along. Effortless. Easy. The lack of trying is what makes them lovely. We all try too hard. Striving wears down our edges, dulls the best of us.

I take those women in like air. I breathe hard. My heart is squeezing shut. Something about them is like the bracelets of old turquoise. In spite of the secrets of those stones, there are times that I cannot stop touching and stroking their light. In that same way, I must be near those women and know more. I cannot let them alone. I look at my setup—van, tent, awning, beads, chairs, scarves, jewelry, folding tables, a cashbox, the turtles—and I sit as calmly as I can at my trading booth among these things. I wait. But when they don't notice me, I decide I must act bold. I trade store-minding with my neighbor, a family from Saskatoon, and then I follow the women.

Tiptoeing just behind at first, then trotting faster, I almost lose them, but I am afraid to get too close and be noticed. They finish circling the arbor, enter during the middle of an intertribal song, and dance out into the circle together. I lean against a pole to watch. Some dancers, you see them sweating, hear their feet pound the sawdust or grass or the Astroturf or gym floor, what have you. Some dancers swelter and their faces darken with the effort. Others, you never understand how they are moving, where it comes from. They're at one with their effort. Those, you lose your heart to and that's what happens to me—I sink down on a bench to watch these women and where usually I begin to drift off in my thoughts, this morning I am made of smoothest wood. They dance together in a line, murmuring in swift, low voices, smiling carefully as they are too proud to give away their beauty. They are light steppers with a gravity of sure grace.

Their hair is fixed in different ways. The oldest daughter pulls hers back in a simple braid. The next one ties hers in a fancy woven French knot. The hair of the youngest is fastened into a smooth tail with a round shell hairpiece. Their mother—for I can tell she is their mother mainly by the way she moves with a sense of all their consolidated grace—her hair hangs long and free.

Dark as heaven, with roan highlights and arroyos of brown, waves deep as currents, a river of scented nightfall. In her right hand she holds a fan of the feathers of a red-tailed hawk. Those birds follow the antelope to fall on field mice and gophers the moving herd stirs up. Suddenly, as she raises the fan high, my throat chills. I hear in the distance and in my own mind and heart the high keer of the stooping hawk—a lonely sound, coldhearted, intimate.

BACK AT MY TABLES, later, I place every item enticingly just so. I get provisions of iced tea and soda and I sit down to wait. To scout. Attract, too, if I can manage, but there isn't much I can do about my looks. I'm broad from sitting in my foldable chair, and too cheerful to be considered dangerously handsome. My hair, I'm proud of that—it's curly and dark and I wear it in a tail or braid. But my hands are thick and clumsy. Their only exercise is taking in and counting money. My eyes are too lonesome, my lips too eager to stretch and smile, my heart too hot to please.

No matter. The women come walking across the trampled grass and again they never notice me, anyway. They go by the other booths and ponder some tapes and point at beaded belt buckles and Harley T-shirts. They order soft drinks, eat Indian tacos, get huckleberry muffins at a lunch stand. They come by again to stand and watch the Indian gambling, the stick games. They disappear and suddenly appear. The mother is examining her daughter's foot. Is she hurt? No, it's just a piece of chewing gum that's stuck. All day I follow them with my eyes. All day I have no success, but I do decide which one I want.

Some might go for the sprig, the sprout, the lovely offshoot, the younger and flashier, the darker-hooded eyes. Me, I'm strong enough, or so I think, to go for the source: the mother. She is all of them rolled up in one person, I figure. She is the undiluted vision of their separate loveliness. The mother is the one I will try for. As I am falling into sleep I imagine holding her, the delicate power. My eyes shut, but that night I am troubled in my dreams.

I'm running, running, and still must run—I'm jolted awake, breathing hard. The camp is dark. All I've got is easily packed and I think maybe I should take the omen. Break camp right this minute. Leave. Go home. Back to the city, Gakaabikaang, where everything is set out clear in lines and neatly labeled, where you can hide from the great sky, forget. I consider it and then I hear the sounds of one lonely passionate stick game song still rising, an old man's voice pouring out merciless irony, no catch in his throat.

I walk to the edge of the rising moon.

I stand listening to the song until I feel better and am ready to settle myself and rest. Making my way through the sleeping camp, I see the four women walking again—straight past me, very quickly and softly now, laughing. They move like a wave, dressed in pale folds of calico. Their pace quickens, quickens some more. I break into a jog and then

I find that I am running after them, at a normal speed at first, and then straining, putting my heart into the chase, my whole body pedaling forward, although they do not seem to have broken into a run themselves. Their supple gait takes them to the edge of the camp, all brush and sage, weeds and grazed-down pastures, and from there to alive hills. A plan forms in my mind. I'll find their camping place and mark it! Go by with coffees in the morning, take them off guard. But they pass the margin of the camp, the last tent. I pass too. We keep looping into the moonlighted spaces, faster, faster, but it's no use. They outdistance me. They pass into the darkness, into the night.

My heart is squeezing, racing, crowded with longing, and I need help. It must be near the hour that will gray to dawn. Summer nights in high country are so short that the birds hardly stop singing. Still, at dawn the air goes light and fresh. Now the old man whose high, cracked voice was joyfully gathering in money at the gambling tent finally stops. I know him, Jimmy Badger, or know *of* him anyway as an old medicine person spoken about with hushed respect. I can tell his side has won, because the others are folding their chairs with clangs and leaving with soft grumbles. Jimmy is leaning on a grandson. The boy supports him as he walks along. Jimmy's body is twisted with arthritis and age. He's panting for breath. They pause, I come up to him, shake hands, and tell him I need advice.

He motions to his tired grandson to go to bed. I take the medicine man's arm and lead him over tough ground to where my van is parked. I pull out a lawn chair, set it up, lower him into it. Reaching into my stores, I find an old-time twist of tobacco, and I give it to him. Then I add some hanks of cut beads and about eight feet of licorice for his grandkids. A blanket, too, I give him that. I take out another blanket and settle it around his back, and I pour a thermos cap of coffee, still warm. He drinks, looking at me with shrewd care. He's a small man with waiting intrigue in his eyes, and his gambler's hands are gnarled to clever shapes. He has a poker-playing mouth, a head of handsome iron-gray hair that stretches down behind. He wears a beat-up bead-trimmed fedora with a silver headband and a brand-new denim jacket he's probably won in the blackjack tents.

I'm an Ojibwe, I say to him, so I don't know about the plains much. I am more a woods Indian, a city-bred guy. I tell Jimmy Badger that I've got a hunting lottery permit and I'm going to get me an antelope. I need some antelope medicine, I say. Their habits confuse me. I need advice on how to catch them. He listens with close attention, then smiles a little crack-toothed pleasant smile.

"You're talking the old days," he says. "There's some who still hunt the antelope, but of course the antelope don't jump fences. They're easy to catch now. Just follow until they reach a fence. They don't jump over high, see, they only know how to jump wide."

"They'll get the better of me then," I say. "I'm going to hunt them in an open spot."

"Oh, then," he says. "Then, that's different."

At that point, he gets out his pipe, lets me light it, and for a long time after that he sits and smokes.

"See here." He slowly untwists his crushed body. "The antelope are a curious kind of people. They'll come to check anything that they don't understand. You flick a piece of cloth into the air where you're hiding, a flag. But only every once in a while, not regular. They're curious, they'll stop, they'll notice. Pretty soon they'll investigate."

NEXT DAY, THEN, I set up my booth just exactly the same as the day before, except I keep out a piece of sweetheart calico, white with little pink roses. When the women come near, circling the stands again, I flicker the cloth out. Just once. It catches the eye of the youngest and she glances back at me. They pass by. They pass by again. I think I've failed. I wave the cloth. The oldest daughter, she turns. She looks at me once over her shoulder for the longest time. I flick the cloth. Her eyes are deep and watchful. Then she leans back, laughing to her mother, and she tugs on her sleeve.

In a flash, they're with me.

They browse my store. I'm invisible at first, but not for long. Once I get near enough I begin to fence them with my trader's talk—it's a thing I'm good at, the chatter that encourages a customer's interest. My goods are all top-quality. My stories have stories. My beadwork is made by relatives and friends whose tales branch off in an ever more complicated set of barriers. I talk to each of the women, make pleasant comments, set up a series of fences and gates. They're very modest and polite women, shy, stiff maybe. The girls talk just a little and the mother not at all. When they don't get a joke they lower their lashes and glance at one another with a secret understanding. When they do laugh they cover their lovely calm mouths with their hands. Their eyes light with wonder when I give them each a few tubes of glittering cut beads, some horn buttons, a round-dance tape.

They try to melt away. I keep talking. I ask them if they've eaten, tell them I've got food, and show them my stash of baked beans, corn, fry bread, molasses cookies. I make them up heaped plates and I play a little music on the car radio. I keep on talking and smiling and telling my jokes until the girls yawn once. I catch them yawning, and so I open my tent, pitched right near, so nice and inviting. I tell them they are welcome to lie down on the soft heap of blankets and sleeping bags. Their dark eyes flare, they look toward their mother, wary, but I fend off their worry and wave them inside, smiling the trader's smile.

Alone together. Me and her. Their mother listens to me nice and gentle. I let my look linger just a little, closer, until I find her eyes. And when our eyes do meet, we stare, we stare, we cannot stop looking. Hers are so black, full of steep light and wary. Mine are brown, searching, anxious, I am sure. But we hold on and I can only say that for what happens next I have no adequate excuse.

We get into the van while she is still caught by the talk, the look. I think she is confused by the way I want her, which is like nobody else. I know this deep down. I want her in a new way, a way she's never been told about, a way that wasn't the way of the girls' father. Sure, maybe desperate. Maybe even wrong, but she doesn't know how to resist. Like I say, I get her in my van. I start to play a soft music she acts like she never heard before. She smiles a little, nervous, and although she doesn't speak, uses no words anyway, I understand her looks and gestures. I put back the seat so it's pleasant to recline and watch the dusky sky and then I pamper her.

"You're tired, sleep," I say, giving her a cup of hot tea. "Everything's all right with your daughters. They'll be fine."

She sips the tea and looks at me with dreaming apprehension, as though I'm a new thing on earth. Her eyes soften, her lips part. Suddenly, she leans back and falls hard asleep. Something that I forgot to tell—us Anishinaabeg have a few teas we brew for very special occasions. This is one. A sleep tea, a love tea. Oh yes, there's more. There's more that Jimmy Badger told me.

"YOU'RE SHIFTY LIKE all those woods Indians," Jimmy Badger said. "I see that trader's deception. If you're thinking about those women, don't do it," he said. "Long time ago, we had a girl who lived summers with the antelope. In the winters she brought her human daughters to the camp. They could not keep up with her people as they moved on in the bitter cold, the frozen pastures, scattering across the plains. Don't go near them if that is what you're thinking of doing. We had a man who did once. Followed them, wrestled one down. Made love to her and was never the same. Few men can handle their love ways. Besides, they're ours. We need them and we take care of these women. Descendants."

"They might be," I said. "Or they might just be different."

"Oh, different," agreed Jimmy. "For sure."

He looked at me keenly, grabbed me with his eyes, kept talking. His voice was remote and commanding.

"Our old women say they appear and disappear. Some men follow the antelope and lose their minds."

I was stubborn. "Or maybe they're just a family that's a little unusual, or wild."

"Leave," said Jimmy Badger. "Leave now."

BUT IN MY HEART, I knew I was already caught. The best hunter allows his prey to lead, not the other way around. That hunter doesn't force himself to figure and track, just lets himself be drawn to the meeting. That's what I did.

Suddenly I have her there with me in the van, and she is fast asleep. I sit and watch her for a long time. I am witched. Her eyelashes are so long that, when the light from the outdoor flood lamps comes on, they cast faint shadows on her cheeks. Her breath has the scent of grass and her hair of sage. I want to kiss her forever. My heart's a panic on my sleeve.

I drive off. Yes, I do. I drive off with this woman while her daughters are breathing softly, there in the tent, unconscious. I leave the girls all of my trade beads and fancy pawn and jewelry, everything that was stored in the corner of the tent. The miles go by, the roads empty. The Missions rear before us, throwing fire off sheer rock faces. Then we're past those mountains into more open country. My sweetheart wakes up, confused and tired. I tell her jokes and stories, list for her strange or valuable things people throw away. Trading is my second nature, but garbage supports me. I'm in the waste haul business. Me and my partner, or boss I suppose you'd have to say, contract with the city even, big companies, little ones. I drive through the day. I drive through the night. Only when I am so exhausted that I'm seeing double, do I finally stop.

Bismarck, North Dakota, center of the universe. Locus of space and time for me and my Niinimoshenh. We turn in, take a room at the motel's end. I lead her in first and I close the door behind and then she turns to me—suddenly, she knows she is caught. *Where are my girls?* her eyes say, their fear sharp as bone. *I want my girls!* When she lunges, I'm ready, but she's so fast I cannot keep her from running at the window, falling back. She twists, strong and lithe, for the door, but I block and try to ease her down. She pounds at me with hard fists and launches straight into the bathroom, pulling down the mirror, breaking a tooth on the tub's edge.

What can I do? I have those yards of sweetheart calico. I go back. I tear them carefully and with great gentleness I bandage her cuts. I don't know what else to do—I tie her up. I pull one strip gently through her bleeding mouth. Lastly, I tie our wrists together and then, beside her, in an agony of feeling, I sleep.

I ADORE HER. I'll do anything for her. Anything except let her go. Once I get her to my city, things are better anyway. She seems to forget her daughters, their wanting eyes, the grand space, the air. And besides, I tell her that we'll send for her daughters by airplane. They can come and live with me and go to school right here.

She nods, but there is something hopeless in her look. She dials and dials long-distance numbers, there are phone calls all over the whole state of Montana, all of these 406 numbers are on the bill. She never speaks, though sometimes I imagine I hear her whispering. I try the numbers, but every time I dial one that she's used I get that Indian answering machine—that out-of-service signal. Does she even understand the phone? And anyway, one night she smiles into my face—we're just the same height. I look deep and full into her eyes. She loves me the way I love her, I can tell. I want to hold her and hold her—for good, for bad. After that, our nights are something I can't address in the day, as though we're wearing other bodies, other people's flaming skins, as though we're from another time and place. Our love is a hurting delicacy, an old killer whiskey, a curse, and too beautiful for words.

I get so I don't want to leave her to go to work. In the morning she sits at her spot before the television, watching in still fascination, jumping a little at the car chases, sympathizing with the love scenes. I catch her looking into the mirror I've hung in the living room and she is mimicking the faces of the women on the soap operas, their love looks, their pouting expressions. Their clothes. She opens my wallet, takes all my money. I'd give her anything. "Here," I say, "take my checkbook too." But she just throws it on the floor. She leaves off her old skins and buys new, tight and covered with bold designs. She laughs harder, but her laugh is silent, shaking her like a tree in a storm. She drinks wine. In a pair of black jeans in a bar she is approached by men whenever I turn aside, so I don't turn aside. I stick to her, cleave to her, won't let her go, and in the nights sometimes I still tie her to me with sweetheart calico.

Weeping, weeping, she cries the whole day away. Sometimes I find her in the corner, drunk, marvelous in frothy negligees, laughing and lip-synching love scenes to the mirror again. I think I'll find a mind doctor, things cannot go on. She's crazy. But if they lock her up, they'll have to lock me up too. She'll rage at me for days with her eyes, bare her teeth, stamp on my feet with her heeled boot if I get near enough to try for a kiss. Then just as suddenly, she'll change. She'll turn herself into the most loving companion. We'll sit at night watching television, touching our knees together while I check the next day's schedule. Her eyes speak. Her long complicated looks tell me stories—of the old days, of her people. The antelope are the only creatures swift enough to catch the distance, her sweeping looks say. *We live there. We live there in the place where sky meets earth.*

I bring her sweet grass, tie it into her hair, and then we make love and we don't stop until we're sleeping on each other's pillows.

Winter, and the daylight dwindles. She starts to eat and eat and puffs up before my eyes, devouring potato chips and drinking wine until I swear at her, say she's ugly, tell her to get a job, to lose weight, to be the person she was when I first met her. That tooth is still cracked off, and when she smiles her smile is jagged with hatred but her eyes are still dark with love, with amusement. She lifts into the air in a dance and spins, spins away so I can't catch her and once again she is in my arms and we're moving, moving together. She's so fantastically plump I can't bear it all, her breasts round and pointed, and that night I drown, I go down in the depth of her. I'm lost as I never was and next morning, next afternoon, she drags me back into bed. I can't stop although I'm exhausted. She keeps on and she keeps on. Day after day. Until I know she is trying to kill me.

That night, while she's asleep, I sneak into the kitchen. I call Jimmy Badger, get his phone through a series of other people.

"It's her or me," I say.

"Well, finally."

"What should I do?"

"Bring her back to us, you fool."

HIS WORDS BURN behind my eyes. If you see one you are lost forever. They appear and disappear like shadows on the plains, say the old women. Some men follow them and do not return. Even if you do return, you will never be right in the head. Her daughters are pouting mad. They don't have much patience, Jimmy says. He keeps talking, talking. They never did, that family. Our luck is changing. Our houses caved in with the winter's snow and our work is going for grabs. Nobody's stopping at the gas pump. Bring her back to us! says Jimmy. There's misery in the air. The fish are mushy inside—some disease. Her girls are mad at us.

Bring her back, you fool!

I'm just a city boy, I answer him, slow, stark, confused. I don't know what you people do, out there, living on the plains where there are no trees, no woods, no place to hide except the distances. You can see too much.

You fool, bring her back to us!

But how can I? Her lying next to me in deepest night, breathing quiet in love, in trust. Her hand in mine, her wicked hoof.

7

The Ojibwe Week

Giziibiigisaginigegiizhigad

Klaus lives in exactly half of the bottom floor of a duplex built in 1882 and owned now by his friend and boss, Richard Whiteheart Beads. His main room, once the dining room, has a ripply old window topped with a stained-glass panel. Even though the old window looks directly into the window of a brand-new lower-income housing unit built smack on the property line of Andrew Jackson Street, just off Franklin Avenue, an occasional shaft of morning radiance sometimes stirs in the prisms of glass. When that happens, bands of colored light quiver on the mottled walls. The bed, a savage hummocky mattress laid on top of an even older mattress and box spring, which in turn is nailed right into the floor, sometimes catches the rainbows in its gnarled sheets and blankets. The rainbows move across the bodies of late sleepers. Klaus watches the sheaf of colors waver slowly through Sweetheart Calico's hair and then across her brow. The rainbow slides down her face, a shimmering veil. When she wakes up, she doesn't move except to sag with disappointment. Her eyes are dead and sad, killing the rainbow, catching at his heart.

"We are codependent," he says. "I read it in a newspaper. We are at risk, you and I. Well, you most of all since you are the one tied to the bed."

A curtain tieback solidly bolted into the wall acts as a hitching post for Sweetheart Calico. A web of makeshift restraints binds her ankles, wrists. There is even a cord around her waist, tied with complicating rosebud cloth and functioning as a sort of sleep sash. Klaus unties her and she rises, naked, yawning. She rubs one ankle with the side of her other foot and stretches her arms. She floats to the bathroom breathing an old tune—she doesn't talk to Klaus but she's always whispering songs much older and more powerful than any powwow or sweat-lodge or even sun-dance song he has ever heard. There are flushing sounds, water, a shower. She loves the shower and will stand beneath it smiling for half an hour and would stay longer if Rozin, wife of Richard Whiteheart Beads and monitor of hot water use in this joint living space, didn't stop her.

"I need some hot water for cleaning," she calls from the kitchen.

Giziibiigisaginigegiizhigad is the Ojibwe word for Saturday and means Floor-Washing Day. Which tells you that nobody cared what day of the week it was until the Ojibwe had floors and also that the Ojibwe wash their floors.

We are a clean people, Klaus thinks. He knocks on the bathroom door. He opens the door and when he sees the bathroom window is wide open, in spite of the child safety locks he installed, he knows already without looking behind the shower curtain that she is gone.

SHE LOPES CRAZILY through the park. In the lighted shelter where the street people drag her, she curls up on a flea-funky pallet in the corner and sleeps, not forgetting all of her daughters but taking them back into her body and holding them.

At night, she remembers running beside her mother.

Her daughters dance out of black mist in the shimmering caves of their hair.

When she touches their faces, they pour all their love through their eyes at her. Klaus? She never dreams about or remembers him. He is just the one she was tied to, who brought her here. But no matter how fast or how far she walks, she can't get out of the city. The lights and cars tangle her. Streets open onto streets and the highways roar hungry as swollen rivers, bearing in their rush dangerous bright junk.

Anama'e-giizhigad

Although the Ojibwe never had a special day to pray until mission and boarding schools taught how you could slack off the rest of the week, Sunday now has its name. Praying Day. Klaus spent all day yesterday walking the streets and bushwhacking down by the river and questioning. Questioning people.

"Have you seen a naked beautiful Indian woman hanging around here by any chance? Or she could be wearing just a towel?"

"Bug off, asshole."

"She's mine," he says. "Don't touch her."

Yesterday he walked a hundred miles. At least he felt like it. Today on Praying Day he takes out the pipe that his father was given when he returned home safe from the war. Which war? The war so shadowed out by other wars that nobody can recall that it was the war to end all wars.

"I'll be asking the Creator for some assistance," he says to his father's pipe as he fits it together and loads it while singing the song that goes along with loading a pipe. He takes from a slip of cardboard a feather that he uses to fan the ember at the heart of a small wad of sage. The smoke rises and rolls. He has disabled the smoke alarm.

"I pledge this feather to my woman if she returns of her own free will," he says between smokes.

The feather is very special, a thunderbird feather, a long pure white one that dropped one day out of an empty sky.

Dropped into my life just like you, my darling sweetgrass love, Klaus thinks. The smoke curls comfortingly around his head. But he smokes his pipe too much. He smokes it again and again until his head aches and his chest is clogged. He will cough for the rest of the day and every time he does, a puff of smoke will pop from his lungs.

Dizzy, he breaks down his pipe, cleans it, puts it carefully away. He rolls the pipestone bowl in his father's sock—all besides the pipe and his deaf ear that he's got left from his father. Oh, wait, you could count his libido, too, and of course his lips.

"You got a lip line a girl would kill for," one of his not-girlfriends had said to him. Those plush yet sculpted lips were his father's lips. Many times they fit around this pipe stem, this okij. His father was so old that he died of old age when Klaus was six. Klaus is the same age as his nephews. He rolls the okij in a red-and-white buckshot bag. He puts the feather back into its fold of cardboard and stashes these sacred items on the highest shelf of the kitchen cabinet. He feels much better. He goes out to talk with Richard Whiteheart Beads. He coughs. A puff of smoke.

"Is that a smoke signal?" Richard says. "What are you trying to tell me?"

"Have you seen a beautiful naked antelope lady running through the streets?"

"She escaped? That's good. You can't just keep a woman tied up in your room, you know. Rozin suspects. If she finds out she will get in touch with the women's crisis hotline. I don't want the police coming around here. Plus, my girls. What kind of example for them?"

Klaus coughs.

"Oh, I got that signal," Richard says. "Me fucked."

"That is the problem," says Klaus. "She has enslaved me with her antelope ways."

"You one sad mess," says Richard. "Let her go."

But Klaus goes out into the night and continues to search the streets, which are quiet and peaceful and empty.

Nitam-anokii-giizhigad

First Work Day. Proving that the names of the days of the weeks are the products of colonized minds. What a name for

Monday. Rubbing it in that work starts early in the a.m. with Richard. Today they are ripping carpet out of the soon-to-be-renovated Prairiewood Rivertree Mall, next to the Foreststream Manor.

Carpets in malls are always the color of filth. In the petrochemical nap, the hue of every excrescence from shit to trodden vomit comes up beneath their prying and ripping tools. They carry roll after roll of the stuff out to Richard's fancy yellow pickup truck. Even Klaus thinks it's way too visible. They are being paid to dispose of a toxic substance and Richard has the perfect place.

Land checkerboard was one gift of the Dawes or General Allotment Act of 1887, which dispossessed most tribes of 90 percent of the lands that were left after the red-hot smoke of treaty signing. The checkerboard. Their reservation which they drive to from the city is a checkerboard—white squares and red squares—denoting ownership. One red square still belongs to Klaus's foremothers. On one white square a big farm stands, owned by a retired Norwegian couple who winter and sometimes spring and even fall in Florida. Richard has rented their farm under an assumed name. He and Klaus are now quickly filling the barn with carpet, which it costs a pretty penny to dispose of in an EPA-designated hazardous waste site or costs nothing to put in a barn.

"They won't mind. They won't even notice. They never go out to the barn."

"You sure?" asks Klaus. They are unloading the ripped-up carpet. Roll after noxious roll. The rolls are bound with the same cord hanging from the hitching post next to Klaus's bed. Klaus and Richard have made meticulously neat stacks, filling the cow stalls level. They make certain that each layer is completely solid, filling in the gaps between rows with carpet scraps.

We are doing a bad thing, but we are doing it well, thinks Klaus.

For his part, Richard uses compartmentalization. Its extreme usefulness cannot be overestimated. Richard first learned the term from Rozin. He was surprised to find there was a word for what he had been doing all his life to accommodate the knockings of his conscience.

Oh, on some level, he says to his conscience, this is certainly wrong. Not only will the old couple be stuck with hazardous waste, but the checkerboard is reservation board and thus eligible for tribal homeland status if the casino ever turns a profit. Theoretically there might be enough money in the tribal coffers one day to repurchase this old farm and add it to our reservation, only first there'd be the problem of disposing of as many tons of carpet as this barn will hold and it looks like it will hold an awful lot.

Wall. Wall. Wall. Compartment.

Meanwhile, Richard is pocketing the money paid him to dispose properly of righteous poisons. Some of it he pays to Klaus.

Even if this land is owned by Norwegians it is still Mother Earth, thinks Klaus. Nookomis, please forgive me. I am sorry. I am doing a very tidy job of hurting you, if that makes a difference.

He takes his gloves off and says that a beer would go down good.

"Let's hit a bar on the way home," says Richard. And so they do. And they are finished with Nitam-anokii-giizhigad.

Niizho-giizhigad

Life is hell without her tied up next to me. Klaus mourns all night and dismally wakes on the Second Work Day. All the Ojibwe do is work, you would think. Work and pray. Again the carpet ripping and the fetid stink of concrete underneath and again the thoughtful cerebral work of stacking in the barn. Stacking for the future so that the two can climb onto the neat floor from the stairs up to the hay loft and not die in a carpet quake or be swallowed up in a carpet-roll crevasse.

Sweetheart Calico, Sweetheart Calico. My bitter black heart is bursting open. Klaus whispers. His chest still hurts from the intense smoke-praying that he did two days before and from all the secular inhalations in the days since. There's been no clue, no lead, no sighting of the woman he kidnapped—no, she went willingly, didn't she? It's all unclear. He put her in his van at the powwow and took her home and got addicted to her.

Your sex love should be declared a controlled substance, he thinks now. I am experiencing severe withdrawal. He shakes as he stuffs ripped carpet down the seams of the next layer of carpet-roll floor. He should not have done what he did—stolen her, gotten her drunk, loved her, tied her up—except she asked for it with her eyes. Which Rozin will tell him should get him ten to twenty years in Stillwater Pen.

"She never asked for nothing with her eyes," Rozin says

when she finds Klaus's sweetheart. "Except for you to let her go. You compartmentalized. You put your mental processes in only part of your brain so you can enjoy yourself. Even when what you are doing is a crime."

"But she tied me up, too," says Klaus. "She tied me up with those same ropes."

"And left you there, right?"

"Yes," says Klaus in a small voice. "I thought something else was going to happen that time. She came back though of her own free will because she loves me."

"She came back because she has nowhere to go. Where did you steal her from? Where are her people?"

"They are nomadic."

"Tell that to the cops."

"They roam Montana," says Klaus.

Out where the barns are filled with hay, not carpet. Though he knows from the great rolls of carpet glued to floors of acres of malls all through Montana that this is not true and conceivably there could even be two Indians like Klaus and Richard out there disposing of old carpet on their own federal trust land where special rules apply.

Aabitoose

Halfway. How is it that with all the lovely names for the months and seasons and the lyrical possibilities in the origins of this most extraordinary language, the best that can be done for Wednesday is Halfway? To where? To the end of the week or to the day of fun where we wash the floors?

Aabitoose is the day Rozin goes to the bakery owned by her cousin Frank. Frank's Bakery is a real old-fashioned independent little bakery, the kind there used to be, with hand-fried doughnuts—not donuts—the *ugh* makes them Indian and heavier. Rozin goes to the bakery after the girls are on the school bus because she needs a coffee lift before her second job. There is also Frank himself, who has a crush on her. She likes pretending that his flirting annoys her. She doesn't go because she wants to find Klaus's girlfriend, whom he claims in his emotional confusion is part antelope.

But there she is. A dog lolls next to her.

Sweetheart Calico and the dog sit side by side on the curb just outside the shop. A car could run right over Sweetheart's tiny feet. The dog is gray, shaggy like a coyote, nondescript. Sweetheart Calico is arrestingly graceful, but tired. She is a tired, tired woman with tangled hair, wearing a huge pair of jeans belonging to Klaus Shawano and a shirt that could belong to anybody in the neighborhood as it is a huge black T-shirt with an airbrushed buffalo stampeding away from an American flag and through a hoop of fire with an eagle screaming at its shoulder and beneath its hooves a wolf and bear also running for their lives and all of the animals surrounded by thunder and lightning. You see that exact T-shirt on every other person on the street but this particular shirt belongs to Klaus.

"Oh, my god, here you are. Are you all right, Sweetheart? Come and have a coffee with me."

Sweetheart Calico holds in her hands a fragrant, tawny, puffed-up ball of dough with a saddle of lemon jelly that quivers when she takes a bite. She throws half the pastry to the dog, who snarfs it midair. Mouth full, she follows Rozin into the bakery, where there are three tables with two chairs each that fit right against the window. Frank has a Bunn coffeemaker—just decent old-fashioned coffee—one dollar a large mug or free with any pastry.

"You forgot your free coffee," he says now to Sweetheart Calico, though he gave her the pastry too, free, and now gives her another lemon jelly doughnut.

The dog waits alertly right outside the door. Frank just smiles because all of the awkward semisuggestive lines about fresh buns and long johns were used up long ago.

"Niinimoshenh, what can I get for you?"

Rozin ignores that word, which means my sweetheart but which can also mean my sex-eligible cousin. She examines the trays of chocolate éclairs, bismarcks, long johns—no scones or lumpy vegan muffins here. She buys a cup of coffee and selects a loaf of bread. Gives it to Frank for slicing.

Rozin and Sweetheart Calico sit down with their coffees at a table in the sun of the window.

"Are you okay? Why did you run away from Klaus? Is that sucker mean to you?"

Sweetheart Calico shrugs and licks sugar off her fingers. *I am lost*, her look says. *I don't know how I got here.*

She stuffs the jelly doughnut into her mouth. The lemon filling has real lemon in it, sweet and tart.

"Do you want to come home with me? I'll let you in downstairs. You can sleep. You can shower."

Sweetheart Calico glances out the window at the dog. Rozin makes a face. "Okay, it can come too."

Frank gathers the slices from the machine into a tight

transparent bag. He walks over to them holding out the loaf, so fresh it sags between his hands like an accordion.

HALFWAY DAY. If it was All the Way Day things might have gone much differently. But Rozin walks only halfway into the downstairs apartment. The dog, too, halfway in. Then it settles on the floor. Sweetheart Calico is halfway glad to get home. The twins, Cally and Deanna, do halfway well at school and make it halfway home on the bus before they sort of fight and pretty much make up. Rozin halfway wants to quit work as usual, but does not. Klaus and Richard work hard and the barn is half full when they leave. Unfortunately at home the meat is halfway cooked because the electricity has gone out and the Crock-Pot is cold when Rozin touches it. Then Richard and Klaus are cleaning up at the same time and you can hear them yell halfway through their showers when cold water hits their skin.

Later, Rozin is halfway through with sex with Richard when she thinks of Frank Shawano holding that bread. She tries to push the picture out of her mind. What's he doing there? Get away, she thinks. No, come back. The picture makes her feel something she was not feeling before. Richard has been drinking with Klaus after work but he is not even halfway drunk. He has been patient about the half-cooked meat. He has listened with half an ear to all that his daughters did during the day. So Rozin should be at least halfway into sex, which is all it really takes to satisfy Richard. But she isn't. She is somewhere else. Afterward she turns away with the sudden feeling that her heart is breaking right in . . . not half—it is shattering into golden infinitesimal fragments. It is bursting and the grains are flying fast against the sun. Her heart is pollen glinting on the wind. No, it is flour, blowing toward Frank's bakeshop wanting to get mixed into his batter with eggs and sugar and formed into a doughnut. Her heart travels faster and faster, toward Frank's deep fryer, and all the time Richard thinks she is asleep, weighted firmly in the dark that will become tomorrow.

Niiwo-giizhigad

Pragmatical disappointment! Day Four. And so many other choices for this poetic day—a day near the freedom of the weekend yet not the frantic rush to get your work done . . . not yet. A day that can almost stand by itself because of its special ceremonial associations in Ojibwe teachings. Anyway, Day Four. Day of new existence. Day of anything can happen. Day of pollen on the wind. Day of Klaus half awake tied to his own bed by Sweetheart Calico and thinking in his dream that he hears the clatter of her hooves as she runs wildly back and forth bashing into unfamiliar walls and believing that when he opens his eyes his sheets will be covered with her inky cloven erotic tracks.

Actually, she is outside playing with her new dog. Well, not new. That dog is definitely secondhand, thinks Klaus. It is a used dog, a thrift dog, at best a dollar-store animal with its skinny legs, big belly, scraggy pedigreeless fur. And its head is way big for the rest of it, like a sample fur toy that was never mass-produced but thrown into a discount bin.

I don't like that dog, he thinks. There is definitely something sinister about its big, round, grinning head.

And it growled when he took the rope out last night.

Forget about locking me in the bathroom, its look said. I'll shit on the floor.

Then it growled worse and worse until he handed the rope to Sweetheart Calico.

AT LEAST DAY FOUR is about four, the number that the Ojibwe love best of all. Every good and sustaining thing comes in fours—seasons, directions, types of people, medicines, elements. There are four layers of the earth, four layers of the sky, four push-ups to a song, four honor beats, four pauses of the great megis on the way to Gakaabikaang and hereabouts. So why shouldn't today, which partakes of that exquisite number, be an extremely lucky day, thinks Klaus, eyes still shut, although I can feel the cords that bind my wrists and ankles tightly and I remember somewhere in the night that she wrapped her long tense legs around my body and used special antelope knots on me.

"Oh no," Klaus speaks but still doesn't open his eyes. He tries to move but can't. He whispers, "Sweetheart? Are you there?"

DAY FOUR BEGAN so well for Cally and Deanna. Instead of iron-fortified and vitamin-enriched sugarless multigrain cereal flakes, instead of the stinky-boy cackling bus, their mom brings them to the bakery for anything they want and drives them to school in her car. And says, glowing happily, "Girls, we should do this more often!"

Blood sugar peaking from the cracked glaze on the doughnuts and the éclair custard, both of them swear thrillingly that they will become A+ not B- students if this regimen is followed by their mother. Twinklingly, she laughs. They stand on the sidewalk in front of the bank of school entryway doors, waving until her car is down the street.

They look at each other and both say at once, "Is Mom okay?" Then they say in unison, "Get out of my head." They scream with laughter and walk to the doors doubled over. When the sugar wears off and smacks them to the harsh floor of the gym at 9:00 a.m. and they profess to be ill, both are sent to the school nurse, who takes their temperatures with fever strips and gives them each a plastic cup of high-fructose-enhanced orange juice. Jacked up for another few hours, they return to class and do a prodigious pile of pre-algebra equations, which they both love. An affinity for numbers! They were born on the fourth day of the fourth month, at 4:00 and 4:04. So no wonder they are not to be mistaken for ordinary twins at all. They are mystic twins, like the twins who created the world. Only those first twins inarguably messed it up and if Cally and Deanna had a chance they would make the world properly. In fact, they make the world up all of the time. It is their favorite thing to do when they get home from school.

Cally and Deana start to draw the world after school on Niiwo-giizhigad, but the dog brought home by Sweetheart Calico interrupts. It barks as it chases Sweetheart Calico around and around in the weedy yard. The antelope woman laughs silently as she leaps on high heels, evading its teeth and paws. The dog jumps and twists in the air looking like a big gray wind-tossed rag. It isn't a very good-looking dog. Couldn't be called any one particular breed of dog. Yet a sympathy for humans shines out of its eyes and the girls fall instantly in love, not knowing that this very dog is the fourth dog of the fourth litter of the forty-fourth daughter of the dog named Sorrow.

They join in running and playing tag with the dog and with the woman whose great-grandmother on her human side slit the throat of that ancestor dog and boiled its meat so that her daughter would have the strength to travel into the blue west, wearing the same blue beads that Sweetheart Calico hides now as she leaps away from the dog, laughing that wild and silent laugh. She screams noiselessly, even as poor Klaus, whom she has freed to go to work that morning, creeps into the apartment and showers off the greasy grit of random Minneapolis citizens whose shoes mashed every form of personal grunge into the mall carpeting and transferred that human scurf to Klaus, so that he's covered utterly with the invisible populace—including refugees from every tribal and oil war in the world. And it won't wash away. Twin Cities people have entered his very pores and he has breathed them in also, so that Klaus is now inhabited by the world's thousands. Dead and living. Brand-new and ancient. Bargain-hunting ghosts inhabit Klaus on Day Four of the week as Rozin too returns from her work and says, *What the hell is going on it this madhouse* but wearily smiles as her daughters are whirling and chasing and full of life and if Rozin half closes her eyes and watches them through the blur of eyelashes, she sees the inutterable grace of antelope children galloping midair.

Naano-giizhigad

Oh please, you wouldn't name this day sacred to the now Ojibwe workplace just . . . Day Five. There are so many other good names for this almost-there day when you wake and think, *Tomorrow I can sleep.* The morning will bring the rainbows on again like the week before and Klaus can watch them cross the elegant wild structure of her face. Tomorrow for Cally and Deanna there will be drawing and a dog to play with and no more teacher's dirty looks or locker-slamming-on-your-fingers boys who suck dead rats and pretend that Cally and Deanna are Chinese or Hmong or Mexican and sneer, *Go back where you came from.*

"That's just boys," says Rozin. "Go back where you came from! How can you say that to a Native person?"

"I'll fix 'em. I'll go right in there," says Richard.

But here it is Day Five and he and Klaus must pull up the last of the carpet.

"Go then," says Rozin.

The girls watch for a kiss between them but are disappointed. They have noticed that their mother likes to talk to Frank at the bakery and that their father's eyes follow Sweetheart Calico even though she is the girlfriend of Klaus.

And all of these grown-up doings make them sick, sick, sick. They'd rather make the world over in girl image. The world would be only girls and animals and no boys or disappointing grown-ups except perhaps their mother visits bringing favorite food once every two weeks and long hugs but I could last a month, says Cally.

"Nobody mean can live on our planet," says Deanna.

"And the dog will be our brother."

"We won't take husbands."

"Obviously."

WHY CAN'T THIS be the day of the otter, the kingfisher, the coot, the loon, the balsam tree, the moccasin flower, or the trout? The Ojibwe words for all of these lovely animals and plants are original and fluid words but in all probability some lackluster hard-assed missionary Jesuit like maybe Bishop Baraga the famous Snowshoe Priest put those names down in his Ojibwe dictionary in the hope of making the Ojibwe people into hard-assed lackluster people like him by forcing them to live every day of their lives working or praying or halfway to nowhere. Many days of the week in English go back to various ancient pagan gods (Thor's Day, Frigga's Day, Saturn's Day, etc.). Naano-giizhigad would be so much better as Nanabozhoo-giizhigad. As Nanabozhoo was a great teacher who taught lessons via foul hilarity and amoral idiocy, so the day could celebrate and commemorate the great lessons learned from fools like Klaus.

For he knows he is a major doof to work for Richard on

this scam, which becomes every day more deadly and strange as the carpet mounts in the barn and the checks get written out and Richard signs his name on government paperwork.

"That's *government* paperwork," Klaus notices.

Richard winks a movie-star wink, an old-time black-and-white-movie lip-hanging-cigarette wink. Thank god it's Naano-giizhigad and they can get the hell out of the barn before the ghost carpet swallows them.

"It's all over, my friend," says Richard. "Let us cash these obscenely fat checks and treat our wives to a fancy dinner."

"My lady don't sit still," says Klaus. "She likes to take long walks. We buy food on the way. We keep walking."

"C'mon, say it, Klaus. She likes to graze."

"Shut up," says Klaus.

"You should bring her back to where you got her. She's trouble. She's a goddamn ungulate."

"I know," says Klaus. "But I can't let go."

Neither of them remarks on Richard's use of a high school vocabulary word, which he has carefully saved up until this moment. He had also saved what he thinks is a Zen saying.

"You can hold more water in an open hand than in a closed fist," says Richard.

"That's ridiculous," says Klaus. "You can hold the neck of a bottle in your closed fist."

"I hadn't thought of that. You're not tying her up anymore. . . ."

"No, she's got a dog now and it bites."

"Well, okay."

"Now she's the one who ties me up."

"I don't think I'd like that," says Richard.

"It's pretty good though," says Klaus. "Except when she runs away and leaves me there."

They drive up to the divided house built twenty years after the murderous year when the starving Dakota were told that their dying children should eat grass and some lost patience with the settlement of their homeland by people who hated their guts and so killed some and were killed worse in return and their leaders hung and the rest driven out and the women and children hunted down and kept in a concentration camp which was the same Fort Snelling Scranton Roy started out from at the beginning of this book. The house now inhabited by the Whiteheart Beads and Roys and one antelope woman and a dog was built by another soldier who'd come home from the Civil War with a sickened heart that he could numb only by pounding nail after nail. Pain made the house solid. Klaus and Richard park the car on the beaten-down part of the yard that has become the driveway. Cally and Deanna, looking out of their window, watch them remove a case of beer each from the trunk.

"Let's leave them out of our world," they say in unison. "Jinx!"

They slap hands, spin hands, rap their hands up and down, and ruffle the air four times to seal in the luck of words spoken together. Rozin walks out the door and says to Richard, "Watch the girls. I have to go buy a loaf of bread." The descendant of Sorrow slides along the foundation to the alley dense with buckthorn and mulberry. The dog ambles close to and settles down by Sweetheart Calico, who stands very still in the leaves, believing she is invisible.

8

Why I Am No Longer Friends with Whiteheart Beads

Klaus

When people ask me why I am no longer friends with Whiteheart Beads, I hedge around and come up with a neutral type of explanation. I say something innocuous, to keep things going on the surface. I have to do that. The reason is I'm afraid. My fear is this—if I ever begin to tell the story it will all flood out of me. It will be gone, unfixed, into the mouths of others. I'm afraid the story might stop being mine. Which would be dangerous. I rely on the story, you see. I keep it inside me because without it I might forget or dismiss the reason I no longer trust him. And once I did that, there is no telling what could happen.

Richard Whiteheart Beads, I've thought so often, foe or friend? I decided on the first because he cost me everything

I had. I did manage to keep my life, but aside from that—my clothes, my savings, and even, yes, my wife, Sweetheart Calico. My Antelope Girl. Gone. Due to Whiteheart.

Now you'll say to yourself there is no human on this earth with power of that magnitude. None. You wouldn't believe it surely if you did meet him. He has a handsome, bland, forgettable face. Forgettable unless of course he has ripped out your heart. So me, I remember his face just fine.

SOME THINGS HAPPEN easy, and you feel like they were meant to be. And some things, oh god, they come so hard. The party we attended together, put on by the regional waste collection association, that was the easy part that led to the impossible.

I am standing before the salads and cheeses and deli meat with Richard Whiteheart Beads. We start loading our plates. While we are selecting food, he tells me about yet a newer truck he is thinking of buying—he's always thinking of what he can acquire. This truck, it is just another example of Whiteheart's imaginary surround. I know that. But I listen as though I believe in its pinstripes and refurbished engine, its Thirstbuster cup holders.

"Wish I could get an automatic sunroof, too," Whiteheart Beads is saying. "Then you could travel with the wind in your hair."

"What hair?"

I'm an Indian with a buzz cut now. I got it when she left the first time. I cut my hair for sorrow. She left again. More sorrow. And again. Yet shorter. Anyway, now that she's back my hair says to her, I hope, what I have reformed myself to believe. Plain living. Hard work. The simple life, unadorned, ridding the world of waste. "People You Can Count On." My new motto in garbage management. My belief.

"You should grow it out again. Long. Women love it."

Whiteheart Beads is referring to his own ponytail, a serious thick rope reaching halfway down his suit-jacket back. We, the two of us, present a very different image and I must admit that his is probably the more selling look in terms of women. And for sure, since from our association raffle he has won two Appreciation Top Prize all-expense-paid tickets to Maui, a fact revealed shortly after the soda pop stops flowing at this lunch, his ponytail might bring good luck.

We mill around. We eat more. Used to be us Indians had nothing to throw away—we used it all up to the last scrap. Now we have a lot of casino trash, of course, and used diapers, disposable and yet eternal, like the rest of the country. Keep this up and we'll all one day be a landfill of diapers, living as adults right on top of our own baby shit. Makes sense to me. Of course, our main business is that we deal with EPA staff. Richard aims to be the first Native-owned waste disposal company in the whole U.S. He's already proud of it. Proud of our imaginary management expertise and good old-fashioned ability to haul shit. Not to mention stabilize it. Let's not talk about carpet.

A cake is wheeled in and it is shaped like a collection vehicle with bright colors of thick frosting, the lard and sugar kind, heart-stopping artery paste.

"You want 'em?"

Whiteheart holds the tickets out casually in the lucky

presentation envelope. I take the envelope: pictures of windsurfing Barbies and Kens, a couple of sea turtles winging through the gloom. Native Hawaiians dressed in flowers, holding torches, paddling a huge wooden canoe.

"Right," I say, reluctant to hand the envelope back. I notice it's not transferable, his name is filled in the blanks.

Whiteheart waves his hands at me, fanning out his fingers.

"Keep 'em. Keep. My wedding present."

"Wedding?" My heart jumps.

"Or pretend wedding honeymoon only. It's up to you."

Whiteheart looks at me and shrugs, very modest, as though any gratitude will just embarrass him, as though it makes him very nervous, which I notice he has been all along, that day, through the cheese and crackers, fruit, cold meats, the cake. He's been looking over his shoulder, staring into corners, behaving in this distracted and jumpy fashion I know so well. Woman trouble.

"Whiteheart, Whiteheart my friend." I put my hand on his shoulder. "Who is she? You can tell me."

His smile snaps across his face like a banner pulled tight.

"Not a woman. Not a woman. You take those tickets, Klaus. You can borrow my ID. You have a good time—hey, I mean it."

Then, with surprisingly little fuss or bother, Whiteheart exits through a side door, disappears almost. Unlike him until the eleventh hour.

Next thing I know, my sweetheart and me are getting ready for the trip. Maui. Glorious. Tropical. Hotel on the beach. We decide to go immediately in case Whiteheart's mind changes or he comes along, a thing he is fond of doing on our dates. I was always the one who minded those lopsided occasions worse than Sweetheart. I think back on that now. I should have known from the beginning, but love blinded me the way it does. She probably would have rather been with Whiteheart even then! But no, no. Don't get ahead of the next event.

It all happens bang right out of the gates. These guys. Two guys at the airport looking us over in that special way I am familiar with from getting kicked out of the army. Big guys. In suits. Four words to cause concern. *Big guys in suits.* I'll never look at life the same.

We check in.

Apparently there is some sort of seating arrangement that goes with these tickets, and it involves my wife and I split up in separate seats. Not only that, but the middle row seats.

"Hey, this can't be right. We're together, on our honeymoon," I tell the check-in personnel—exotic-looking woman, nails to here.

She chews her lip and fiddles with the keyboard, scowls at what blips up on the screen, and then looks at us with a blank, closed expression. Lots of purple eye shadow.

"I can't do a thing about it." Her declaration is such that I don't even think to argue. She stamps our tickets, asks us if anyone had given us anything to carry on board the plane, waves us on.

"We'll switch once we're on the plane," I say to my lady love, reassuring her. "Someone will be glad to change places with a couple newlyweds."

I like your faith in human nature, her look tells me. I am proud of her pessimism, read it as an answer. And she is right about those guys. One of them sits next to each of us. I ask, politely, lying. "We're newlyweds. Our seats got screwed up. Would one of you fellows mind switching?"

Like asking a favor of a set of bowling balls. These guys are muscle-bound and thick of neck, ponytailed like White-heart. One with a gold ring in the chunky lobe of his ear. The seatmate I address is the color of a Hereford, too, red-dish and whitish. Dull eyes of a slab of meat. And you know what it's like in the middle seat of an airplane anyway, that stuffed-in-a-cat-carrier feeling, claustrophobic. I am directly behind my love and to take my mind off my panic, I watch with longing the only part of her that I can see—top of her head and dark hair ponytailed in something I've heard called a scrunchie, a purple satin cloth band thing that bobs and slides up and down as she nervously mimics the flight at-tendant's demonstration.

It concerns me, her sitting next to that guy.

Quite apart from the weirdness in the first place, she's that sort of taut-bodied, fine-boned woman who arouses instant lust. From the back, especially, one of her most at-tractive angles. She has a sloping deer-haunch bottom. I am glad it is pressed against the seat. Her mouth now that her tooth is broken always looks as though she's just bit into a sweet tart candy, pursed together like her scrunchie. When she smiles, though, it looks real witchy. I find her broken tooth something to adore, though I admit it is not to every man's taste. Anyway, what I'm trying to say, politely, is that her front side, grinning, though lovely to me, is not her most attractive to the less discerning. I hoped she wouldn't have to rise, say, to visit the bathroom, putting that lovely rear of hers within a handsbreadth of that ape.

No chance of that, I later find.

I was in perfect agony, she communicates, slumping against me once we have deplaned, *and do you think they would so much as let me stir? Pretended to speak another sign language, or not understand me. I ended up pointing you know where and hissing.* I wince. *They didn't get it.* She shrugs. *Pretended not to. What's going on?*

This is at the car rental place, in Maui herself, where we find ourselves waiting a mere ten hours after boarding that plane. We are standing in the patient headlights of those guys in suits.

"Something odd about those guys," I mutter, tired, fed by a prescient insight. "Something that has to do with Whiteheart."

Sweetheart always perks up when his name drops from my lips. She peers at me now through her tattered hair. Whiteheart. These burly types in suits. I keep not getting it even as we drive through the booming night air, light and sugary, blowing a pale salt through the windows of the car. They are going along the same road, it appears. I still don't get it when they make the turnoff, directly behind us. When they park, next space. When they emerge just as we do and form an escort phalanx around us like Roman guards. Then, as we march into the huge waterfall-running Bird of Paradise lounge and check-in desk, I do get it. They're going to kill us. They're assassins.

ONCE I UNDERSTAND THAT, I'm okay. My mind is clear.

The hallways of this big elaborate jungle hotel lobby contrast with the long white light tunnels to the stacks of rooms. Walking toward our number we are of course accompanied off the elevator by the big guys in suits, whom I am tired of seeing at every turn. So tired of it all, in fact, so clear in my read, that without thinking or caring about the consequences I confront them.

I whirl, annoyed to the point where I do not have fear. I face them with stony resistance. They sweep right past, whereas I thought they'd halt, we'd speak, have words. No words. At least an exchange where I could ask who on earth they thought I was—a man worth pursuing and killing? How come?

"Hey"—I take on the smaller, bullnecked one—"what's the rush?"

Both stop and look, eyes like marbles.

"You're sent to kill, I know," I say, amiable. "Obvious. So why not enjoy yourself first?"

"We're not here to hurt you," says the shorter one after a pause. "It's nothing like that."

The bigger one laughs. "Worse."

My heart thumps. My voice comes out scratchy and small.

"IRS?"

"Not exactly. We're here because of dumping practices. You're part of a major sweep. It's okay to tell you, we just got the word."

"Might as well do the honors," says the big guy.

"You're under arrest." It is the smaller one who shows his badge.

"You have to say his name," the larger guy prompts, underneath his breath.

"Oh yeah," says the newer cop, officer, whatever.

"Whiteheart. Richard Whiteheart."

"Beads."

"No! I'm not him!" A sudden wave of relief gushes through me. I start to laugh, to explain. "He gave these tickets to me for my honeymoon. He sent us here, made us a gift, changed our lives."

"Oh, right." They both grin little tight shark smiles and remind me that I'm on an island. We'll leave in the morning. They'll accompany me to the airport.

"Really, though. I'm not Whiteheart. *Look.*"

I take out my wallet, open it, slip my license from the interior of its pocket, and to my complete sincere suddenly remembering shock I find that I am carrying the ID pictures of Whiteheart—he gave them to me, of course, to present for the tickets. We look enough alike, I guess, being both the real thing Anishinaabe men.

"Wait," I say, digging for the real me, which I can't find. Where is it and where am I and worst of all who?

SO THAT IS ABOUT the extent of our honeymoon, me and Sweetheart. I decide, since we've got one night in paradise, to make the most of it. I purchase my babe mai tais in a big plastic cup. We go down in the elevator to the tile whirlpool hot tub, a hidden glade unit surrounded by flowers. Of course, the big guys follow.

We get in, her and me. She's wearing a suit covered with blue hibiscus flowers. Something I bought her back in Gakaabikaang. And oh man, but is it ever good, this whirlpool bath of heat and chlorine. The hot jets rumble up and down my spine and the presence of my lady is all but too much for me. I'll never forget this, never, I think, her face in the rushing blue lights. Her hair in smooth snakes and curlicues floating and drifting on the surface of the medicinal waters. The booze, which I suck down in order to enjoy the present moment, disremember the past, meet the stupid future, both knocks me down and buoys me up. The night progresses and the heat intensifies. Of course, there is a certain restraining factor in the presence of the gorilla.

"You have to sit there in that suit?" I say at last to the big boy in the shadows. "How come you don't just hop in here?"

"Yeah, wish I could."

"Why don't you guys pretend not to catch me for a while and stay here, I mean, hang out and absorb some rays. Snorkel. Beachcomb. Hot tub. Swim."

"Oh, shut the fuck up," he says, but in a wistful tone.

My dear one and me stay up all night, and I tell you it is a night to remember. A night I won't forget. Sensations abound that haunt me even now in the underpasses and the park undergrowth and old abandoned boat shacks of Gakaabikaang. There is something very pure and old that happens when we're on, together, moving like we're running over distances, floating like swift clouds. The next morning, breakfast, and by nine o'clock we're hustled off. We're boarding. We're gone. It's like we dreamed the night. I can't tell you with what a sense of desolation and purpose I look down on that green beauty and blue sea from on high.

Maybe I know then, and maybe I'm just starting to understand, that life will always be like this around Richard Whiteheart. One minute high in Maui and the next minute yanked from bliss. I'm heading back now to tell my story before the judge, and I don't even know what my story is, though I'm certain it involves waste carpet. I decide, right then, as we pass into a cloud, whatever else happens I won't take the blame I can sense waiting at the terminal. No, that will be Richard. I won't pay. Will not be held responsible. I'll rat. I'll speak. Things get dumped, terrible poisons in deep old wells. Or barns. Nothing's endless, though. Every place has limits. And everybody.

9

The Deer Husband

The Autumn Rose Dress

The air is pink and golden, smelling of fresh rain. The girls' canvas high-top shoes soak through as they run over wet grass to the time tunnels, the monkey bars, the fenced plain of deer. Early fall. The late roses are blooming, their petals flimsy, trembling, floppy silk and tight furled centers. They see a woman in an autumn rose dress just like their mother's. She is walking across the rose garden with a man. With Frank, of course. The girls see that the woman is their mother. Rozin. They are with their father, Richard, because he has been bullied into taking them somewhere, anywhere. They grab him by the wrist, bring him to the rose beds. They point across the grass to make him understand that it is Rozin. He returns their excitement with a calm gaze, chin tipped down. His eyes clouded and hard.

"No, that isn't her."

"Look!" The girls pull on his sleeves.

"No"—he speaks indifferently—"that isn't your mother. I know she looks like your mother."

"She is! She does!"

"I know she does."

"But Daddy"—they are together in this now, persuading him—"she has the same *dress*."

"A lot of women bought that same dress." He speaks with deliberate and now forceful gravity. "Like I said, that's not her."

It is only when the two walking people get close enough for the girls to clearly see her face, laughter fading in their mouths, that they decide, as she bends to the other man, touching his chest with the flat of her hand, that their father is right. They are looking at some other woman whose face, alight and radiant and still with anticipation, they have never seen before.

CALLY AND DEANNA turn away from their father and away from that woman who looks like their mother. They begin to slap each other's hands in a complex, nimble patty-cake.

I don't wanna go to Hollywood
No more, more, more.
There's a big fat Michael Jackson
At my door, door, door.
He grabbed me by the hips
And made me kiss his lips.
I don't wanna go to Hollywood
No more, more, more.
Shame on you!

Then they laugh hysterically and do the rhyme over and over all the way home and keep it up until Richard thinks he'll lose his mind.

Love and Relocation

Get them off that land! Away from one another. Split apart those families just getting to know one another after boarding school. Relocation is the main reason fewer Indians now live on reservations than in cities—like Klaus, like his cousin Frank, like Rozin, and like Richard Whiteheart Beads, whose mind is a bright rubber-band ball twisted of bewildered jealousy.

He keeps taking the colored bands off the ball, his emotions, and shooting them into space. Green fury, white disbelief, yellow hurt, purple rage, brown embarrassment. Also, he gets served with papers. Right after he returns from the park, two men come into the yard. The dog doesn't even bark. It only laughs. The men are there to serve him with papers. Not divorce papers, yet at least! These papers are a court summons. If he does not appear in court he will be arrested. The legal paper servers wear gray suits. They always wear gray suits. No ties. Maybe they think the person who accepts the papers will reach out and grab them by the tie. Do they carry mace? Do they carry weapons? Do they carry tissues or handkerchiefs for people to cry into?

I won't do any of those things, thinks Richard as he takes the papers. They needn't fear me. But maybe Klaus should!

"Klaus!"

"Yes, I told them."

Klaus gave Richard up. Just like that. He told the men, whom he said were big and scary and wore black suits, where Richard lived. Klaus cracked. Klaus squealed: *Richard lives on Andrew Jackson Street in Minneapolis.* It doesn't matter, though. Klaus is up to his neck. Implicated. Richard reads the papers, then he sits down on the front step and begins to chain-smoke. No matter whether he goes to court or whether he is arrested he will be served with divorce papers. No, he decides. From all papers, he will flee. Damn Relocation! None of this would have happened without the proximity of all those many acres of carpet, which could only be so proximate in the city, which is why Relocation sucks so bad, thinks Richard. If I had been educated on my home reservation and lived with my family and received instruction in our traditional ways, I would have probably been a medicine man.

Whiteheart Beads, Medicine Man

Richard keeps thinking about the future that he might have had but for government programs. The War Department program for Indian eradication in the beginning, then treaty-making or removal. If his reservation had not been clipped back severely his family would have had more land, perhaps enough to live on and farm. Then every kind of sickness. If the few left had not had their children forcibly removed and shipped off to boarding schools where they either died of fresh diseases or died of loneliness or survived and got drunk and run over in the road . . . then . . . And if the few left after that hadn't sold their land during the allotment years and become completely homeless and got tuberculosis sleeping on the ground, then . . .

If my ancestors had not got so sick from sleeping underneath that grand piano, maybe I would still have deposited toxic carpet in that barn, thinks Richard. Or maybe I would have healed people with my ceremonial knowledge.

He visualizes himself in his natural state. Not naked. He is wearing a loincloth. One of nicely tanned buckskin that his woman has chewed until soft. Sad. Her teeth are all worn down. His imaginary loincloth is smooth as silk from all of Rozin's chewing. He laughs and cracks a beer. Early in the day to drink, but he's been served with papers, is no medicine man, so needn't stand on ceremony.

Did a man just dangle under that loincloth, he wonders, or was there some sort of diaper arrangement? A ball band, he decides. There had to have been a soft buckskin jockstrap underneath the loincloth. He sees his flowing braids, his stomach hard as a pine board, his biceps tough and stringy. Racing around curing people keeps him in shape. He is a shaman. Not a *sham* man, as Klaus always calls them, but the kind of shaman white people search the Internet for now and, when they find one, worship.

WHEN ROZIN COMES home later on, after the girls have seen her in the park, she doesn't show that face with the beauty and ecstasy painted across her features. She is the very same mother as before. Calmer. Irritable. But in the old familiar ways. But then she drives off with their father and they stay away for the weekend. The girls can tell that something has happened that is not love, not getting back together. It is some sort of panic over looking happy with Frank for Mom and breaking a law for Dad. Cally and Deanna heard their mother shout that they could lose the house. They heard their father angrily deny it as she'd kept it in her name. They heard the name Frank and they ran up to their room.

It is a small room with bunk beds and the paint on the windowsills has been tested for lead. The top layer is perfectly acceptable now, but the woodwork has been in place since 1882, so the mustard-colored, the black, and the bitter-red paint under the fresh white coats is toxic. Cally and Deanna have been instructed never, ever, to chip away at the paint on the walls and woodwork and especially not to eat it.

"Let's eat it now," says Cally. But Deanna does not understand the logic.

"They'll have to pump our stomachs," she explains. "That will bring them together."

"Can't we do it without getting our stomachs pumped?"

"No!" says Cally.

So she and Deanna chip off a bit of paint, put it on their tongues, swallow, and wait to die.

"First we'll have convulsions, that will tip them off," says Cally.

"Where are you getting this information?" says Deanna.

Nothing happens. They forget about having eaten the paint after a while. Then Sweetheart Calico bolts outside with the dog. They run downstairs and whirl through the yard playing tag and hide-and-seek.

Nookoomisag

They emerge from the truck with their hard little suitcases, and cast their cold eyes around the house and yard to check for enemies. They see Cally and Deanna and their eyes turn into grandma eyes, black and warm. The grandmothers are both round-shouldered, powerful, small women. Their little hands are tough and splayed. They heat up cans of beans and corn for the girls that evening and let them watch TV while they sit at the table with the harsh light on them. From cheap plastic bags they draw silky deerhide, needles in wooden cases, little fan-shaped boxes of quills, and spice jars full of colored beads. Grandma Noodin pricks up beads and sews calmly. Grandma Giizis wears moccasins. They have traveled down from the reservation to care for their granddaughters in the city, while Rozin and Richard work things out.

Grandma Noodin hopes they work it out and Grandma Giizis does not like Richard and says he is a snake. She thinks that Rozin and the girls should move back and live with them anyway. Forget about these no-good men and forget about the noisy, crowded, ugly, tangled-up, bewildering Gakaabikaang.

Sweetheart Calico

Grandma Noodin catches a glimpse of Sweetheart Calico playing with the girls the next afternoon and says to Grandma Giizis, "Something is not right with that woman."

They both begin to watch her, to spy on her, to question the girls all about her. They are awake that night when it rains and they open the curtains to peek outside. There she is with her clothes off, running around and around the yard. In the morning, hoof tracks.

Grandma Giizis nods at Grandma Noodin. "One of those," they agree.

The Girl Who Married the Deer

Their gitchi-gitchi-nookomis was a peculiar girl known for her tremendous appetite though she stayed thin as a handful of twigs. During berry season, she went picking many times a day, filling her birchbark makak over and over but eating it empty before she ever made it to the house. Not only that, but she couldn't keep her hands off mushrooms, food of the dead. She robbed the wild rice caches. Ate all the boiled meat. It worried people to see that she was always eating, always hungry, but never full.

A voice.

I've been watching this girl. Maybe she's a wiindigoo.

No, said her mother. She's only that hungry. Nothing wrong with her.

Still, the other people ignored her or gave her shaming looks when she approached a food pot. Hungrier than ever, she took to the woods. More and more time, days even, passed with her gathering and cooking out there in the heart of the dense bush. You could smell the steam, the good smells, you could smell the smoke rising.

She's cooking out there. Wonder what she's making? Wonder if a little child disappeared, we would find it in the cooking pot? Great-Great-Grandmother ate the whole rabbit. Ears too. She wanted to eat her own arm.

And then she was joined out in the woods.

The girl was cooking up a fine pot of dried corn stew when a deer approached, stood by the edge of her camp. Just waiting. The girl thought, Should I eat him or should I share with him? Which? She picked up her killing hatchet but when she finally advanced toward the deer and looked him in the eye, she felt ashamed. She knew hunger when she saw it. Just walked past the deer and chopped a little more wood for the fire. Finished that stew.

She put the stew onto the plate, set the plate down in front of the deer, got her own plate full, and ate sitting before him. He never moved. She ate the whole stew, mopped up every trace of it with bannock, then sat quietly looking at him, crescent of horns, waiting. Unafraid. She had this feeling. Full. So this was what other people felt. She looked over at the deer. His eyes were steady and warm with a melting black light. His heart shone right out of his eyes.

He loves me, she thought. He loves me and I love him back. Right down to the ground. Who he is. No different. Of course, too bad that he's a deer. That night, she made a bed out of young hemlock branches and curled against his short, stiff pelt. She began to live with him, stayed with him out in the woods, and traveled with him on into the open spaces. Became beloved by his family, too. Got so that she knew how to call the hooved ones toward her. They came when she stood in the open. Her song was peculiar, soft, questing.

THE GRANDMAS LIGHT their small red-bowl kinnikinnick pipes. They sit in the corner, smoking and brooding.

They are wondering what to do about Sweetheart Calico and what to do about their daughter, Rozin, and about the twins, Cally and Deanna, who say they have eaten lead paint off the windowsill. They are wondering what to do about Frank, who's come by with sugar on his pants and flour in his hair. There was in his hands a large box. In the box, between layers of wax paper, an assortment of fancy sugar cookies cut into the shapes of carrots, trees, dolphins, stars, moons, dogs, and flowers. Each type of cutout is decorated with a different color of hard icing trimmed with a rickrack of frosting, studded with edible foil-sugar beads or blue-black raisins. Grandma Noodin puts down her pipe. She puts the head of a pink dog into her mouth and bites it completely off. As the crumbly cookie dissolves grain by grain on her tongue, she understands that Frank loves her daughter. She believes that Richard Whiteheart Beads will run from prosecution and try to hide. She hopes he'll take Klaus along with him. Those two are a couple of bums.

Grandma Giizis puts her pipe down, too. She eats a carrot-shaped cookie frosted orange with green piping leaves.

"My doctor said carrots are good for me," she says.

Cally eats a dolphin and Deanna eats a flower.

"So what happened to the girl who married the deer?" asks Deanna.

"Wait until I finish my carrot," say Grandma Giizis.

THE GIRL DIDN'T want to leave her deer husband, but her brothers came to get her one brilliant spring. Shot her man with three arrows, one bullet. Brought her back to her family, her village, her people. She was not hungry anymore, and she was grown. They named her for the flowers that stretched past her shielding arms and were spattered with deer's blood, blue flowers scraped from patches of sky. Blue Prairie Woman.

She married one of the Shawano brothers, even though that family was said to be descended of wiindigoog. She lived winters on the traplines with his father and brothers. Spring through late fall they stayed in a village where she could be with her woman relatives, talk all night, cook, laugh. She never used her medicine to attract the hooved ones. Never. But everyone knew what she could do.

Sometimes the deer people came to her, anyway.

One slender doe did on the morning of the big knives. Told Blue Prairie Woman to leave, go now, tie her baby on the back of the dog, and run. Too late, though. Just as she started out a tornado of bluecoat men. Everything scattered, lost, burned, murdered. She saw the same man who killed her great-aunt leap forward suddenly and run, uttering inhuman cries of loss, from the swirl of death into the distance. He was following her baby. Her baby tied in the dikinaagan. Riding on the back of the dog-mother of six fat, fine puppies. One, Blue Prairie Woman would nurse with her own milk. The others grew too weak to save.

10

The Gravitron

THEY ARE GIVING out free figures of gods of the underworld along with Happy Meals at McDonald's. Driving up to the window, Rozin buys the meals. Cally gets Hades, a sinister blue guy with skinny arms, and Deanna gets two plastic halves of the three-headed dog Cerberus, which makes the twins wonder immediately whether, if Hades went into a pet parlor to get the dog clipped for the summer, he'd have to pay triple.

"Cerberus has one body. That's definitive," says Cally.

"But the heads represent separate thoughts, separate dogs," Deanna points out.

"With my crummy job we've got enough to worry about," Rozin tells her daughters.

She laughs shortly but the supermarket checker job she took again, temporarily, is turning out to last a long time and still no benefits.

THE TWINS' ROOM has a rattling old window. Their outlook on the world. The trees are black locust and tree-of-heaven trees that grow everywhere, tough, with small, oval pointer-finger leaves that flip over in a breeze. Sometimes the girls watch the dull underside roil. They bathe their brains in showers of four-o'clock gold, streaming from the west. Sometimes a branch tosses high, like a horse against the bit. They think of riding the branch, hair flying against the wind. The thought of that same wind ruffling leaves and heading north along no highway to ruffle the leaves of their grandmas' trees pulls at them with longing. Some days, the twins feel that pull more than others. Summer has been comics and bakery and turning almost ten. Already leaves are turning on the driest trees. Some mornings are quick and cool. A low wind rides, trembling in the stiff grass, unwinding and slowing their steps. The gravity tugs harder. School looms too close. The girls turn to each other with wide eyes.

Will they take us on *rides*, anyplace there are *rides*, if we dance, if we cry, if we hold our breath? How about we reasonably ask.

THAT IS WHAT almost being ten is about. They ask to go to the state fair and their mother says yes. End of August. It is night, the cheese-curd stands frying curdled milk, the Australian batter-fried potatoes, the chili con carne bars at war, the dip cones, and the beer gardens. Eating something long, snakey, and blue, the twins, Cecille, Rozin, and Frank watch the show horses practice outside the arena in a sawdust ring. So delicate. So fine. Hooves like sewing machine needles, they do fancy stitch work up and down the sides of the metal fence. They pass so close the girls can feel the breath off their velvet noses and smell the warmth of their glossed hides, braided manes, sense the determination of their stiff little riders.

Here is Frank, so kind, his hands plucking cotton candy off a paper cone to hand first to her, then the girls. And so unassuming. He looks at the prize rabbits of every shape and size, and the bread sculptures and the Elvis faces made of beans and seeds, and he makes no jokes whatsoever about the size of the prize boar's sexual equipment. Nor does he look as though he feels entirely outclassed in that matter, like some men, staring back over their shoulders at the pig in envy and fascination. Frank might be good for me, Rozin thinks, walking behind the girls, who hold hands with him. Cecille walks ahead of them all. Rozin follows as they make their way zigzagging to the sizzling zipper lights of the midway. They walk past the howling bungee jump, over the Chinese bridge, on and on until right before them the Gravitron rears.

CALLY AND DEANNA stand in the drama of light and music and fair noise watching people move like happy zombies to the entrance of the ride, a big crowd. Just over their heads, they see the exit and entrance of a new bunch of people slightly nervous and chattering as bored attendants strap them in. The operator of the ride looks way too young—

brushstrokes of a soft yellow beard, hair in a braid, earring. Vacant. He disappears for a minute under the equipment and then jumps to his music monitor control panel and begins rattling some strange Wolfman Jack spiel into the microphone.

The Gravitron starts slowly with the purr of a giant motor and a lurch of gears. The deep bass throbs to life, heavy rock beat, a flame of guitars. Strapped in standing, hands at their sides, the riders are hugged by welded bars to the inside of a gigantic pie plate that starts turning now, turning against the night. Green lights in refracting bands. Rippling blue. Pink. A maddened cake stand that swivels on its base! Tipping side to side, it spins faster, faster, gravity a hand flattening the faces of the screamers to one green dimension. . . .

"Looks like fun," says Cecille.

"Yes!" says Rozin.

The twins think they must be hearing things. Rozin says it again. Her tone so dry the twins think she must definitely be kidding, but she's actually not. This is how on the next run the girls find themselves watching with Cecille, astounded at Frank and their mother. They walk up the ride stairway and climb into the cages that close over them like alien claws. Again the Gravitron comes to life, now, Frank and their mother clinging to the bars and straps, blurring into one unit as the ride commences. The girls' faces are serious with worry. Cecille tells them not to worry and she turns away for a moment. Turning back the other way around, she casually catches the eye of the operator, or not his eye so much as the strange fixed grin that he is shooting right through her from the little cage he inhabits next to the gears and motors.

He stares at Cecille and she stares back at him until she realizes he's not seeing her. Staring through her as though he's disordered, his whole body fixed and frozen, he's a shirt-store dummy.

High, Cecille thinks in total understanding.

"Hey you!" She waves her hands at him, yells. He whips his head away and with a screech of Wolfman laughter only crazier and nastier, he accelerates the ride. Faster. Higher. Cranked up and down with fire shooting from their eyes, the riders scream. The operator starts to blow froth bubbles. Rabies! An overdose! And he's garbled, makes no sense. There's only this overarching manic howl that penetrates the Hendrix "Purple Haze" lick and funk. The girls cling to Cecille in terror. She is certain he's hit the far edge. She starts forward. Others, concerned, do the same. Cally and Deanna grab each other and watch as people surround the lighted booth and start to knock, and then find that his door's wedged shut. The people start to claw and beat and yammer. He's spouting chilling warbles and declaiming as he revs the inner body of the Gravitron.

What follows from above is frightful, the riders understanding now that something has gone most horrifically wrong and the ride, a killer to begin with, now juiced up to unbearable, is whipping them mercilessly through time and space. They're roaring. Puking. Blurred. They're like those tigers turned to butter. They're all one face of horror smeared across the inner circle of the Gravitron. They'll die. Brain damage, inner organs turned to mush. The girls are so terrified they grab a railing and begin, with another desperate and grounded loved one, to wrench the bar from the walkway. They think they will use it to batter in the Plexiglas window, flail against the door, somehow jam the mechanism. But no, someone is there before them. With a tire iron swung with swordlike precision, Cecille smashes the window. People jump to the marked controls and now, at last, the ride is slowing. Each rider, coming into focus, is the very picture of sick and dazzled terror except for one.

Rozin. She steps out of her cage, doesn't falter, not a single misstep. She helps a wobbly, limp, gray-green-faced, sweating Frank off and leads him to a place in the grass where he sits in grateful wonder with his eyes still spinning. She strokes his hand. She holds his shoulder, puts her arm around him, and holds him lovingly, the way the girls cannot ever remember her holding their father. The way she acts is so different, so natural, so real, so warm and naked that they suddenly have this picture of what has just happened to her.

Their mother has been scaled. All the scales of convention and ironic distance have been scuffed off her. All the boney armor she affects against the world. She has been stripped by centrifugal force and jumbled up inside. The wrench of gravity has undone all her strings.

HE CALLS, THAT night. The twins hear them long on the phone and put their pillows over their heads, laughing at them. Juvenile! The next day is Saturday and he calls again. She's jumping up and pacing back and forth. Strewn with a blasted weight of emotion. The girls can sense waves of feeling, banners with cutting edges, huge sensations ranging from her, all set loose. Dressed, but awkwardly, her collar turned inside, she bats away their hands when they try to fix it. Goes to a corner of the room. And it is there from watching her back and shoulders tremble that the girls understand it is too big for her, too much. It is pulling at her with inexorable weight. She's falling into it. Gravity. They don't know what to do. Already in the other room, the phone is ringing. As their mother walks toward the receiver with her hand outstretched, she seems to shrink and fall into the steady pull.

11

Yellow Pickup Truck

ROZIN WAITS FOR the school bus alongside her daughters. They stand close together on the street corner, watching traffic. Her hand brushes down her daughters' slippery brown hair. The girls ask about the deer husband and Blue Prairie Woman. Is it true?

"That old story," says Rozin. She holds their slim shoulders against her. Their heavy backpacks clunk against her hips on each side. The bus bumbles to a stop and the doors sigh open.

"Is it true?" Both of the girls look back as they are getting on. They pause on the black school-bus steps.

"Don't worry," says Rozin. "It will be all right. It will be okay."

"What will?"

"The divorce," hisses Cally.

Deanna halts as the door swishes shut and the bus drives off before they sit down, completely against safety regulations. Now they are waving from the backseat. Rozin watches until the bus turns down the street and then she walks into the kitchen and puts the old blue kettle on to boil. Standing tall in her black yoga pants, in which she will do the same jumping jacks and sit-ups she learned in high school, hands pressed on the pale tiles of the counter, unsmiling, she gazes out the window into the festooned yard. She leans forward and frowns as though looking for something hidden.

When her husband steps into the kitchen, yawning, rubbing his chest, and pulling down a thick sweatshirt, she drops her gaze. Unspeaking, she sets out spoons, milk, slices a grapefruit, rattles a cereal box, takes down a pair of white lotus bowls. Richard pours the steaming water into the plunger coffeepot and then he stands with her in a drowsy suspension.

"Klaus and me are going to take a lot of heat on this. Bad stuff is going down," he says.

"You never talk like that anymore," says Rozin. "Why are you talking like that again?"

They fell in love at an American Indian Movement protest and her mother told her she had a sinister feeling about the future. But did Rozin listen? No, she ran off with those people and lived here and there, but fortunately not on Pine Ridge during the years it had the highest per capita murder rate in the USA. Being in AIM was frustrating since the old ways were taken up again, the ceremonies and the pipes and the berets . . . wait, those berets were French?—but they looked cool. AIM was complicated for women because for instance if you had your period you couldn't be around any of the good-looking men and couldn't cook or touch their pipes or any sacred objects but had to stay in a moon lodge, which was usually the apartment of a sympathetic white person. Rozin had rebelled against her mother's traditional ways, but once they were AIM ways she felt spiritual.

Richard cheated on her many times while she was in the moon lodge. She never knew it at the time, but it later became a reason she felt justified in drinking coffee with Frank.

Eventually, Rozin tried to put her politics into practice. She went to school to be a social worker but didn't finish her degree. Sometimes she does community work. Other times she's laid off and works at the supermarket, or for temp agencies. Anyway, she is steady and was able to buy and rehabilitate this very old house. As for Richard, all he's got left of AIM is the ponytail.

Richard is always participating in some scam or another. She has gotten used to this. He was the treasurer for AIM for one month and money vanished. He was actually kicked out, but things were getting very dangerous and he felt lucky not to have been executed by some former friend whose mind was poisoned by Cointelpro agents. Handsomely, charismatically, he flunked out of college and cast about for other ways to live. Once he was a telemarketer, he said, but he was actually part of a group that invested old people's money in a nonexistent Indian hot springs resort. Another time he took a casino job and commuted. That worked out pretty well and he made enough to buy the yellow pickup truck that everybody knows him for driving.

"That pickup truck was never a good idea. So easy to spot," says Rozin.

"Easy to repo," says Richard.

She nods, but does not answer.

As always, she pours the coffee into his pottery cup. As always, he takes his first drink and winces at the stinging heat.

"Does it even bother you that I am going underground?"

"Underground, isn't that for radicals? You're an illegal carpet dumper."

"I suppose you're glad. I suppose that you'll be messing around with Frank."

"Yes," sighs Rozin. "I suppose so."

During a recent receptionist break she read a magazine article about the brain chemicals that are released in the beginning of romantic love. Wow, has she ever got them, and to spare.

"Are you in love?" says Richard poisonously.

"Madly," says Rozin flatly. She succeeds in tamping down a warm flutter.

Her matter-of-factness deflates Richard. He thinks of how he could refer to Frank's unhealthily sweet pastries and tell her he hopes they both get diabetes. But he just doesn't have the energy. Maybe once he and Klaus are on the move his outlook will improve. He will call her on the phone with a slashing comeback. He will leave eloquent and withering messages.

"Are you changing your identity?" asks Rozin. "I'll want to know when I get the divorce papers. I'll want to know so I can serve you with divorce papers."

"Make those guys who bring the papers wear neckties. And of course we're changing our identities. We are going to masquerade as homeless guys who can't remember who we are."

Rozin is alarmed and sits down across from him, frowning.

"That's stupid, Richard, and so dangerous."

"What do you care?"

"I still care for you."

"You won't have sex with me."

"That would be crossing a boundary."

"It was a boundary we once loved to cross, like the state line, like the Forty-fifth Parallel, like the line between Central and Mountain time."

They are both very quiet and sadly sit drinking their coffee and remembering that they'd had many good and crazy years before these bad years.

"Aren't you worried about Cally and Deanna, about how they'll take this?"

"I have the grandmas here."

"They never liked me. They'll talk bad about me."

"No, I won't let them."

But they both know the grandmas are out of anyone's control and that they have always said that Richard would end up homeless in the streets being hunted down by the authorities. Sure enough, that afternoon, the grandmas are watching when two of those very authorities come up to the house and repossess the yellow pickup truck. The repo men ask for Richard, but he is gone, because by that time Richard and Klaus are crawling around in the bushes down by the Mississippi River. They flip for who will buy the first bottle and Klaus loses. They roll out their sleeping bags and take the first burning swig. The sky is clear, slate blue. Soon enough, the air chills, dusk comes on, the brightest stars show, and the moon is nearly full.

"It's not so bad," says Richard.

There are deer in the leaves. A head pokes through once; a young doe stares at them meltingly and disappears.

12

The Ojibwe Holidays

GRANDMA NOODIN AND Grandma Giizis call the city Mishiimin Oodenang, Apple Town, because of the sound of the word—Minneapolis. Many Apple Us. They call Thanksgiving Day Gitchimiigwechiwegiizhigad, which means the Day When We Give the Big Thanks. It is not an original holiday, but the Ojibwe are big on feasts. Noodin and Giizis still live on the reservation homestead, the allotment that belonged to their grandmother, now a farmed patch of earth and woods and mashkiig from which they gather their teas and cut bark for baskets. The tribe gave them a brand-new prefabricated house, two bedrooms, slate blue. They can sit on the deck with their backs to the lake, and watch the road. Noodin can fold and sew a ricing tray or a makak without looking at her hands, but both she and Giizis prefer to construct and quill fancy boxes bearing animal icons—bear, loon, deer, and bear. They are hard-packed women with wise nimble fingers, heavy ankles, and legs that run straight down like fence posts into their shoes. Their faces originally had the same wide, plain soft beauty, but as twins will they have grown into their differences. They are like two cookie sheets. Noodin's is the newer sheet, relatively unmarred, while Giizis's is a pan baked on, burnt, shaded into character.

Noodin and Giizis are arriving early because Rozin has made a doctor's appointment. This was made for Noodin because she confided a set of feminine symptoms to her daughter, the sort of thing for which it was felt that she should be seen by what she calls "a woman's expert." Noodin is furious that she must see a doctor. But none of her own medicines work.

Sitting in a rocker
Eating Betty Crocker
Watching the clock go
Tick, tock, tick, tock
Shawallawalla
Tick, tock, tick, tock
Shawallawalla
ABCDEFG
Wash those boy germs off of me!

The twins are smacking their hands together and singing and rubbing off boy germs. They are not interested in what the grandmas will be angry about or what foods they will tell everyone they prefer—the burnt heart of the turkey to the white breast meat, cranberry sauce made from fresh berries only. Mincemeat pie gives Giizis the runs. Pumpkin stops Noodin's bowels. Wild rice must be prepared with no salt, and garlic gives both an instant cramp.

Misty snow, plump clouds, occasional breaks of sun. Ice on the sidewalks slick and treacherous under the white dusting. Rozin is just returning from a long emergency run to a convenience mart, when she sees her cousin Cecille back Frank's delivery truck with expert care into a space across the street. Inside the truck, both grandmas are sitting high and proud on grass-blue vinyl, their stunning Miss Indian America profiles on display in the watery dark of the window. The truck is white. The snow is neat, a new fall outlining the shoveled walk and steps. Rozin breathes blue air stepping out of her car to meet them.

"Take this. Here!"

Giizis opens the truck door. She holds a casserole pan in her lap, a meat-fragrant oblong warming her knees through her red-and-white trader's-blanket coat. Rozin takes the food carefully. There is the night before Thanksgiving meal to feed everyone and Giizis has arrived with her famous wild rice and duck hot-dish. The grandmas don't even get out of the truck—they're too busy reminding Booch Jr., Cecille, and Rozin of their complex digestive needs, which change every year.

"Noodin takes no salt. I eat the whites of eggs only, yolks will kill me. Plus Noodin's got that sugar in her blood. She craves it, though. Try not to tempt her," Giizis whispers. "Don't leave the cookie plate alone in the kitchen. She'll make a pig of herself behind your back and then she'll lapse into a coma. Me, you know I'll eat whatever."

"No you won't," Cecille tells her. "You're picky as your whole family put together. And the yolks of eggs will not kill you! Rozin has already fried the onions and celery for tomorrow's stuffing. You'll have to divide it out."

"She is making the stuffing already? That's ours to make."

Noodin is nervous about her appointment and scurries

into the house. She locks herself in the bathroom. She only has a few minutes, Rozin calls through the door. They are going to be late unless she hurries.

"I am hurrying," shouts Noodin, her voice thin with anxiety.

"Don't pressure her," says Cecille. "After all, she's never been to a gynecologist before. She's very upset about this."

"It's unbelievable," says Rozin. "Well, I'm taking her to Doctor Carr. He's very nice, really. I have seen him a couple of times."

"Him? I would never have a *him*."

"How ridiculous," says Rozin sharply. "They are professionals. They've seen a million of 'em."

"'Em?" Cecille laughs. "And isn't he young?"

"Okay, he's seen thousands of 'em."

"'Em." Cecille walks off. "Booch," she calls, "how many of 'em have you seen?"

"How many of what?" Booch asks.

"'Em," says Cecille.

"Oh stop it," says Rozin.

Noodin is still in the bathroom. The water is gushing and there are frantic sounds of hurry.

"Just relax," says Cecille. "I'll call and say you're running fifteen minutes late."

But they are at least half an hour late by the time they get Noodin into the car.

AN HOUR PASSES. Noodin slams into the house and Rozin follows.

"What's the problem?" asks Cecille, her hands deep in flour.

"She won't tell me."

Noodin throws her purse in the corner, glares at everyone, and then thumps into the kitchen. She microwaves a heaping bowl of her own hot-dish, eats it. Without a word to anybody else she begins to tear up loaves of bread for her own stuffing and to chop apples. She likes apples and raisins and sausage in her stuffing. She takes a big package of sausage from the refrigerator and dumps it into a frying pan. Noodin broods as she cooks it, breaking it with the edge of a spatula.

"What's wrong with you?" asks Cecille.

No answer. Cecille shrugs. "What's wrong with her?" she asks Giizis.

"She's like that," says Giizis.

Eventually Noodin stomps off to bed, still without a word to anyone.

"What was the diagnosis?" asks Cecille once Noodin is sealed in the bedroom.

"Normal," says Rozin. "Everything benign! Except her! Maybe she's just mad because she went to the doctor for nothing?"

ROZIN'S KITCHEN IS a long, sunny galley with three windows over the sink and a chopping board built into the side opposite the stove, underneath the cupboards of dishes. Out in the other room Cecille sets the table with Rozin's holiday cloth—turkeys, pilgrims, and golden-eyed deer—and plates with the border of twined green leaves. Cecille has brought her own special water glasses. Beautiful rummage-sale cut glass of an elemental blue that does not match anything.

Just like her, Rozin thinks, annoyed but also obscurely pleased. Everything else on the table is red, orange, or gold. I've set it carefully, and here comes Cecille insisting on her blue water goblets.

Cecille is slender as a dancer. She shows off her breasts and shoulders by wearing leotard tops. Her eyes are wide, deer-brown, caramel-cream, and she has grown her hair long, thick, and wild. She likes to streak it with henna. The twins are proud of her. Sometimes her earnest and pedantic air as she discusses her martial arts annoys everyone. But she is a second-degree black belt now, tae kwan do, she is going to school to become a drug counselor and holding down a regular job selling food supplements. Cecille is a success. Her apartment over Frank's shop is filled with textbooks, meditation mats, and bowls that sing when struck with a wooden mallet.

Rozin sugars the rhubarb Noodin brought, frozen from last June. Following Frank's recipe, she spreads it on the bottom of a baking pan with strawberries and then mixes the butter, oatmeal, brown sugar, and crushed walnuts for the topping. Spreads the sweet stuff evenly across. She slides the pan into the space below the turkey, which is almost ready, its small red-plastic timer button half extended. Cally and Deanna hold out spoons to baste the tender, crackling skin. The heat fans their faces and they suddenly think of their mother's face brushing against Frank's. They put down the spoons and flee.

Miss Mary had a baby
She named it Tiny Tim

She put it in a bathtub
To see if he could swim
He drank up all the water
He ate up all the soap
He went down the drain
In an envelope

"Nothing makes sense about that drain," says Cally.

"The envelope would dissolve and anyhow a baby wouldn't fit," says Deanna. "Let's spy on Sweetheart Calico."

She is in the small apartment watching Klaus's television and trying out colors on her toenails. She takes the polish off with pink acetone, then paints them a new color. She must have a hundred little bottles of color. They are scattered everywhere. The room reeks.

Cally and Deanna are worried.

"Let's not spy," says Deanna. "Let's paint our nails too and show her how to put the tops back on the nail polish."

So the twins spend Thanksgiving preparation time screwing the tops on the bottles and arranging them in a row along the side of the mattress where Sweetheart Calico curls. They have heard their mother worry about bills and say that Klaus has paid enough rent for the rest of November but after that Sweetheart Calico will have nowhere else to go. They will open the big door that divides this part of the house from the rest, and she will then live with them.

"She'll have to get a job," Rozin said, looking doubtful.

"THE GROWN-UPS ARE sitting down," Cally tells Sweetheart. The girls comb her hair out and blow on her fingernails and find a pair of thongs for her feet. They find a white shirt for her to wear over her tight push-up bra low-cut tank. They take her hand and lead her to the table.

Cecille is talking about Klaus and Richard.

"They're on the streets, looking like hell warmed over. Making signs that say they are war veterans! For which they could get arrested!"

Booch Jr. hands Frank the gravy pitcher, pretending not to hear Cecille talk about Klaus, his favorite uncle, like a father to him. Frank's face is pained, he is searching for the right tone, stalling. Frank has eaten with the family before, but never with Richard out of the picture, never with the potential to be Rozin's man. He wants to make sure that everyone knows he isn't taking Richard's place. That he has no hostility. That he doesn't want to hear gossip. He takes the pitcher in two hands and leans over to Cecille.

"He's the girls' dad, so have some respect."

"Yeah. Give it a rest," Booch says to Cecille. She pauses, but only to gather momentum. Even with no marriageable male attention, she preens in her short skirt, folds her arms against her breasts. Her eyes are perfectly lined and shadowed and her neck is sultry with a thick gardenia perfume. She bends her mouth into a seesaw smile of irony and does not give any satisfaction. Does not back off her subject.

"I know. It's not in the family, maybe our culture even, to speak out, to mention these sad, hard topics. I know that.

But how much better if we all accepted truth and spoke with honesty, from the heart! For instance, Cally and Deanna are at a higher risk for depression and substance abuse because their role model exhibits self-destructive behaviors. I'm saying it. Because I want them to realize!"

"They're not depressed," says Booch Jr., "but all of us could get temporarily deranged, by you."

Booch grips a salad bowl of honey-colored wood. He stares back at Cecille and slowly, imperceptibly at first, then with increasing force he trembles, mildly jittering, from the feet up, from the ground, then with more vigor until his head tips to the side, his eyes roll back to the whites. The mass of dark leaves jumps. He grips the bowl even tighter until he is shaking all over in explosive starts and jerks.

"Quit it, Booch," laughs Rozin.

Giizis starts forward, scared. Booch stops. Looks around at the table, blank. "Where am I?"

Cally and Deanna think he is hilarious.

"Booch?"

Cecille's voice is instantly suspicious. "What was that?"

Grandma Giizis shakes the serrated knife she's using on the bread. "Get out of here, you crazy boy, or I'm gonna take this to you!"

Noodin unfolds her arms and goes back to fluffing her wild rice, puts the lid back on the pot, carries it in to the table with two dish towels wrapped around her hands as mitts.

"You egg him on," she says pointedly to Cecille, in passing. Cecille gives a pleased shrug. The twins and Sweetheart sit looking at the table. The turkeys and pilgrims and golden-eyed deer race along the borders of the tablecloth. Red candles. Ivy plants. Gold paper napkins. The unexpected blue glass.

THE TABLE IS long, with boards to add and with extra wings at the end. A table made for big gatherings and doings. It's a good thing, because the topics of conversation at the table tend to polarize. Especially the things the grandmas say. Past a certain age the Roy women believe that they have earned the right to talk about sex, birth, blood, the size and shape of men's equipment, the state of their own, even at the holiday dinner table. But at this Thanksgiving, Noodin is strangely subdued. Still fuming and filled with secret hostility.

"There should be no salt on this table!" cries Grandma Giizis. "In the early days we had no salt. We didn't know of it. We had no taste for it. Now look at us." Her blood pressure medication keeps her dizzily alert.

"I can eat as much salt as I want—" says Cecille.

"If you're pregnant—"

"I'm not."

"Eat the head of a skunk," advises Giizis. "In the old days, that was the way to make sure the baby's head would be a little head, easy to push."

"Did you have morning sickness with Cecille?" Booch asks. His mouth stitches together in anxious amusement. "That skunk head might not sit too well."

Giizis continues on with implacable deliberation.

"I knew a woman with that morning sickness. She ended up in labor for two weeks!"

Helping herself to mashed potatoes, Noodin takes up

the theme now, in a darkly relishing tone of voice. "The pain was constant, too, hard labor for a total of twenty-four times fourteen hours. Plus, all the while she screamed. No, it was more a yodel. So pitiful. And people heard her—this was before they set up the soundproof room in the hospital."

"A big baby?" Giizis purses her lips in knowing fashion.

"They couldn't stitch her back together in the right order. And yet she somehow lived."

"Only to die the next time, probably."

Noodin shrugs.

"On that note," says Booch, his face sunken and pale, his voice catching, "shall we toast an easy labor and healthy outcome? Toast!"

"I'm not pregnant," Cecille says uselessly. "I don't even have a boyfriend."

But Booch desperately raises his mug of apple cider and downs it like a pirate tossing back hot grog. Still, the grandmas are not finished.

"That's a bad way to go. And they had to bury the baby in a little shoe box. Me, when I go," brags Giizis with a long slow wave of her hand across the heaping plate, "you won't have to take up a collection. My funeral is all paid up."

"Whose isn't?" Noodin shrugs her sister's boast down. "Those vultures. They come around the reservation with those sales handouts—"

"Brochures."

"Catalogs. They make the rounds and you sit paging through those pictures of the caskets—"

"Mine!" Giizis says loudly. "Mine is frosted, I tell you, frosted!"

"Oh, that sure is wonderful." Rozin rolls her eyes. "Like a cake."

"Please," says Booch, "do we have to—"

"If you must know," Noodin loudly interposes.

"We don't need to know," says Booch, and Frank looks at him gratefully.

But Noodin's eyes flare with indignation. She ignores him. "I am paid up, too, with money from my checks. I put a small amount away each month. I got the cardinals, red cardinals painted on my casket and it's made of real oak, not cheap pine board. A cheerful woodsy scene on front. Spared no amount of big expense! I even got the dinner paid for and no jelly and no peanut butter—oh you bet, no commodity funeral for me!"

"Ticking. Mattress ticking. Railroad cloth. I like that on the inside of a casket, though," Giizis reflects.

"Homey-looking."

"Like you were really going to sleep or something. And then the sheets."

"Mine are satin."

"Don't you think," Rozin breaks in again from her corner place, where she's filled and refilled her plate, picking through her food with furious dispatch, "if you're going to spend for satin sheets, you could at least get enjoyment out of them in life?"

"You would," says Giizis sternly, spearing Frank with a look. But her attempt at embarrassing Rozin falls flat, for Rozin just nods and as though struck by some ecstatic thought smiles openly and suddenly at Frank, right across the table. Everyone can see her and notice that smile, too, which is the sort of curious and gloating smile a teenage girl turns on the first boy she's shown her breasts to in a parking lot. Returning her look, Frank's is grave and intent. Their look holds, and then, with quiet attention, tenderly, he dips some small morsel of dark meat into the scarlet of cranberries. Placing the tart, reddened flesh in his mouth, he casts his eyes down and chews.

Giizis has removed the slender forked bone from the breast meat already and stripped it clean, handing it to Cally, who has vowed with Deanna never to be tricked into pulling apart a wishbone. She gives it back to Grandma Giizis and has the presence of mind to say, "Share it." Giizis holds out the wishbone, and Noodin touches it. The bone is cool and faintly slippery in her fingers. The tiny strips of meat cling to it tenaciously. Looking into each other's brown, sorrowful eyes they seem lost, unguarded. The bone is fragile between them. They know from childhood that to break a wishbone to your advantage you must hold your thumb higher than that of your opponent, your sister.

And so Giizis tries. But Noodin has been harboring some secret anger and her thumb creeps higher. Giizis twists her hand to try wrenchimg the wishbone from her sister. Noodin stands with a cry and snaps off the longer piece of the bone. The two old twins pant and glare at each other and throw down the pieces of the wishbone. They bare their teeth murderously and then, still staring directly into each other's eyes, they change expressions and slowly, sheepishly, secretly, begin to laugh.

Noodin wipes her eyes. They sit. The pie is coming out, the rhubarb crisp, the cake, the coffee, the swamp tea, the cookies and Jell-O mold salad with peaches set in star shapes. And the men are talking to each other. They have outlasted the women's hold on the conversation and they are talking about their cars. They are discussing the insides of their cars the way women discuss their own insides. Pre-labor. Post-labor. Just the same except instead of doctors the men talk about their mechanics. Opinions, prognoses, prescriptions, and probabilities.

Dishes clatter. Coffee scents the air. The house is too warm, though, so the girls decide to cool themselves at the back door. They have sneaked out a plastic bag of turkey scraps. With it, they step out onto the tiny porch and stare from the steps out at the frozen gray yard and garage.

The dog appears instantly and smiles lovingly at them as they dump the scraps into his bowl.

THERE ARE TIMES in the city, rare times, when the baffle of sound parts. Cally and Deanna listen for those times of transitory silence. No cars. No planes' roar. No buses or distant traffic. No spatter of television noise, even people talking. Now, just as the twins define the moment by the absence of all it isn't, someone laughs, a car door slams, there is a screech of tires. It is gone, their moment of baseless peace.

The noise that brings them back is the muted plastic thump of a city garbage Dumpster and then crisp, slow steps. Rozin and Frank round the corner of the garage but they don't notice the twins because their eyes rest upon each other. Cally and Deanna can see their mother's warm three-quarters profile as she gazes seriously up into Frank's face. He is turned from them, but although they cannot view his expression they know it.

The grown-ups are staring at each other with moon-glow sitcom eyes!

"They are acting like two cows," says Cally.

The girls laugh in a mean and outraged way. They have also got a parcel of turkey bones they were told to throw in the sealed garbage container and not give to the dog. They give the bones to the dog.

Giizis takes a sip of the coffee, a bite of pie, and holds up her tiny piece of the wishbone. Noodin laughs, but then her face goes dark as she remembers. She finally speaks to the women sitting at the table.

"Yesterday," she announces. "Yesterday. That young doctor was forward with me!"

"What?" says Rozin.

"I knew there was something," says Giizis.

"How?" says Cecille.

All of the women put down their coffee cups and look at Noodin.

"The nurse came and told me to take off my clothes and put the robe on. So I do that. So I was lying there covered with that sheet," says Noodin, "and he came in for the exam. When he lifted that sheet for the exam he said, 'My, aren't we glitzy today!' "

" 'Glitzy'? You're kidding!"

Rozin and Cecille say this practically in unison.

Noodin frowns. "I hate when you say that. Of course I am not kidding. That is the way it was, the phrase of words, 'My, aren't we glitzy!' I said nothing, of course. Why in the world do you think he said it?"

"Maybe you're"—Cecille tries to think—"unusually better than normal down there!"

Giizis and Noodin look aghast.

"Did you wear some fancy underwear or something?"

"I had none on, of course," says Noodin. "None on at the time. No, it was simple rudeness, or worse. . . ."

"Did you wear some, ah, maybe some perfume?"

"Oooo," says Giizis.

"That neither," says Noodin. "I just, well, I used some of that feminine hygiene spray they advertise. I took it from your bathroom, that's all."

Rozin looks at her quizzically.

"I don't have any of that stuff."

"You don't have any?"

"No."

"Then . . . well, it looked like a can of what they advertise. Same color."

"Mom!"

"What?"

Noodin gets up and goes to check the bathroom. They hear her rummaging through a drawer, and finally she brings back the can. She holds out the can and shows it to Rozin.

"Is this what you used?" Rozin asks.

She nods. Rozin hands her the close-up pair of reading glasses that the twins share. The can is left over from Halloween. She did up Cally and Deanna's hair with a frosting of gold spray-glitter.

"Read the label, Mama."

Noodin does, then rears back, thoughtfully blinking.

13

Rozin

It is not so simple being Rozin Roy. You have a missing carpet stasher for a husband, an ardent baker who keeps dropping off boxes of ginger-frosted gingersnaps, a mother with a secret glitzy place, a job you must go to every day even if the week after Thanksgiving weekend one daughter wakes up with a headache and the other has a sore throat and both are experiencing a sense of loss because their father will soon be divorced from their mother. No matter that he was not around much, or when home, dimly lit or even smashed. He is their father.

"I never thought you'd be divorced," Cally weeps. "We hate Frank."

"No," says Deanna, "we love him, remember? But as our uncle, okay, Mom?"

Deanna quietly broods on her cereal. Both are mourning with reversals of mood. Rozin looks at the clock and thinks how when she was late just a week ago her supervisor gave her one of those looks of cool skepticism that signal the beginning of lack of trust. It was wrong for Rozin to have spent her three-month perfect record of goodwill. She had coffee this fall, too often, with Frank. All that dependability she'd built up, spent now that her children need her. She should certainly have anticipated this, but she made the mistake a so-called functional parent makes about a so-called dysfunctional parent. Yes, they do miss him! Of course the girls are sad! And now the grandmas have returned home saying they couldn't eat more of Frank's cookies. The cookies kept appearing once Grandma Giizis said she liked them. Irresistible cookies. Irresistible like Frank. But perhaps like Frank overbearingly sweet, Rozin thinks, an unworthy thought. He has become her lover. Their blood sugar has also shot way up into the heavens.

"I have to go to work now," Rozin tells her daughters. "I just have to. I'm going to get in trouble!"

Cally and Deanna look at each other and big burps and bubbles of sobs come up as they feel the same thing together. The feeling bounces back and forth, getting larger. This happened to them when they were babies. Rozin had to separate them to calm them.

They hear a flamenco tattoo, as if a tap dancer was merrily clicking across the floor on the other side of the wall. It is Sweetheart Calico. Tapitty tap tap, tapitty tap tap. Faster and faster. Tapittytaptaptap. The girls' sobs turn to fascinated hiccups. A door slams. They walk to the window as Sweetheart Calico, now silent, flashes across the weeds. Rozin bolts out the door.

"Wait! Come back!"

Sweetheart turns, eyes wide, and walks back toward Rozin's beckoning hand. Sweetheart is dressed in tight jeans and a flowing pale pink shirt. Her tiny black boots have steel clips on the toes and heels. Her hair is combed and braided on one side. It loops long down the other. Rozin doesn't tell her about the lopsided hairdo—maybe she's got only one hair band.

"Could you please, oh please, babysit the girls? They are too upset to go to school. They won't get on the bus. It is weirdly hot today! They need time to have their emotions. And I have to go to work."

Rozin's pleading rivets Sweetheart Calico and she stands very still and cocks her head forward in order to understand what Rozin is telling her. Rozin goes on, throwing her arms up and down, pointing at the car. Sweetheart's dog cocks his head side to side as Rozin swishes her arm at the door where the girls stand together, dressed alike as they do for comfort, and sad.

Yes, of course! Sweetheart Calico's look says. *I'll take care of them the same way I would take care of my own daughters!*

She nods and walks up to the girls, takes their hands in hers. Now the three are standing in the doorway and Rozin is waving good-bye.

"Good-bye, Mama, we'll be okay."

The girls cling to Sweetheart Calico. The dog sits steadfast at the doorstep. Rozin has many doubts but she drives off anyway, afraid of cool skepticism. Afraid of lack of trust. Afraid to offend her supervisor, who could take away the job that pays the mortgage and feeds them and buys all they need to live.

The Spaces

As soon as Rozin drives away, Sweetheart Calico lifts the girls' hands. She looks from one to the other. The cracked-off tooth in her smile makes her look homely and goofy, but also she is beautiful in her pointy boots and swirling blouse. She has a lot of makeup on—bubble-gum pink lipstick, happy blue eye shadow, blaring black eyeliner.

"You forgot one braid," says Cally.

"Yeah, you look weird like that," says Deanna.

Oh this? Sweetheart Calico touches her flowing hair uncertainly. *Wrong?*

"But it's not so bad," the girls decide. "It's a look."

Sweetheart Calico rolls her eyes, happy. *Here we go!* She swings their hands as she steps down the steps.

"Wait!" says Cally. "We never finished our breakfast!"

"We don't have jackets! Plus we're supposed to be sick!"

So what? Her arm swinging makes them laugh. *We'll find food. You're not really sick. It's weirdly warm today. Time to move, to go, to walk, to tap along, to jump and run!* The girls take jackets anyway because they do not trust the warm sun and they follow Sweetheart down the lumpy old sidewalk with the tree roots bulging up out of the earth. They run past her once they get to the park; they leap and scurry through the swing sets, monkey bars, and field of grass, where they find half an old Frisbee. They toss it awkwardly to the dog, who gamely chases along after it as if he is doing them a favor. Which he is. He is worried about where they are going. Sweetheart Calico always gets lost. He laps all the water he comes across. Pees everywhere he can. He does his best to leave a trail, in the manner of Hansel in the forest, but this has been a dry fall and there are few puddles. He pees like a frat boy. Everywhere. But can't reach fountains to replenish. They pass the lake and he gulps at the toxic shore until his stomach bulges. They are foraging on and on into the city, into the downtown area near the bus station, past the Irish pubs, music bars, and old buildings made of reddish purple stone dug from the northern Minnesota quarries or fawn-colored Kasota stone dug from the southern Minnesota quarries. Farther yet until they hit the river. There on its banks, the dog smells an entire two-day-old novel that Richard and Klaus have written with their scent in the leaves, on the sidewalks, on the ground, on the benches. They are not here anymore.

The dog tries to communicate with Sweetheart Calico: Let's go back now, it's time. Let's go home. They are not like your daughters. They can't run forever. They are not as swift, not as strong, and they are human, not like you.

The dog leaps at her, snapping at her one braid. Sweetheart Calico catches his jaw with her pointed steel toe. He yelps and crumples. Gets up showing his teeth. If only I were still a wolf, then I'd hamstring and eat you! The girls are slowing down, slumping over. They sit down on a curb. They are so hungry and thirsty that can't even cry. Desperate, the dog barks, lolls, leaps at everyone who passes in his most appealing way. Which is not appealing. Someone says, "There are leash laws, you know." Sweetheart Calico stands watching, twitchy and annoyed. She does not like to stand still. The girls droop on the curb some more. At last a man comes out of the pizza shop behind them with sodas and slices. He can't stand it anymore. The children gobble up their food with big eyes and he tells Sweetheart Calico that she should take them home. He keeps talking, trying to impress the gravity on her. They shouldn't be around here. This is not a good neighborhood for children as they could get picked up and drugged and either sold to a Wayzata businessman or trafficked up to Duluth to service the freighters—and it is dark, anyway, and who are they and maybe he should call the police?

Sweetheart Calico gives her most human nod and saunters off. The dog and the girls follow her. The man shrugs and walks back inside. It's getting cold. Around the corner, Sweetheart leaps high and cuts a little caper. It's time now! The lights are going to ride up and down! The signs pulse on: There's girls hot, hot, hot! And free drinks for pretty women! Just past Augies she forgets the twins. But that's all right because they're gone, anyway, following the dog, who is following the trail of his own piss marks down the streets and through the alleys and across the parks and backyards and church landscaping across the bus station sidewalk and along old park benches and over the walking bridge that spans I-94 and its torrent of noise.

And do their feet ever hurt. And their sad little hearts feel ever sadder. And will they get back to their mother?

A COOL FALL NIGHT on Andrew Jackson Street. Dead cottonwood leaves clattering and traffic a dim snarl to the west. Rozin sits with her back to the open window. She watches her phone as if staring at it would make it ring. She imagines the police voice, We've found them. We've found them. The police told Rozin to stay home and wait because missing children usually show up. They usually do! They will! But nothing happens. Her heart's flamenco tattoo taptittytaptap. Hating itself. Adrenaline floods her like poison. She's alert and leaden. There is the phone, ringing with some crazy new ringtone. But no, that's just chatter of sleeping sparrows in the leggy vines. She hears the girls outside! But no, that's the fan in the next room, sifting fire through its sleeves. The light socket with the bulb out grows a new bulb. What thoughts. Stupid thoughts.

Rozin wakes to the telephone's persistent ring. Downstairs, in the yellow wash of light over the kitchen sink, she raises the phone to her aunt's voice.

"Did you find them?" Giizis asks.

"No."

Rozin lowers the receiver into its cradle. She passes her hand across her face, crumples a fist to her mouth, and wonders what she will feel next. Nothing comes. Just nothing, though her blood roars and her skull suddenly feels tight as a helmet. Her brain overstuffed with too many thoughts. She is just about to lift the phone again and call somebody, anybody, when Deanna's voice floats down from the top of the staircase.

"Mama . . ."

Rozin steps back out into the hallway, stands at the bottom holding the worn curl of the banister.

"Mama?" Deanna asks. "We're lost."

Cally says, "Shut up, Deanna. She knows."

They aren't up there. The house is empty.

Rozin freezes. An excuse, a little laugh, shoots up inside her and then her throat shuts. If she lets her daughters keep talking, they will never stop. They'll go on talking. She'll talk them all the way home. The air at the top of the stairs is thick as black cotton and she can't see where they went. Her knees give.

"Come home," she whispers.

Dread like an ice cape. Silence. The dread passes over and a lighter feeling sails in. Her heart bobs and the longing is a stitch in her side. She gasps painfully.

"Come out, come out, wherever you are," she calls out, hopeful and afraid. But there is no answer. Wax leaves clatter against the side of the house. She crouches on the bottom step, motionless.

She won't call Frank. Perversely, she thinks he got her into this mess. He poured the coffee that kept her from going to work all those times, which made her paranoid about missing work this morning. And Sweetheart Calico. Her. Her. Why did Rozin ignore her best instincts and leave her children with a woman who has never spoken a word out loud, a woman weird and wild or FAS or learning disabled or suffering a form of autism or some undiagnosed ADD or ADHD or who is off her medication for some mental disorder even though she sometimes seems so pleasant and willing and kind and playful.

Rozin begins to pray to the great and kind spirit. The earth tips its farthest shoulder to the sun and the dark goes solid. Cold air seizes in bands along the mopboards. She sits there, waiting. Incrementally, the dark motes thin to gray. The air stirs with the cold soupiness of dawn. She doesn't shift her weight. She doesn't lean or twist to move again, not until the starlings begin to whistle in the tattered cedars.

Rozin rises and slips her arms into an old shirt. One of Richard's that she kept, a black-and-white checkered shirt that reaches almost down to her knees. For he is a tall man, and she is more her mother's size. She removes a heavy iron pot from its cupboard place and brings it over to the bowl of the kitchen sink. Into the pot, she pours an inch or so of wild rice. A fine sweet dust rises off the rice like smoke, smelling of the lake bottom, weedy and fresh. Next, she runs water into the pot, swirls her hand among the ticking grains. Black-green, brown-green, dotted with paler speckles and very fine. Uncultivated. Not the fake stuff. Knocked into the bottom of Noodin's beat-up aluminum canoe. A few small hulls, sharp and papery, ride the surface. Poured off, the water carries away green clay, powdery silt. Another water. Five waters altogether, until the last comes clean and she sets the pot aside. Onions now. She holds a kitchen match tight between her teeth so the juice won't make her eyes water, then she crosshatches the onion from the root end, slicing the tiny cubes into a pile she keeps neatly triangled with the flat of the knife.

Broth will slowly cook the onions into the rice. Before she sets the top on the pot she adds a tiny pinch of white pepper but no more. The twins like simple foods, no spices. Odd they never got their dad's complex food tastes. Basic foods. Potatoes and cheese for Cally. Rozin remembers the stubborn genius of Richard's ways and sees him, now, before her suddenly. Dark brown hair and brown eyes with a curved smile and hollow cheeks. Shuts her eyes against the picture.

He is a magnet, Richard Whiteheart Beads, with a prickly and unappeasable energy some people resent and others worship. Around him, she was like that herself, never doing things the easy way, always finding the method of most resistance. Even now, she prefers to cook food she'll have to guide and watch over. A soft vanilla pudding from scratch. Stewed turkey. Creamed corn still from scratch, though she can't use fresh cobs, only frozen this late in the year. She butters and creams them, pours them back into a plastic bowl. It is good, though, the care she takes with everything, for the smell of this food is going to bring them home.

She sets two places carefully. A paper napkin folded once. Knife, fork, and spoon all on one side. She fills the plates with the wild rice in a heap beside the turkey, the milky, buttery corn, a bit of fruit salad containing strawberries, and, beside them, a large bowl of vanilla pudding.

Come on now. Come home. Eat it, eat it all up, now, she thinks vehemently, heartsick. You've been out all night. The sooner you eat the sooner you can go to sleep.

The minute hand flicks down the face of the clock. 7:30. The phone rings. The caller ID says it is Frank so she does not answer it. At 7:36 she hears the dog scrabbling up the steps and then the tired dragging footsteps of her daughters. She's out the door and holding them. They smell like salt, pepperoni, leaves, garbage. They smell like the only meaning in life. They slept in the park, they tell her in amazement, underneath the heaviest bushes. They had their jackets! There was a thick layer of newspaper down on the ground, so they curled up because they couldn't walk farther and the dog curled with them to keep them warm you should have heard he growled a horrible growl if anybody came near the bush. They don't know where they were. Where Sweetheart Calico was. And no, she didn't kidnap them. No. They just went with her. For the fun of it. And then it wasn't fun and they were lost and a man gave them pizza and the night covered them. Then to get back here they followed the dog. And what's that smell? It smells good. Is there some food? They sit at the table shoveling in the food with concentration. As Rozin watches them, her being fills. She gets up and walks to the refrigerator. She takes out a pound of hamburger, which is all the meat she has, unwraps the meat, and puts in on a plate on the floor. The dog comes over, inhales the meat. Laps fresh water from the bowl she sets beside it. Rozin slowly lifts the phone.

"Did you find them?" asks Noodin.

"Yes," she says.

Rozin knows that they have been smoking their little pipes and praying all night long. They learned the words to their prayers from their grandmother Peace and their grandfather Waabizi, The Swan, during the years those two raised them. The words call the spirits by name from each direction, from the sky, from the earth, from the night, from the day, from the sun, from the moon, from the winds, the flocks of birds and the solitary birds, from the clans, from the animals that give themselves as food or are sent to delight us or to help us, like the dog, from the rivers, from the lakes, from the rain, from the water in the mother's body and the water in the snow, from the stars and the mysterious place the stars came from, and the fire, the original fire.

14

Almost Soup

Now, my brothers and sisters, having retraced my urine with stunning accuracy, snarled at bums all night, snarfed a bowl of hamburger, and having guarded and saved my young humans, I will resume the story of my life. I begin shortly after I received my name. As you know, I started my life in the vicinity of Roys and Shawanos. There I lived among my relatives, who all descended in some manner from the dog named Sorrow, who was nursed by Blue Prairie Woman and bequeathed to us our eternal protective connection, the devotion of Sorrow's descendants to hers. I was brought down to this place by the theft of Sweetheart Calico. We dogs sensed that danger and chaos in her form could threaten the twins.

I like Gakaabikaang. I've made it my home. Here on the ground where I now sprawl and scratch, I intend to live out my years of strength, fertility, and purpose. As you see, I have survived into my tranquil middle age. But not by chance. Not by luck. I have the dog skills of the ages in my blood.

Survival Rules for Animoshag

It is jokingly said by Anishinaabeg that those Indians who live on the plains eat dogs while they, the woods Indians, eat rabbits. However, it is my dog experience that this is not entirely true. I tell you now, relatives and friends, it is best to beware. Even in Ojibwe country, we are not out of danger.

There are the slick and deadly wheels of reservation cars. Poisons, occasionally, set out for our weaker cousins the mice and rats. Not to speak of the coyotes, the paw-snapping jaws of clever Ojibwe trapper steel. And we may happen into the snares set as well for our enemies. Lynx. Marten. Feral cats. Bears, whom we worship. I learned early. Eat anything you can at any time. Fast. Bolt it down. Stay cute, but stay elusive. Don't let them think twice when they've got the hatchet out. I see cold steel, I'm gone. Believe it. And there are all sorts of illnesses we dread. Avoid the bite of the fox. It is madness. Avoid all bats. Avoid all black-and-white-striped moving objects. And slow things with spiny quills. Avoid all humans when they get into a feasting mood. Get near the tables fast, though, once the food is cooked. Stay close to their feet. Stay ready.

But don't steal from their plates.

Avoid medicine men. Snakes. Boys with BB guns. Anything ropelike or easily used to hang or tie. Avoid outhouse holes. Cats that live indoors. Do not sleep under cars. Or with horses. Do not eat anything attached to a skinny, burning string. Do not eat lard from the table. Do not go into the house at all unless no one is watching. Do not, unless you are absolutely certain you can blame it on a cat, eat any of their chickens. Do not eat pies. Do not eat decks of cards, plastic jugs, dry beans, dish sponges. If you must eat a shoe, eat both of the pair, every scrap, untraceable. Always, when in doubt, the rule is you are better off underneath the house. Don't chase cars driven by young teenage boys. Don't chase cars driven by old ladies. Don't bark or growl at men cradling rifles. Don't get wet in winter, and don't let yourself dry out when the hot winds of August blow. We're not equipped to sweat. Keep your mouth open. Visit the lake. Pee often. Take messages from tree stumps and the corners of buildings. Don't forget to leave in return a polite and respectful hello. You never know when it will come in handy, your contact, your friend. You never know whom you will need to rely upon.

Which is how I come to my next story of survival.

Avoiding Sacrifice

Within the deep lakes of the Ojibwe there is supposed to live a kind of man-monster-cat thing that tips boats over in the cold of spring and plucks down into his arms the sexiest women. Keeping this cranky old thing happy is the job of local Indian humans and they're always throwing their tobacco in the water, talking to the waves. But when the monster takes a person in whatever way—usually by drowning—there is some deeper, older, hungrier urge that must be satisfied by a stronger item than tobacco. You guessed it. Lay low, animoshag. I tell you, when a man goes out drunk in his motorboat, hide. Say he's just good-timing, lapping beer, driving his boat in circles, and he hits his own wake coming at him. Pops out of the boat. Goes down.

Humans call that fate. We dogs call that stupidity. Whatever you name it, there's always a good chance they'll come looking for a dog. A white dog. One to tie with red ribbons. Brush nice. Truss in a rope. Feed a steak or two. Pray over. Pet soft. Not worth it. Stone around the neck. Then, splash. Dog offering!

My friends and relatives, we have walked down the prayer road clearing the way for humans since before time started. We have gone ahead of them to present their good points to the gatekeeper at that soft pasture where they eat all day and gamble the night away. Don't forget, though, in heaven we still just get the bones they toss. We have kept our humans company in darkest hours. Saved them from starvation—you know how. We have talked to their gods on their behalf and thrown ourselves in front of their wheels to save them from idiotic journeys, to the bootlegger's, say. We're glad to do these things. As an old race, we know our purpose. Original Dog walked alongside Nanabozhoo, their tricky creator. The dog is bound to the human. Raised alongside the human. With the human. Still, half the time we know better than the human.

We have lain next to our personal human shrouded in red calico. We have let our picked-clean ceremonial dog bones be reverently buried in bark houses. We have warned off bad spirits from their babies, and talked to the irritating ghosts of their suicide uncles and aunts. We have always given of ourselves. We have always thought of humans first. And yet, for me, when Fatty Simon went down I did not hesitate. I took to the woods. I had puppies, after all, to provide for. I had a life. Next time, there was a guardrail accident way up on the bridge and Agnes Anderson met her end that way. Again, not me. Not me tied like a five-cent bundle and tossed overboard. Nor when the lake took Alberta Meyer or the Speigelrein girls, not when old Kagewah fell through that spring sitting in his icehouse or even when our track star Morris Shawano disappeared and his dad's boat washed up to the north. Not me. Not Almost Soup. That is my name and I refuse to give it up for human mistakes or human triumphs.

I refused, that is, until my girls weakened and got sick.

As I told you, a girl saved my life, but also saved me from worse—you know. (And now I specifically address my brothers, the snip-snip. The Big Fix. The words we all know and watch for in their plans and conversations.) Cally and Deanna hid me whenever their mother tried to drag me to the vet. Thus, they saved my male doghood and allowed me full dogness. I have had, as a result of their courage, the honor of carrying our dogline down the generations many times. For this, alone, how could I ever thank them enough? And then they got sick, as I say.

Visiting their grandmas for Christmas, it happened. One foul night in a blizzard they got sick with a fever and a cough. It worsened, worsened, until I sensed the presence of the black dog. We all know the black dog. That is, death. He smells like iron cold. Sparks fly from his fur. He is the one who drags the creaking cart made of sticks. We have all heard the wheels groan as they turned, and hoped they would keep on past our house. But on that cold late winter night, up north, he stopped. I heard his hound breath, felt the heat of his lungs of steam and fire.

15

Lazy Stitch

Almost Soup

Curled underneath the beading table with the shoeless feet of women, you hear things you'd never want to know. Or things you do. Maybe it's the needles, Pony Number Twelve, so straight and fine they slip right through the toughest hide. Maybe it is my own big ears that catch everything, and more. Maybe it's the colors of the seed beads that work up in stitches so intimate and small—collect, collect—until you have a pattern to the anguish.

We dogs know what the women are really doing when they are beading. They are sewing us all into a pattern, into life beneath their hands. We are the beads on the waxed string, pricked up by their sharp needles. We are the tiny pieces of the huge design that they are making—the soul of the world.

See here, Rozin says, holding out her work with a trembling hand. We dogs know already what happened down in

Gakaabikaang and why she left for her mothers' house. After her children ran off with Sweetheart Calico, after her lover, Frank, left boxes of cookies that the dog willingly wolfed, after Rozin was late the entire next week and the week after the trauma and the celebration of Cally and Deanna's return into her arms, she was laid off. She applied for unemployment and was given enough to live on if she used her savings bit by bit as she looked for the next job. But not enough to pay the mortgage on that house.

Frank suggested that, as the girls were out of school for Christmas break, why not go up north and stay with their grandmas for a while? "I'll fix up your house," he said, "and we can live there when we get married. I'll even help with the mortgage."

That last line seals it (although Rozin ignores the when-we-get-married part). She takes the girls up to her original turf for a visit. And then she stays. And Frank travels up and travels back. Up and back. And whatever is happening down in Gakaabikaang just happens without Rozin. Her cousins up north, Jackie and Ruby, who figure they have a say in Rozin's love life, counsel her to go back down and snap up Frank. He has a job, they say, fully employed! And pleasant enough looks and is maybe insecure but that's a plus in an Indian guy. He doesn't appear to drink to excess. Wow! He is also known to be one of those rare men who was faithful to his wife until he left her. So what is Rozin waiting for? Why the hesitancy? Why the chilled feet? Why enroll her daughters in the tribal school and disrupt their learning process? She even has a house down there! Is it that you miss the grandmas? They will visit you. Is it that you fear commitment after Richard? Just get over it. Do you guys lack chemistry?

"No," says Rozin, "there's too much of it."

"There can't be too much," says Ruby, looking puzzled at Jackie. They are both large, happy women who laugh often and make anything, everything, into wild rice hot-dish.

ROZIN CAN'T SAY exactly what "it" is and so cannot be helped. She just wants to stay where she is, living out by the lake with her mother and her aunt. Even though they drive her crazy, she just wants to stay with them and learn things, oh, cultural and spiritual things, maybe, and she wants her daughters near and she does not want to rely on a man to make her happy. Frank. Though she misses him. Well, but she can live with it.

Here's the real reason: Getting her children back feels like all the luck in her life is now used up. She doesn't want to take any more risks.

But I could have told her that from a dog's point of view life is nothing but risks.

Wild Rose Pattern

"Let me tell you about this flower," Rozin rambles to her mother now, "this leaf, this heart-in-a-heart, this wild rose, these girls of mine."

"Cally knows everything about me. Deanna knows everything about everything."

"What things, for instance?"

"Ridiculous things!"

Rozin lowers her velvet and the old twins' eyes glide over at the swimming vines, the maple leaf in three blends of green beads, the powerful twist of the grape tendril, and her four roses of hearts that she's finishing in a burst of dangerous pinks. Rozin is becoming tiny and bird-boned. She has developed a drooping eye. You could think this eye was giving you the curse. Or you could think it was giving you the come-on.

"So how, ridiculous?"

"Just listen!"

"My girls and I get confused about one another. It happens with mothers and daughters, you know it does. Deanna. Cally. We think the same things sometimes. They don't mind if I am nine years old again. Will they even like me three years from now? Will I embarrass them? Will they hate me like the other girls all hate their mothers? Was I like that to you?"

Noodin and Giizis exchange a look that says, *Whatever they deal to her she's got it coming.*

"Eya', indaanis," says Noodin. "Don't worry."

CALLY AND DEANNA are always outside. It's good for them, Rozin thinks. Cally stomps massive clearings out on her snowshoes and throws her jacket off, her hat, for me to run with and toss. We see a mink flash by. Deanna loses her mittens for me to find. The girls play hard then tear into the house, faces dark with joy, cheeks blazing, the raw cold and sweat of icy breezes swirling in their hair.

Rozin paints their fingernails a golden satin pink. Cally burns her mouth on hot bread behind her back.

"Ow, Grandma!"

But Cally is laughing, fanning off the tip of her tongue, taking the next piece of dough her grandma fries with more care. Instead of eating once it cools, however, my girl suddenly sets down the golden crust, unfinished. Cally coughs hard and then she is tired. She curls up by Deanna. They wrap together in one blanket beside the stack of old newspapers that the grandmas keep by their easy chairs. They don't want to play with the dog anymore. I sneak under the edge of the couch-cover fringe. They usually don't let me in the house—the girls have to hide me.

Just like her great-grandfather Augustus, Giizis reads all of the summer news through long winter nights. She calls out to Noodin or Rozin occasionally, exclaiming over a visit from the Pope, another shooting, the practices of cults and movie stars. Now she shades Cally and Deanna from lamplight as they curl into a knitted afghan. It is only later when the girls wake, flushed in their first misery, that anyone except me even knows they are sick.

Their fevers shoot up abruptly to an identical 103. Rozin takes the steel bowl and washcloth. She wrings the cloth reluctantly, sloppily, and bathes down the fever, wiping slow across her daughters' arms and throats. Faster, faster! I think desperately, whining. She touches the girls' stomachs and they both cry out. Their faces wrench suddenly.

"Mama!"

Rozin bundles off the knitted blankets, brings fresh sheets and remakes the couch. All that night they are up, then down. I am constant. Under the couch, I keep faith and keep watch. Rozin falls asleep on the roll-away in the next room and Noodin sleeps beside the couch in the recliner, covered up with an old hunting jacket and a giveaway quilt. Giizis sleeps down on the cold floor. Every hour, Cally or Deanna cries out and is sick with nothing in her stomach, her whole body straining, her face fiery with heat again.

There are eight inches of new snow on the ground next morning. Rozin wakes to a still brightness in the tiny bitterly cold closet where she slept as a child. She curls for a moment into the blanket, deeper, then rolls wearily over when she hears the girls. She closes her eyes, aching for the warmth again, waiting for Noodin or Giizis to respond. Cally and Deanna continue to cry softly. Rozin rips the covers down with an almost angry gesture and hops out, stretching. Shit, she mumbles, walking into the next room. Her hand, though, touches down gently on Cally's forehead and cheeks as she strokes. She refills the basin, then sponges each daughter's blazing gold forehead, throat. She lifts Deanna's head and puts the cloth against the back of her neck and again rubs Cally's chest, again waits out the dry heaving.

Noodin goes out to shovel. An hour passes, and then Rozin pours a little ginger ale into a cup and sits down, careful not to jostle her daughters. She feeds them teaspoon by teaspoon, waiting for each spoonful to settle. Their lips are dry. Rozin puts a bit of Vaseline on her finger, rubs their deep and punished color. Cally lies back in the pillows, impossibly still. Deanna turns over and stares dully at the wall.

When Noodin comes in the door, Rozin turns.

It's no good, Noodin's look says. The phones were unreliable anyway, now cut off.

Then the girls can't keep down even those precious teaspoons of ginger ale and the whole miserable process begins again. They'll get dehydrated, Rozin says. Now Giizis comes in from outdoors, from the old lean-to where she's been searching through rolls and bags of bark for the best slippery elm, the strongest sage to boil to make a healing steam. Noodin goes back out and all morning they hear her shovel or the regular fall of her ax as she builds up the woodpile. I go out to encourage and guard her. Slip back in, dart under the couch. Hardly eat. By the end of the afternoon, Giizis's eyes narrow, her lips crease with worry. The smell of cooking upsets the girls. More snow falls and all day they take turns sleeping and eat cold food.

Cally is shrinking, thinning, hardening on her bones, Deanna is coughing in explosive spasms that shake the springs just over my head. Weeping tiredly. Cranky. Then they lose the energy to fight and grow too meek. I lick the hand that hangs over the edge of the couch. I call upon my ancestors and their old ones for help. That night, the girls seem even worse. They stare blankly at Rozin, who takes a sleeping bag and sleeps in the chair and sends Noodin to sleep on the roll-away. Rozin coaxes her daughters back to sense after that odd stare. Falling instantly into my own sleep, I dream of hissing cats.

Bad omen! Bad things! I wake at Cally's cry and Rozin jumps to her. Cally thrashes her arms and legs, but then silently and rhythmically. The regular movement of the seizure stiffens Rozin to a calm horror. She holds Cally as best she can until the climbing movements of her arms and legs cease. At last Cally sags, unknowing, her face at her mother's breast, eyes staring out of the whited mask of her features.

"Cally."

Rozin's voice is deep, from a place in her body I have never heard. Cally. She calls her daughter back from a far-off tunnel path. Cally's mouth opens and she vomits blood into Rozin's hands, into a towel she holds beneath her daughter's mouth. She calls until her daughter stops looking through her mother and brings her troubled gaze to bear. She regards her mother from a distance, then, with eyes that soften in a grown woman's pity.

Rozin wipes her daughter's mouth, her forehead, her twig wrists, the calves, so fine, burning, dry. The soles of her feet. She wipes and wrings and wipes again until Cally stops looking at the ceiling. Rozin keeps on stroking with the cloth, finds herself humming. Slowly singing, she wipes up and down the pole arms. The forehead, her daughter's beating throat. She wipes until Cally says, I'm thirsty, I'm so thirsty, in a normal voice.

You have to wait. Just wait a little bit. Rozin's voice shakes.

Cally falls back. Her eyes shut. Her lips have darkened, cracked in fine, bloody lines, and her skin dries the wet cloth. Rozin keeps on wiping the fever away. I know she feels it underneath her hands, swirling, disappearing, but always coming back. After a while, I can see the fever itself, a viral red-yellow translucence creeping behind the blue of the wiping cloth. The exact same thing happens to Deanna next. Rozin puts the fire out, all night she puts the fire out, wiping until the sweet blue trembles in her daughters and she herself is light, lighter, rising to her feet to get the teaspoon again, fetching the ginger ale, the cup. She adds more water to the boiling kettle on the stove, more bark. The air is steaming, the windows a solid black with frost, a heart-rent blue, a dim gray, then white when Noodin rises to take her place.

Rozin sleeps, but her nerves are shot through with adrenaline. She lasts one hour and then rises strong with fear. She washes her face—the water icy from the tap—brushes her teeth. Her eyes in the mirror are staring, young and round. She slicks her hair back into a tail and chews a nail impatiently.

"Go to bed."

Giizis sends her back, fierce, almost slapping at her. And so a day passes. Another evening. Another night in which Rozin and Cally and Deanna do as before, the same routine, no change, except that the girls are weaker, Rozin stronger in her exhaustion.

You get too tired, you'll get sick too.

The grandmas send Rozin to bed with hard words, but their eyes are warm and still with a mixture of worry, sympathy, and something Rozin has not seen in their faces before. Drifting away she wonders at it, but then the dark well opens and she drops into an unconsciousness so profound she does not hear the four-wheel-drive winter ambulance finally groan and whine down the road that Noodin is killing her heart to shovel.

The ride down to IHS is complicated by new drifts and whiteouts. I jump in the back and hide just as they swerve off. No way that I'll get left behind. The dark comes on quickly as the EMT drives along, silent. In the back Rozin holds our girls. Snowlight flicks through the branches as the wheels grind and tear and the ambulance swings patiently along. Rozin stares into her daughters' faces and whispers. Cally's skin goes white as wax. Deanna's dark eyes bore into her mother's face, intent and strange. Their skin is rough as velvet when cool, then slides up to the skid of wax again when hot. They finally get there, carry the girls into the emergency room, into the hands of the nurses and doctor.

One look at their blood pressure and the doctor orders IVs. Cally has surprising strength. I watch through the hospital window. Hear her yells and shouts. See Deanna tug away, or try to, but Rozin holds her close in a fixed and tender grip saying calm words, calm though wrenched inside out at her daughter's feeble terror. They put a cot up right beside them in the hospital room. At last with Noodin downstairs on the phone, signing papers and arranging things, with Cally and Deanna on the IVs suddenly unhollowed, full of color, strengthening and falling into sleep, Rozin lies still, breathing calmly.

It is then, in the hospital room, halfway asleep, that Rozin feels me put her daughters' lives inside of them again. Unknown to her, I have taken their lives with me to keep them safe. Waiting for her daughters to return, Rozin feels some confusion, a fall of silver, a branch loaded with snow, the snow crashing through her arms. Then Cally and Deanna are back in their own beds and they are separate, drifting off under different cotton blankets, in sterilized sheets, into deeper and deeper twilight, entering new ravines.

ROZIN IS SEWING the roses onto a shawl of black velvet, a border of madder pink and fuchsia flowers, twining stems, fancy leaves that never grew on any tree except in her mind. She has an odd thought—Cover the whole world with lazy stitch! Then Cally and Deanna walk in the door and say in unison, There's nothing lazy about it! Rozin rubs the corner of her one drooping eye, but she says nothing. It's a small thing, this mind reading that the girls do on her these days, and it's harmless except that sometimes her daughters get big feelings they are not ready for yet. The old, dead, angry love between her and Richard, unfinished sadness so big and devouring that she can't understand it herself. The worry at what he has become. The lonely wish to walk small between her mother, her aunt again, their arms curving over her like tree branches, making a smooth dim path for her to travel.

She takes agonizing stitches. Uses harrowing orange. They almost shoot fire in the dark room, these pinks. The word for beads in the old language is manidoominensag, little spirit seed.

Though I live the dog's life and take on human sins, I am connected in the beadwork. I live in the beadwork too. The flowers are growing, the powerful vines. The pattern of her daughters' wild souls is emerging. With each bead she plants in the swirl, Rozin adds one tiny grain.

Part Three

Niswi

Sounding Feather, great-grandma of first Shawano, dyed her quills blue and green in a mixture of her own piss boiled with shavings of copper. No dye came out the same way twice. According to her contribution, always different. The final color resulted from what she ate, drank, what she did for sex, and what she said to her mother or her child the day before. She never knew if she'd end up with blue dye, green, or a dull combination. What frightened her was this: One morning, after she had lost her struggles, done evil in the night, resented and sought revenge of her sisters, slapped her husband and screamed at her child, the quill worker peed desultorily and finished her usual dye. Dipping the white quills into the mixture, she found that the blue she made that day was unusually innocent, lovely, deep, and clear.

16

The First Mix-up

WHEN CALLY AND DEANNA were born, the new assistant nurse who clicked the stopwatch twice, as each twin emerged, and later cleaned up after the birth had then to deal with Grandma Noodin.

"Where are their birth cords?" Grandma asked the nurse.

The young woman thought she hadn't heard right. "They don't get cards, they get certificates."

"I said cords, like the thing between the baby and the mother. Where are they?"

"The umbilical cords?"

"That is right, smarty-pants."

"I guess I threw them out. They're in the trash!"

"The trash?" Grandma Noodin swelled in alarm. "Go get them," she cried.

The nurse hustled to the hazardous waste bins, filled with bloody paper birth pads and rubber gloves. She knew already that this must be one of the cultural issues surrounding birth that she had read of in her maternity textbook. She was preparing to keep a straight face if Grandma Noodin wanted to fry the birth cords. She imagined telling her roommates about it. Good thing she remembered how she'd carefully wrapped the two long cords that the father had severed. Cutting the babies' cords was not his idea, but the mother said it was the father's job and he had taken it on, reluctantly. He had tried not to shut his eyes. The nurse found the cords and showed them to Grandma Noodin in triumph.

"Here they are!"

"Which one goes to which baby?"

"Oh, I don't know. Does it matter if you're going to eat them? Here."

The nurse had wrapped each piece of umbilical cord in a new length of gauze. Grandma Noodin glared at her in new outrage.

"We don't eat them, you fool," she said. "The babies play with them."

"*Play* with them?" The nurse's voice betrayed her disquiet and she tried to hide it by clearing her throat. "Play with them." She said it again to make sure.

"Yes, that's right," said Grandma Noodin sternly. "So you need to have the right cord for the right twin."

The nurse now looked fascinated. "Because if one played with her *sister's* cord . . . ," she prompted.

"She could get sick later on."

Grandma Noodin took the cords in their clean gauze wrappings, frowned at them, compared them, shook her head, and put them in a cigar box already filled with tobacco and sage. The herbs would dry the cords out and then she would sew each one into a buckskin holder shaped like a small turtle. She and Grandma Giizis would bead those little turtles using precious old cobalts and yellows and Cheyenne pinks and greens in a careful design. Grandma Noodin pretended that she knew which cord belonged to each baby. She labeled each roll of gauze because she did not want to upset anyone. It was a heavy responsibility. And ever after that, she secretly worried. If the cords were mixed up right from the beginning, all sorts of things could happen.

Indis

The turtles hung off the curved headbands of the babies' dikinaaganan, then off their belts. Just as Grandma Noodin had said, the indis was each baby's first toy. Some believed that an indis was supposed to be placed off in the woods. Others said the person was supposed to have it all their life, even to get buried with it back on reservation land. But one day the twins came in from playing and their beaded turtles were gone. Grandma Noodin breathed a sigh of relief. No longer would the girls be mixed up, too mixed up maybe, the way she and Giizis had always been ever since they were young.

Why They Needed Names

Rozin thought differently when she knew they had lost their beaded turtle pouches. Slowly, over time, the absence . . . it began to tell. The girls began to wander from home, first with Sweetheart Calico. Then they flew away on fevers and she was afraid they would not return. Where would they go next? Rozin wanted to keep them here on this earth.

"I fear the spirits are trying to take them away from me. What should I do?" she asked Noodin and Giizis.

"Isn't it obvious?" said Noodin.

"Oh, that," said Rozin.

The girls did not have traditional names. They did not have Ojibwe names. This had always been a sore spot with everyone. One thing or another always intervened. Maybe Rozin had been lazy about it. No, she'd been lazy for sure. One thing was also true. She could ask only Noodin and Giizis to name them, otherwise they would be offended, but then whatever names they came up with everyone would have to accept. Rozin would have to live with their names for her daughters. That was giving her mother and her aunt a lot of power, but now Rozin decided that she had to do it.

Rozin went over to her purse, pulled out a pouch of Prince Albert tobacco, and put a pinch of it in each woman's hand.

"I am giving you tobacco to find names for Cally and Deanna," she said.

The old twins' hard eyes misted over, their hands enfolded the tobacco, they touched the flakes of tobacco with their fingers, and slowly like sleepy birds cocked their heads from side to side. The fact is they had already dreamed long complex dreams in which the names of their granddaughters were revealed. But that night they had short dreams that were like page markers of the other dreams.

The Names

In Noodin's dream she followed Cally into the woods and out of the woods and along a lakeshore out onto the prairie until she met the place where sky met earth and Cally wrote her name in the dirt: Ozhaawashkmashkodikwe.

THAT SAME NIGHT, Grandma Giizis dreamed that an old white man with stringy gray hair approached her and lifted his arm. He held it sideways so that Giizis could read his scar. Gaagigenagweyaabiikwe.

THEY MADE THE mistake of telling Rozin about the dreams before the ceremony.

Objection to History

"Those names are both freighted with tragedy," says Rozin. "I knew it! I just knew you'd come up with names that carried old baggage."

The grandmas stand firm. They have had their dreams and the dreams are definitive. Yes, there was a Blue Prairie Woman. Yes, there was a man named Scranton Roy who killed their ancestor and then appeared on the reservation with that word scored into his arm. Yes, there is history. No getting around it. But the dead exert a protective influence and their spirits rejoice when they know that their names are still used in this world. So Cally and Deanna should receive their traditional names in a family ceremony.

Rozin refuses to give her daughters those names, and the grandmas are shocked and grieved. The dreams are strong. The dreams are correct and it is completely wrong to interrupt the naming.

"We don't like it," says Giizis.

"Something might go wrong now," says Noodin. "Again."

"You're trying to scare me," says Rozin. "Anyway, there's no hurry. The names are the names, right?"

Cecille drives up from Minneapolis for the ceremony and Rozin tells her that there will not be a ceremony. Cecille says, "I drove up here and canceled all of my classes. Everyone has rearranged their schedules. But who cares!"

The grandmas pout and glower. They smoke their pipes and pray to the spirits that gave the names and tell them that no disrespect is meant. They ask the spirits to have patience with Rozin. They pray over Cally and Deanna. They do their best to put their invisible world back into some order. Right afterward the twins run away again.

This time they stow away in the backseat of Cecille's car, so of course the running away is again by accident. Cally and Deanna think she's just going into town to the store, where they'll surprise her and beg her to buy some candy. But the car keeps going and going and they fall asleep underneath a star quilt that represents the ancestors of the Ojibwe who came from the stars.

Cecille keeps driving, oblivious in the scrawl and loop of her favorite music. One road widens into two lanes, then four, then six, past the farms and service islands, into the dead wall of the suburbs and still past that, finally, into the city's complex heart.

Lemon Light

The girls wake up when the car stops at Frank's Bakery, where Cecille is still living in the upstairs apartment. After Cecille gets out and takes things from the trunk to bring upstairs, they slip from the backseat. They walk into Frank's shop, and the bell dings with a cheerful alertness. They have the chance to smell those good bakery smells of yeasty bread and airy sugar. Behind the counter, lemony light falls on Frank. He is big, strong, pale brown like a loaf of light rye left to rise underneath a towel. But his voice is muffled and weak, like it is squeezed out of the clogged end of a pastry tube.

He grabs the telephone, his eyes still on the girls.

"They're down here! They just walked in! They must have been in Cecille's car because she just pulled in! They're okay. They're . . ."

Frank puts his hand over the phone and whispers, "Are you girls fine?"

They nod vigorously.

"They're fine," he reports. "No, you can't kill them. I'll kill them for you."

And he puts down the phone and comes around the counter and sweeps them into his arms.

He holds them and they shake his hair out of the thin dark ponytail that he binds up in a net.

"Just as I'm closing."

His eyes are tearing up. "What will we do with you? I don't know. Maybe custard buns."

He cleans his hands on a towel and beckons the girls into the back of the bakery shop, between swinging steel doors. They know him as a funny man, teasing and playing hand games and rolling his eye, making his pink sugar-cookie dogs bark and elephants trumpet. But now he is serious, and frowns slightly as the girls follow him up the back stairs and into the big top-floor apartment with the creaky floors, the groaning pipes, odd windows that view the yard of junk and floating trees. The girls tap the door open.

Cecille sees them and screams. *"Omigodomigod!"*

"Calm down," says Frank. "The drama is over. Rozin knows."

"Let's put them in the back room, huh?" says Cecille.

This little back room, no bigger than a closet, overlooks a maze of tree branches. There is a mattress on the floor. The girls look out the window and see an old brown car seat below, a cable spool table, spring lawn chairs, a string of Christmas lights.

The room seems safe, the mattress on the floor even has a sheet on it, the blankets, the shelves for things, and the familiar view below.

"Talk to your mom?"

Frank gives orders in the form of a question. He acts all purposeful, as though he is going back downstairs to close up the store, but as the girls dial the number on the kitchen wall phone he lingers. He can't drag himself away from the magnetic field of their mother's voice, muffled, far off, but on the other end of the receiver. He stands in the doorway with the towel he brought from downstairs, folding and refolding it in his hands.

"Mama," the twins say, and her voice on the phone suddenly hurts them. They want to curl next to her and be little babies again. Their bodies feel too big, electric, like powerful bear bodies enclosing tiny mouse souls.

They begin to cry and Frank darts a glance at them, then stares at his feet and frowns. The girls picture everything at Grandmas'. On the wall of their room up north, there hangs a bundle of sage and Grandma Noodin's singing drum. On the opposite wall, Cally taped up a poster of dogs, photos of Jimi Hendrix and the Indigo Girls, a second grade boyfriend Deanna had but doesn't have anymore, bears, and Indigenous, their favorite band, another of a rainbow and buffalo trudging underneath. Ever since they were little, they have slept with a worn bear and a new brown dog with wiry blondish hair and a red felt tongue. And their real dog, too, curled at their feet sometimes, if Mama didn't catch them. Though she lets him sleep with them ever since he rescued them. Now they start crying worse than ever because they realize they left him behind.

The twins never liked dolls. They made good scores in math. They are so lonesome for their dog that they lose track of Mama's voice and hand the telephone back to Frank. He begins to talk in a wistful bantering tone and the girls wander off in their thoughts until he hangs up and says, excited, "I think she's coming back here. Coming down here.

What you girls did was wrong . . . oh so wrong . . . but so right. You didn't mean to anyway. I'll never punish you. What kind of doughnuts do you like?"

And they are extremely confused as they eat a chocolate custard bun and a powdered doughnut and drink a glass of skim milk, which Cecille keeps in her refrigerator to make up for all the doughnuts. They are confused because they miss their father. And yet they like Frank. And they certainly like the unhealthy pastries that he lets them eat although just one, because of how the grandmas left to escape his cookies, which spiked their blood sugar. He knows about that. He sits and talks to them and tells them that he is going to put them to work. To work! They could not be more thrilled.

Sweetheart's Visit

The next morning they start right in and learn the cash register, the prices, how to handle the pastries with a plastic glove or wax-paper tissue. Of course Frank does the real work. There are child labor laws, he says. I'll pay you under the table.

Now, that is an exciting thought! An exchange of money beneath a table. Grown-ups have strange customs. Even so, they sell doughnuts. Also maple long johns, hot pies, raised braids, and crullers. Things go fine until Sweetheart Calico.

They are behind the display case with a spray bottle of lemon glass-cleaner when they get this tickly, hairy, sifty feeling they are being watched. The store is empty, that dead hour just after lunchtime. The air is quiet though the growl of motors on the street barges and recedes. A few passers-by glance in, neutral, no interest in the display of breads or cakes or even the scent of fried dough that Frank has purposely vented where it will attract the casual customer. Deanna hears the scratch of nails on paint, twirls. Nobody. Cally turns back to rubbing the glass and then there is the tap, tap, tap of heels. The girls drop their polishing rags and spring to the door leading back to the ovens. They're supposed to stay behind the counter, but there are tiny noises and a staticky feeling at the napes of their necks. Nobody is there, and they are about to turn back to arranging cookies when a light touch at Deanna's shoulder spins her into the antelope gaze.

Sweetheart Calico.

She doesn't speak. Her lean face is clear, smooth, pale milk-caramel, sweet as a hen's egg; her tea-brown eyes are wistful, sad. Her hair is a powerful wing sweeping down her slim back. She has slender, jutting hips, long legs. On her feet black stiletto heels like shiny fork prongs. Perfectly honed features. The girls smile at her and open their mouths to talk. A mistake. For then she smiles back at them.

When she opens her mouth, her eyes go black. Her grin is jagged, a tooth broken and as sharp as a nail. Her smile is fixed, frightful. Her gaze scrapes over them. The scariest thing of all is this: they can sense she is glad they are here, but not in a good way. Excited. She wants them near and as they stand quiet before her they feel it all—her hating need and eager sly wishing washes toward Cally and Deanna like an oily black wave. She wants them in her part of the world, Gakaabikaang.

She wants to steal them again! They have come to believe as their mother says, that they were kidnapped by Sweetheart Calico. It has all gone vague except for their dog who brought them home. It all goes vague now. Then the wave recedes. She is gone as suddenly as she appeared.

Frank walks in, whistling, a tray of crullers on his shoulder.

Their hands are clumsy as they rub the display glass, smearing it. They are not the same afterward, nor will they ever be until they understand the design. They don't know how to take this, don't know what to make of it, have never known and do not now want to know a person like Sweetheart Calico. For she alters the shape of things around her and she changes the shape of things to come. She upsets the girls, then enlightens them both with her truthless stare. She scatters everyone's wits.

SWEETHEART CALICO STILL lives secretly in Rozin's house, which Frank is renovating. She does not break in, really, just melts through the walls and takes showers, endless showers for as long as she wants. She uses up so much hot water that Frank thinks there is a leak in the water heater. He is even thinking of getting a new water heater. Which would be a hassle. He would have to ask Booch Jr. to help him move the old one out. He never even suspects. She doesn't leave her cloven tracks, now, she is too clever. Nobody is there at night so nobody knows. She hums in her sleep. Sometimes Frank notices the smell of prairie sage, but he thinks that is a wonderful smell and it reminds him of the old days of his youth when he wandered to the place where sky meets earth.

Frank would not be surprised to see Sweetheart Calico in the shop, even though he doesn't know she lives in Rozin's house. Only Cecille knows that he felt sorry for this woman adrift, and hired her to work. Although work is not exactly what she does. If she is around, Sweetheart is sitting in the corner, down in the yard, poking through things in the basement, doing the shop chores somehow not quite right—sweeping with her broom between drags on her cigarette, but then forgetting to pick up the piles of dust. Washing pans but not rinsing them, so next day the maple long johns taste faintly of soap. Dusting the blackboard and the pictures of muffins onto the floor. Leaving them there. Washing the bathroom mirrors with toilet paper so the little papery bits are stuck all over. She takes hours in the bakery bathroom putting makeup on and hours taking it off. She lotions her face. Sits on the top of the toilet, at peace. Often, just before she leaves, she tries to get Frank or Cecille to go with her. Tries to pull them out the door. Frank and Cecille never go, though her face is desperate. They are pretty sure she walks and walks, sometimes for days, going places nobody knows. Returning with a silent, baffled, pitiful look on her face.

She likes to sit in the back of the bakery kitchen, listening to the radio and watching the telephone to see if it will ring. The next day she is there when the girls' mother calls.

"I'm on my way."

"Okay, Mama."

Frank takes the phone, turns his back on them all as he speaks to Rozin.

Meantime, Sweetheart sits in the corner smiling her shark-tooth smile and smoking a Marlboro. She blinks her hexing eyes slowly and openly stares.

The girls don't want to get her attention, make her grin. That scares them. Cally turns away after a quick, weak smile. Deanna too. But she feels immediately, right in the small of her back, the calm prickle of Sweetheart Calico's gaze.

Sweetheart Calico veers close and gives them each a hug. It is a strange, boney, upsetting, long stranglehold that twists Cally in her own sleeves so she can't speak. Sweetheart Calico is gone before Deanna can untangle her sister. All that is left upon the girls is the scent of her perfume and they find that they can't get the green smell off. They can't stop thinking of her. They see her in their deepest thoughts. Her perfume smells like grass and wind. Makes them remember running in the summer with their hair flopping on their shoulders. Her scent is like sun on their backs, like cool rain, like dust rising off a waterless, still, nowhere-leading road.

Cecille

The twins also get their first real jolt of Cecille. She's like a caffeine surge. She teaches in a tae kwan do school right down the block from the bakery shop. Through this, and peroxide, she has made herself a bicep blond-dyed Indian with tiny hips and sculpted legs that she shows off by wearing the shortest shorts. She has the glitteriest, most watching eyes, with green glints.

Some bloods they go together like water—the French Ojibwes: you mix those up and it is all one person. Others are a little less predictable. You make a person from a German and an Indian, for instance, and you're creating a two-souled warrior always fighting with themself. There are Swedish and Norwegian Indians who abound in this region, and now, Hmong-Ojibwes, those last so beautiful you want to follow them around and see if they are real. Take an Indian who shows her Irish like Cecille, however, and you're playing with hot dynamite.

Rozin thinks it's the salt.

When Rozin drives up with the dog in the passenger seat, when she jumps out and runs into the shop and starts scolding and crying, Cecille thinks she'd better calm her sister-cousin down with lunch. She takes her to a café and tells her to try meditative breathing. Rozin breathes deep and slow and begins to focus. First thing, Cecille gets the saltshaker. She salts before she tastes. Rozin has read that's a habit can lose you a job in an interview lunch. This salting before tasting is supposed to indicate some kind of think-ahead deficiency. Some lack. To Rozin, the pre-salting indicates this notion that the world is automatically too bland for Cecille. Something has to be done, in big and little ways, to liven things up and bring out all the hidden flavors. Something has to be done to normal everyday life, time spent, to heighten and color the hours, to sprinkle interest.

As salt is to food, so lying is to experience.

Or not lying, that sounds too bald. How about sprucing up, spicing, embellishing reality? At first as people get to know Cecille they think everything that happened *happened* just the way she says. But even after lunch, which is simple—health food for Cecille, nuts and carrots and a swipe of peanut butter—she sits back and tells Rozin stories of her students, their progress, then lectures Rozin on all of the amino acids she's imbibed. On the legendary qualities of the naked almond and the undisclosed secret of ginkgo.

"My memory," says Cecille, "used to be a blip. Now I recall every single thing that happens hour by hour, minute by minute. Things I've read, even license plates. My memory is getting close to photographic." She doses herself with more grainy pressed oval pills and swallows bottled water by the gallon to clean her liver.

"I'm all set," she informs her cousin, "to live a hundred years. I want to be around to see my grandchildren."

She has no kids as yet. Rozin stares at her.

"I have looked into our genealogy," she says. "It appears we don't start menopause until well into our fifties. And then, since we're running around with a two-year-old upon our hip, we just don't notice. We don't have time for that hot-flash shit. We bear late."

She gives Rozin a little curious look.

"So are you taking the girls back?" she asks. "I mean, not that I'm criticizing you, but shouldn't they be in school or something?"

"I don't know what to do," says Rozin. "They get into trouble here. But they get into trouble up there. Should I stay here? Should we give the girls those old names our mothers dreamed of? Those old names scare me. As do my feelings. Should I live with Frank? Should I move back into the house? Should I marry Frank? Should I get another job? Where should I be, what should I do? Where is my ex?"

"Whiteheart Beads?"

"Who else?"

Cecille eyes her cousin significantly.

"I know where he is," she says.

Rozin opens her mouth to ask where, but she can't put what she really wants to ask into words. There is this big thing stored up in her, she doesn't know what it is called. Some smooth, round, important piece of data. She keeps tapping the sphere but she doesn't know what's inside. The globe is huge, yellow, sometimes changeable of shape and substance. A weather balloon, sometimes it bobs to the surface of Rozin's day and she must bat it aside, this thing, this ache, this ambition. She shrugs at Cecille now, helpless to describe its bounding weight.

"I think I know what you are feeling," says Cecille.

Rozin looks at her eagerly.

"I have these books," says Cecille, "that belonged to our ancestor Augustus Roy. He was interested in time."

Rozin is disappointed. Time got her in trouble, in the form of being late. Time lost her job for her. Time seems to be trying to steal her daughters from her, too.

"He tried to trace the effects of time on his women. You remember how they hid their identities from him, how he never knew—or at least pretended not to know—which one was whose mother? How this got them into trouble and they were investigated by the priest and that crooked Indian agent? How his children nearly got taken away until they arbitrarily wrote down Mary as his wife, even though we suspect it was Zosie?"

"Yes," says Rozin, keenly listening now.

Cecille goes on, tapping the table with her clipped nail.

"He writes about all sorts of connections in the margins of those old books. He writes about Blue Prairie Woman and about how after she was given the name Other Side of the Earth she walked west looking for her daughter. How she found her daughter and gave her the song that she herself learned from her first husband, supposedly a deer husband. The song that called the antelope."

"I get all that," says Rozin. "Or I remember it, vaguely, the stories."

"But haven't you ever asked yourself," says Cecille, "how this all affects us? Haven't you ever wondered how history is working on us? Don't you sometimes pause in the midst of things?"

"Yes," says Rozin. "I do pause in the midst of things."

"And wonder?"

"Yes, I wonder."

"Think about it," says Cecille. "We developed as a people over many thousands of years. Our culture. Our ways. Our adaptations. Then all of a sudden in one generation—wham. Warp-speed acculturation. And now we're the products of two cultures. Something happened in our family that cannot be explained by the culture we live in now. When our mothers tell the stories they heard from their grandmothers and great-grandmothers, we listen and nod as if we think the stories are true. But we don't think they're true. We don't think they're historical facts. Our minds don't work the same way as our ancestors' minds worked. Our minds sort fact from fiction. We think the stories are powerful, maybe, but metaphorical, merely."

"Yes," says Rozin. "Yet . . ."

". . . yet. I know what you're thinking."

"I can't explain her."

"I can't explain her either," says Cecille. "Do you know I've followed her? To try and figure out if her tracks change?"

"And did they?"

"She walked the whole time on sidewalks and streets. So no tracks. But she walked miles in stilettos, which to me seems inhuman."

"I couldn't do it," says Rozin.

"No woman I know could do it, or at least she'd be limping, which Sweetheart wasn't."

Rozin nods, thoughtful. "I have this feeling . . ."

"Exactly," says Cecille. "It's not the heels, the tracks, nothing you can put your finger on. Yet. It is no accident that Klaus brought Sweetheart Calico here. Her presence is meaningful. History is at work."

"History is random events, not fate, or coincidence." Rozin shakes her head.

"How do you know?" says Cecille.

Frank's Bakery

The bakery has huge steel witch ovens and a concrete floor slippery with grease. There is a dough-pounding table of blocky wood covered with sparkle-shot linoleum. The high windows, coated with years of flour dust, look to Rozin like something from a fable or a movie with their tiny blocks of glass. A tulip, gold stem and leaves, bursts fierce red in the pane. It is an old bakery, much loved and tunneled to by rats, floors creaky with shadows. The doors all set crooked or stuck. There is a built-in deep-fry pit, too, which can be zapped up to bubbling or left to glaze over. It takes up one entire corner of the kitchen. There is a wonderful scent that rises when the grease is fresh. Frank slips in the little slabs of dough and they bob there, bubbling, reminding Rozin of back home at powwows and sweating ladies at the fry-bread stands laughing, pushing those gold rounds at you, hot and welcome.

Rozin, Cecille, and the girls stay in the shop to help Frank the next day. He is absorbed, melting and beating at some transparent substance in his treasured copper pan. The girls asks questions. They can't help but ask questions. They ask questions even though it takes him so long to answer that they have thought of about twenty more before they manage to pierce his distraction.

"What's that pan made of?" Cally asks, just a question to warm him up. But he takes a long time even to answer this.

"This pan is made of spirit metal," he says at last.

"What's that?" Deanna says immediately, so he won't lose his train of thought.

"Miskwaabik," he mumbles, absent in his work. "They say the thunder people sent down this red stuff, put it in the ground."

"Why's it your favorite pot?"

"Conducts the heat real good."

"What about those bowls?"

"Smooth the batter out."

The answers are getting closer, quicker.

"What are you making?" Rozin herself asks, even though she could look into Frank's sweat- and butter-stained recipe notebook, a tattered spiral-bound, and find out for herself. He won't answer for a long while, though, and this makes Rozin naturally curious. So she peeks over his shoulder at the notebook, sees a word she has never seen before, although she has heard of it. Blitzkuchen. Written on top of the lined paper in tired ink.

Blitzkuchen! All of a sudden, he gets talkative. Frank sets the egg timer. He is always timing—this, that—because of course there always is something in the oven to rescue or to check. Anyhow, that day, Frank is working again on his life project. The cake of all cakes. Early in his life, says Frank, he tasted it—light as air with a taste of peach. A subterranean chocolate. Citrus. Crumbled tears. Sweet lemon. A smooch of almond.

"It explodes on your palate," he says, eyes fixed and grave.

"Oh, gimme a break," says Cecille, who has heard this before. "Stick with our daily bread. Or daily doughnut."

Frank considers. An aura of furious effort. Concentrated baker's conversion of heat, light, energy.

"I make the staff of life," says Frank in a dignified and measured voice. "That is my calling. But I will never stop attempting the blitzkuchen."

He's trying to reconstruct the recipe. Trying to capture time. Or at least the punch line of an old family story. The cake is a fabulous thing, he says. The cake is holy. Extraordinary with immense powers of what sort nobody knows. He calls it the cake of peace. The cake of loving sincerity.

Rozin looks at him in wounded skepticism. This is a very different Frank. He has never spoken this way. He has always been down-to-earth. That is something she likes about him. This streak of mysticism, over a cake of all things, makes Rozin nervous, makes him suspect.

For years, he says, he has searched and tested for the exact recipe. In fact, the hunt for this recipe could be called his life quest. Always, between other concoctions, even inventions like his popular rhubarb sludge bars, when he has a little moment to himself, Frank makes a trial cake. Attempts a variation on the length of time he beats the batter. Amount of ground hazelnuts. Type of sugars and butters. Whatever.

"Of exquisite importance," he says to Rozin, waving a darkly wrapped bar of chocolate now, his wide-boned, pleasant face remote and concentrated. "Cocoa content seventy-seven percent. Strong and dark." He writes this in his notebook, scrawls it, and sighs over the batter he is now whipping in the bowl.

"Perhaps," Rozin says, "it is all in the stirring."

He frowns, lost in concentration now, and doesn't answer for the longest time.

"Hey, Frank," Deanna says, wanting to break the spell and change the subject, "why don't you do the nose trick?"

He looks at the twins, shy.

"Come on, Frank."

Frank can push his nose all the way to one side and tape it there. He can also pop his joints, vibrate his ears, and roll back his eyelids. He was the high school clown. He used to be ironic and jolly, always with a sly humor and a broad goofiness. But his fear of losing Rozin has made him serious.

Humor or the suggestion of it reminds him that he might say something to offend Rozin. He is stilted, stunted, stymied by his need to win her. Jokes puzzle and panic him. Put him in a sweat. Like right now, just thinking of a stupid old funny trick that made him look like a big dork, he gets upset. He thrusts his smooth hands deep in the flour barrel. Looks like he'll cry until a teary dough forms around his fingers. Maybe, Rozin thinks, watching him knead and sugar and tenderize, this is how he works through the unresolved grief that Cecille says sociologists have begun to suspect every Indian is born with. Rozin has no idea he has lost his humor because of her.

17

Nibi

KLAUS AND RICHARD have medicine breath from the family-size bottle of Listerine they are drinking. They are sitting by the art museum, half asleep in the heated shank of the day. The air is stifling. The heat is very unseasonable. It is April and should have been cool, but the heat gags thought. The heat makes everyone uneasy. Cars rush by on the other side of the bench.

"Nice to get that breeze from the traffic!" says Richard. "That carbon monoxide. Ah." He takes a deep breath, sits up, and hits his chest. Klaus, a red bandanna wrapped around his head and a T-shirt torn from collar to waist, lies curled, booze-thin, his legs folded neatly as a cat's, his arms a pillow. He opens his eyes and croaks.

"Nibi. Nibi."

"Oh shut up. I got no water, Klaus. Go to the drinking fountain."

"Where's it at?"

"Over there."

They both know it is dry, always is. No fountains work in this part of the city. They share out the last of the Listerine. Richard screws the black cap carefully onto the empty bottle. He sets the bottle on the margin of grass beside the museum steps.

The bench feels good to Klaus, hard but broad enough to curl his knees on. He is so comfortable that he does not move, decides to endure his thirst. He shuts his eyes.

A woman comes out of the museum. She is carrying a huge orange cloth purse slung over her shoulder. It thumps against her as she walks, like a big soft pumpkin. Richard calls out, "Hey, white lady!"

She frowns.

The woman isn't all white. She is something else. Hard to tell what she is, exactly. Richard thinks maybe a Korean or a Mexican or maybe, but probably not, she could be an Indian from somewhere else. She takes some money from her purse and puts it in his hand. Bills.

"Oh," says Richard, "that's very nice of you. I'd like you to meet my friend."

The woman walks away.

"Still," Richard calls after her, "I thank you. I'll put down tobacco for you." She does not turn around. "That's a sacred gesture. We're still Indians."

"You got cigarettes?" Klaus peers at Richard and holds out his fingers.

Richard gives him a cigarette. "That is my last cigarette," he says, although he has more. Klaus holds it lightly in the palm of his hand, in his fingers again. He does not smoke the cigarette.

"How much did that lady give?" he asks.

"There's four here," says Richard, counting the bills over slowly, twice.

Holding the cigarette, Klaus shuts his eyes again and listens. There is music. A sweetheart song playing between his ears. He is still dancing from some long-ago night, as he always does in his dreams. Even now, though her image sags like air is escaping, he pictures his Niinimoshenh and her twenty-six sisters and her daughters in shawls of floating hair. Over and over again they spring into his dreams. Gallop at him. Brandish their hooves like polished nails. He bats them off. She is alone again. There for him again. But he can't stop his mind from turning his sweetheart into a Disney character. The Blue Fairy. Her light increases. Her smile spreads slowly into jag-toothed mercy and then her voice flows, the cool of a river. Once, very drunk, he watched the movie *Pinocchio* eight or ten times in a row with successive nieces and nephews, their friends, their friends' cousins, then the cousins' cousins and friends. By the time the night came on and the children were draped in slumber on the floor and on pillows and heaps of blankets and clothes, he had fallen in love with the Blue Fairy.

"What should we do with this money?" says Richard.

"I'm sick."

Klaus stretches out his arm, too heavy, and then lets it drop. Unconscious again. Two men come out of the art museum. Surprisingly—what day is this?—one of them hands Richard money too. Coins. Then a group of people emerge from the big doors and skirt the men as they pass talking loudly to one another about where to go for lunch.

More people come, the two men go invisible. Some event sponsored by the museum is letting out. No more luck. The streams of people soon disappear into their cars.

"That was exciting," says Richard.

"I'm sick," says Klaus. "Water."

"I wonder if they'd let me in to look at the paintings. Maybe we should make a donation."

"Don't do that!"

Klaus surges to life and props himself against the steps, a big loose-jointed man doll. His lady love is still there in the back of his mind, standing in a ball of blue light.

"I'd like a drink of water," he says to her. She has a glass of water in her hand, too, Sweetheart Calico, but she pours it out in front of his eyes. The molecules dissolve all around him and do nothing for his thirst.

"Did she do that to you, too? Did she?" Klaus is disappointed, outraged.

"What?"

"Pour the water out right before your eyes!"

"No."

"What *did* she do then, Sweetheart?" Klaus asks, jealous. "Tell me every detail or I'll kill you right here."

"With what?"

"My bare hands," says Klaus lazily.

"Klaus," says Richard in a fatherly voice, "you're sick." Gently, he takes the cigarette from between Klaus's fingers. He unpeels the wrapping from the cigarette and begins to sprinkle the tobacco on the clipped grass. Klaus and Richard are very quiet, watching the flakes of tobacco fall to earth. Above them, in the trees, a cicada begins. A long drawn-out buzzing whine. Wait, thinks Klaus, it is only April, that can't be a cicada. It must be the heat in my brain. The day is heating past bearable. When all of the tobacco is shaken onto the grass, they get to their feet. Klaus steadies himself. His knees shake. As they slowly move down the street past the museum, on both sides of the sidewalk the sprinklers set into the sod of the lawn sputter on and then spray out cones of mist. Klaus bends over, puts his mouth on the little holes in the ground, the spigots, and tries to drink.

A museum guard in a dark uniform, a large woman bland and bored, walks down the steps and tells them to leave.

"You're supposed to say," Richard admonishes, "quit the premises. Better yet, vacate them."

The woman shrugs and walks back up the steps.

"Vacate," says Klaus, his face beaded with spray, "I'm still thirsty. It's hard to get much. That spray is thin."

"Well, let's go." They decide, taking themselves back down the street, to find a Wendy's hamburgers. Sneak in a side door to their bathrooms. If challenged, show their money.

"Where is this supposed Wendy's?" says Richard after they walk in the broiling sun over to the other side of Minneapolis.

"I'm thirsty," says Klaus.

They stand outside a grocery store next to a liquor store on Hennepin and they feel good, laugh, making the choice.

"Mad Dog or Evian?" Richard asks Klaus.

"I'm going in there," Klaus says, pointing up at the grocery sign. "I'm asking for a drink of water."

He is in and out the door in seconds and a security guard nodding with satisfaction yells, "Good luck anyway, finding a fountain."

"He didn't want to do that," says Klaus. They walk into the liquor store. "He was just doing his job."

"So was Custer," says Richard. "I opt for a subtle white." He addresses the storekeeper. "Something with volume. I don't get too hung up on the bouquet."

"That's good," says the clerk.

"My circumstances won't permit it." Richard nods. "I can tell the difference between a dollar ninety-nine and a two fifty-nine bottle of white port wine, though, you can't fool me. Don't try."

"I wouldn't."

The clerk scrapes their money off the counter and bags up two bottles, each in its own individual sack, and sets them on the counter for the men to take.

"You wouldn't have a cup of water handy, would you?" asks Klaus.

"Not really," says the clerk.

"Did he mean not as in reality or really not," asks Richard as they go out the door.

"He meant they don't have a glass of real water," Klaus says, gazing back into the window with longing, "just those cardboard pictures on the walls."

"That's all you need," says the Blue Fairy, holding up the bottle before his eyes. Twice, with her glass hoof, she strikes the hollow ground. "Let's mogate."

"To the big water. Gichi-ziibi."

"Howah!"

They walk. Hotter. Hotter. A few times they take a drink from their bottles, but mainly they want to get to the Mississippi, so they walk. Shaking a little, hungry. Go around the back of a pizza place where the manager leaves unclaimed orders every once in a while. Past the Deja Vue Showgirls. SexWorld. Fancy café garbage Dumpster and outdoor bar. Nothing there. A woman exiting an antique store holds out a dollar and the moment Richard touches the bill she drops it like he'd run an electric wire up her arm. She darts away.

"It's that sex thing," says Richard, his look sage. "I have that effect on women."

"They run like hell."

Klaus laughs too hard, furious, thinking of how his antelope girl could take off and sprint.

They reach the broad lawns and paths beside the river, go down the embankment and edge along the shore until they find a clump of bushes, familiar shade.

"We were here a while ago. I remember this place," says Richard. "We should put down some tobacco."

"Or smoke it."

"We just got two cigarettes left."

"Let's smoke it like an offering then. It don't mix with wine, not for religious purposes."

"That's true," says Richard. He slowly decides, and then he speaks. "This afternoon, let's just regard our tobacco as a habit-forming drug."

Klaus sways to his knees and then painfully, slowly, he inches down the bank of the river, leans over the edge to where the water begins. At that place, he lowers his face like a horse. He puts his face into the water, sucks the river into himself, drinks it and drinks it.

"That's Prairie Island nuclear water," Richard yells.

Klaus keeps drinking.

"He can't hear me," Richard says to himself. "Besides, that plant is down the stream farther."

Richard lights a cigarette, takes a drink of wine.

"Or Xcel shit. Or some beaver might have pissed up near Itasca."

Klaus keeps drinking and drinking.

"For sure," says Richard, worried.

Klaus doesn't stop.

"Wowee," says Richard, taking a drink of the wine, swishing it around on his tongue, "full-bodied as my sour old lady."

"How about you?" Richard yells to the river. "Klaus?"

Klaus is still face in the water, drinking, drinking up the river like a giant.

"What do you think he sees," says Richard, helpless without an audience, wishing he could open Klaus's wine already. "What do you think he's looking at? What do you think he sees?"

After another drink, Richard answers himself.

"To the bottom."

And he is right and she is down there. Klaus is watching her float toward him—his special woman—the Blue Fairy, merlady—a trembling beauty alive with Jell-O light, surrounded by a radiance of filtered sun and nuclear dust and splintered fish scales. The water is medicinal, bubbling, hot turquoise. She stops for a moment, flying backward in the great muscle of the current pushing south. It tugs at her hair. She has to go, Klaus knows. Longing for her scorches him through and through. He stretches toward her with all of his soul, but she only looks back at him over her shoulder with her hungry black eyes. Gives a flick of her white-flag tail.

18

Finding Sweetheart

ROZIN FLIPS THROUGH a pile of mail, two paper bags at her knees. One for glossy junk mail and one for plain envelopes and letter paper. Gakaabikaang insists that its citizens sort their business out, and Rozin does this with even more devotion than she used to before her husband created a toxic waste dump in the barn of innocent old people. A story that has been reported in the newspapers she recycles.

A letter with a handwritten address. BIA boarding school script, thinks Rozin. An elder. Indians of the boarding school era have beautiful handwriting—flowing, spikey, and precise. The capitals are rounded and tailed. Rozin looks at the letter and thinks: swollen fingers whacked by rulers and many tears made these letters. These are the well-formed and perfected small triumphs of shame. The name where there should be a return address is Jimmy Badger. The letter is addressed to Klaus.

Rozin opens it because Klaus is gone, and reads:

Bring her back to us. Her daughters are going crazy and are running through our men. They have broke up every marriage and punched out every wife. Our tribal leaders are again locking each other up and the school board is devouring the administration. Gangs are here, the drugs are getting harder, the drinking bloodier. Nobody stops at the gas station and the casino deal is stalled. Birds are falling from the sky. An eagle died in my yard. I have made its tail feathers into a white fan for the woman with the blue beads, the one you stole. Bring her back to us! Bring her back!

Rozin drops the letter on the table. That's it. Cecille is right. History won't let up. Sweetheart's presence has meaning and from Jimmy Badger's letter Rozin now understands that is true. If only the BIA had been more careful about teaching details like a return address! It seems Sweetheart Calico is throwing our world out of whack. She belongs where she was—the stamp is canceled Montana. Since Klaus stole her and brought her here, thinks Rozin, everything there and here has gone downhill. That carpet scam went bad. Klaus and Richard disappeared. I got happy with Frank, but the twins were spirited off by Sweetheart and I lost my job. Then I took them north and they got sick. Finally, they jump in Cecille's car and end up here. At least they're back in school. But we should figure out what to do with Sweetheart Calico.

It seems that Sweetheart doesn't want Rozin to find her, because she won't be found. She has stopped coming to the house since Rozin came back. That is because Sweetheart is busy stalking Klaus and Richard, just out of sight. When they fall asleep, she steals whatever they've rustled together in their day of foraging. She takes it all. The dog has run away to live with her, hunting rabbits in the melted underbrush and through the new spring yards. It's not a bad way to live although it is sometimes so repetitious. Klaus and Richard walk to the same places, collect the same change, buy the same bottles, sleep curled in the same smelly mess of sleeping bags and blankets.

Sweetheart has two sleeping bags. She knows the most deserted hiding places. Finds a house. Creeps into the bag with the dog and both stay warm and also they have scored another old forsaken pizza. Inside the sleeping bag with pizza dog farts, Sweetheart sleeps deeply, happily, even profoundly. She is dreaming of the open spaces, of running and running. She is laughing with her daughters as they charge up and down the hills. She goes to visit Jimmy Badger in her dream and he blesses her with an eagle tail fan and tells how glad he is that she's come home.

Ziigwan

As the days slowly grow warmer, Rozin rises earlier and earlier. She is looking for a job. It isn't going well. She has moved back into her house and Frank keeps bringing by the unsold goodies at the end of every day. Rozin knows she can balloon up fast on day-old muffins, so sometimes she tries to go running with Cecille. The jogging suit Cecille wears, made out of the same silk as a parachute, bright yellow, flares up and down the street and over to the river, her route. With her hair in a ponytail and neat black ribbon, she is a fixated bee. Shadowboxing. Leaping. Posing with her hands cocked and her eyes steady. Man-eating tiger eyes. Irish-Anishinaabe masterpiece woman. Rozin sweats like mad as she bounces slowly along behind her cousin, feeling heavier and madder and more resentful of her joblessness and lack of power in the system. Perhaps I will go back to school, she thinks. Become a lawyer. Hit Richard up for child support. How would that work? You can't hit up a man who has made himself into a wino. You can't garnishee his panhandling take, but I would like to.

She works in the bakery sometimes, but only when Frank is busy. She doesn't sit or have coffee or pass the time of day. Rozin handles the customers and cleans the glass counter and display case of their eternal fingerprints.

Still there are times Rozin rises even earlier, and in those blue morning hours, Frank teaches her everything he knows about the attractions of flours to yeasts to butters. He explains the temperatures that make them brown and rise. Rozin learns to skim with serious efficiency the bits of blackened dough from the Jacuzzi-sized deep fryer full of boiling fat and to run the whip cycle on the mixer that froths up lard and sugar. Her favorite part is to add the food coloring in drops. Instant red, blue, lavender. Killer frosting, whipped high.

All day, people stagger in from the tae kwan do school down the street, exhausted from Cecille's workouts, craving butterfat icing and reflex-slowing caramel-fudge fritters. They have to touch the cases where these things are displayed on doilies. They press close to the delectables, breathe, smudge, cough the air full of predatory microorganisms. Rozin can see their instant relief, after they have paid. Opening the crinkly white bag, exposing sweet deep-fried dough, biting into the spot on the powdered bismarck that holds the squirt of cherry jelly, they sometimes give out a small involuntary moan.

The grandmas drive down to stay a week. Noodin comes into the shop wearing a pair of pink-beaded earrings that Rozin gave her. It is clear from the implacable set of her mouth and her blink at the sight of Frank that she is sneaking away for a jolt of sugar. She is small as ever and her face reminds Frank of one of those squashed-in little dogs. Soft round flat cheeks, heavy chin, a grim wide mouth. Her nose is pug round, brown as a knot of tobacco, and her eyes are dark and yielding with a kind of liquid mournfulness. Her big gaze sweeps over the cakes and cookies. The contents of the lighted case seem to her a tragic puzzle. She sighs over all the choices. She slowly opens her purse. And here's where when Frank knows he is in trouble, not one word yet exchanged. Her little plastic snap purse is held together with a rubber band.

Those rubber-banded snap purses. Watch out, Frank thinks. You see an old lady slowly draw one forth and you know you are going to pay for her lunch and pay beyond that in ways more than money or time. No way you can spiritually afford to charge an old lady with a broken, old, green-plastic snap purse who has, in her pride, saved and used to close it a blue rubber band off a bunch of broccoli she bought to aid her slow digestion. No way you can charge her a dime. Even if she points at the biggest, puffiest, creamiest, most expensive piece of cake in the case you can't charge her.

No way you can get out of marrying her daughter, either. Not that you want to.

"Please," Frank says, sliding the piece of cake at her over the counter, already on a six-inch paper plate, with a plastic fork and napkin beside. "It's on the house." Grandma Noodin rears back as though suspicious. As though she has just recognized Frank.

"Frank," she says, and already her snap purse has vanished.

"I've been hoping you would stop in." Frank comes around the counter to sit down with her, intent on not letting her out of his sight. It is unseasonably hot, one of those wild April heat waves that tell you humans may not last on this planet. Frank has already closed the door and turned on the air-conditioning.

"Miigwech," she growls. "What kind of cake is this?"

He tells her, by pulling out a chair and tidying the corner that he is going to try to keep her in. "This is my attempt at the world-renowed blitzkuchen."

Grandma takes an immediate bite.

"Needs something."

"What?" he asks.

Her face goes intent with thought, trying to discover what spice or ingredient the cake is missing. He watches her sit back, solid as a gray lake rock, chewing in meditation. In the window, looking out as she slowly licks the schlag from her plastic fork, she gives a secret little smile. A familiar expression from up north. Frank is the one suspicious of her now. She's toying with him, this tiny bulldog lady.

She knows, but she won't tell.

"So Nookomis, I've actually been looking all over for you," Frank starts again.

"Oh?" She opens her eyes in what may even be real surprise. "Good thing I came in here then. What did you need?"

She asks Frank, right out, what he wants of her. Just like that. And just like that, faced with the question, he asks not for permission to marry Rozin, which requires many gifts and a longer buildup, especially since Rozin is still married; no, he asks Noodin for the secret ingredient.

"Secret of what?"

"This cake."

Noodin looks down at the crumbs.

"You know the story," she says. "Isn't it obvious?"

"No."

"I'll tell you then."

Frank holds his breath.

"The cake was baked by a man afraid for his life. He put his fear into the cake."

The revelation sets Frank back in his chair. If he were to make the cake, say, as he was misdiagnosed with cancer or if someone held a gun to his head only it was loaded with blanks . . . or if you desperately loved a woman and were trying to think how to marry her when suddenly her husband showed up . . .

Noodin makes significant eye contact with Frank, tips an imaginary bottle delicately to her lips. And there he is.

FRANK DOESN'T RECOGNIZE Rozin's husband at first, for Richard Whiteheart Beads is saggy-skinned, drooping like a week-old helium balloon, and he is sick, with a bruise the green of old cooked liver on his cheek, and puffy eyelids. Around his head a frayed red bandanna. A U of MN Golden Gophers sweatshirt from the Salvation Army with its sleeves chopped off and the gopher just a faded ghost gopher. Shorts sagging underneath a watermelon-tight paunch. Shorts held up with rope. Flapping tennies and no socks. He stands before the counter barely holding himself upright and then he turns. Directly, for he knows, he fixes Frank with such a stare, like looking down into the bottom of a dry well. His mouth opens. A powerful wave of sour breath hits Frank as he croaks three times like a raven, "Cawg . . . cawg . . . cawg . . . ," then stops, gulps dry, and looks even harder at Frank and croaks in a terrible whisper.

"Nibi . . ."

Wheeling backward, whirling his arms like a suddenly light scarecrow tossed by a wind in the air, Richard stagger-skips backward to the door. Frank leans toward him in a tangle of conflicted feeling, but he is out, into the street. Frank, Grandma, and Klaus watch his runaway figure round the corner and vanish.

"That was quick." Noodin returns to her cake, presses up the remaining crumbs with the tines of her fork.

"Aawww . . . we just wanted . . . a drink. A drink of water."

Klaus is still standing in the middle of the store. He

voice is wracked, bone-dry. Klaus tries to speak more words, tapping his throat. He's in an even worse state than Richard. He sways back and forth making small mewling noises of thirst.

Frank steps up to Klaus and catches him before he can pitch down. He pulls Klaus's arm over his own shoulder and drags him back into the bakery. Once behind the swinging steel doors, Frank rolls Klaus gently out on a stainless-steel bread table. Makes him drink a cup of water sip by sip. Turns down the lights. Frank takes an apron or two off the wall hooks and drapes them across his cousin's arms and chest and bare legs.

Rozin walks in with Cally and Deanna. Frank can tell from their faces that they missed seeing Richard, and he's relieved. The girls' eyes go big when they see Klaus sprawled out on the bread table.

"Major disinfection needed there," says Rozin.

"Klaus needs rest," says Frank to the girls, his big face steady. "You come on out to the front. Your uncle needs to sleep."

For an hour or so, Frank works out front, doing nothing more than checking the ovens in the bakery, the specific one in which he's got the next blitzkuchen. Fear! What about frustration? From time to time, he makes sure that his relative is still peacefully passed out. Frank mops down the entry floor and even goes outside and sweeps off the spotless sidewalk. Rozin watches him standing there gazing out at street life, massive from behind, casting a shadow around his feet like a little black pool. She blinks, thinks maybe a dog pauses, just for a moment, out of the searing noon sun.

The hot and sticky day is the reason Klaus became desperate enough to throw himself into the entry of the bakery shop.

"They don't come here much," says Frank when he steps back in.

Rustling, groans. Frank starts forward but the steel door barges open. Klaus has thrown it wide. He is staring at them like a confused scraggly coyote who doesn't know how it got into this body. Or understand why his clothes are covered with filth or what to do with the feet that can't steady the rest of him. His hands reach out, shaking, his face twists like a rag.

"Nibi," he cries, and staggers forward. Frank pours from a plastic pitcher, then gives Klaus the pitcher. Klaus drops the pitcher.

"Oops."

Sweetheart Calico slides in and stands behind Klaus as he staggers forward, and in her eyes there is something Rozin can't name at first. Not kindness, not love. Maybe a savage mercy.

It is really painful when we self-sabotage, her look says to Klaus. *I know where you are at.* Sweetheart grabs his arm. Turns him. In her hand there is a plastic cup of water. Stumbling and reeling, he tries to accept. His hand won't cooperate. He swipes toward the cup and misses. Holds his elbow with the other arm and concentrates. It takes Frank sitting him down on the floor and crouching next to him, holding the cup to his lips.

And all the time Sweetheart is sitting across from Klaus, looking at him, her eyes fixed in his eyes, their minds locked in some form of knowing. They rise in unison. She somehow imparts her grace to him and they float out the door with their arms around each other. Between them, the pilot light of alcohol, dead blue and steady.

Gakaabikaang. That's the name our old ones call the city, place of the falls is what it means from way back when it started as a trading village. Although driveways and houses, concrete parking garages and business stores cover the city's scape, that same land is hunched underneath. There are times, like now, Frank gets a sense of the temporary. It could all blow off. And yet the sheer land would be left underneath. Sand, rock, the Indian black seashell-bearing earth.

Part Four

Niiwin

The red beads were hard to get and expensive, because their clear cranberry depth was attained only by the addition, to the liquid glass, of twenty-four-carat gold. Because she had to have them in the center of her design, the second twin gambled, lost, grew desperate, bet everything. At last, even the blankets of her children. She won enough, just barely, for the beads. And then the snow fell. Gazing into the molten hearts of the ruby-red whiteheart beads, the children shivered, drew closer, chewed on the hem of her deerhide skirt. First one, and then the other, plucked up the beads from behind her hand. Even knowing they were not food, it was the look of them, bright as summer berries, that tempted their hunger. When her fingers finally closed on air, she turned, saw her youngest quickly swallow the last bead. The mother looked at her children, eyes dazed, fingers swollen, brain itching. All she could think of was finishing her work. She reached for the knife. Frightened, the children ran.

She had to follow them, searching out their panicked trail, calling for them in the dark places and the bright places, the indigo, the white, the unfinished details and larger meaning of her design.

19

Wiindigoo Dog

THE DOG IS standing on his chest again, looking down into his face and grinning the same curious, confiding dog grin that started Klaus on this eternal binge. The dog is a scuffed-up white with spooky yellow-brown eyes and a big pink dragging tongue. The damn thing has splayed wolf paws, ears alert and swivel-based like a deer's, and no pity whatsoever for Klaus.

"Boozhoo, Klaus, you are the most screwed-up, sad, fucked-in-the-face, toxic, shkwebii, irredeemable drunk I've talked to yet today," says the dog Klaus calls Wiindigoo Dog.

"Get off me," says Klaus.

Weary. Tired. Klaus had thought wiindigoog were strictly human until this dog came to visit him on a rainy afternoon this summer. Sweetheart Calico has, of course, left him, too. Come back. Then left again. Sent back this dog in her place. Wiindigoo. Bad spirit of hunger and not just normal hunger but out-of-control hunger. Hunger of impossible devouring. Utter animal hunger that does not care whether you are sober or brave or have your hard-won GED certificate let alone degree. No matter. Just food. Klaus is just food to the wiindigoo. And the wiindigoo laughs.

"Shit-faced as per usual." The dog yawns. Its black gums gleam and its ears point straight at Klaus. "I suppose we should have one of our little sessions?"

"No!" Klaus firmly says. "No!" Louder. "Nooooo . . ."

But Wiindigoo Dog is dragging his fat blazing purple killer tongue all over Klaus's face, feet, hands, everywhere. With each tongue lick Klaus shrieks and gags with laughter until he is crying in hysterical hiccups, at which point the dog leans down into Klaus's face and breathes month-old fishhead dog breath on Klaus.

When he is utterly immobilized, then, he leans down and tells Klaus his latest dirty dog joke.

"SO KLAUS, NOT too long ago I overhear these three dogs. A Ho-Chunk dog. A Sioux dog. An Ojibwe dog, too. They're sitting in the veterinarian's office waiting room talking about why they're here. The Ho-Chunk dog says, 'Well, the other day they were eating that good stew they make, just lapping it up right in front of me. That night they put the cover on the stew pot but they forgot to put the pot away. So I sneaked into the kitchen and I took the top of that pot in my teeth, set it down careful, and ate all the rest of that stew. Then I got in the garbage and ate the bones and the guts of everything that went into that stew. Then I wanted to sleep but oh, by that time I had the worst stomachache. I just had to go. I barked, but the Ho-Chunks, you know they sleep good.

They never even stirred in their sleep, so, well, I just went caca all over the house. Now, I guess, they're so mad they're going to put me to sleep. I guess I'll go easy anyways. What about you?'

"'Me,' said the Dakota Sioux dog, 'I have a similar story. You ever heard of the stew the Dakotas make with guts? It's mighty good, and my owner had a big plate of that plus all the makings for Indian tacos in his pickup one day. He was driving home and I was proudly sitting in the cab of the truck when he stopped. He get out, left me sitting there with all that good stuff, and I just couldn't help it. I wolfed it all down. Every bite. Man, was it ever good! But then I waited and waited and my owner, he was having a good time, and he didn't come back. I tried to hold it for a long time but finally, well, I just had to go. I went all over that cab of his pickup. Boy, when he came back, was he ever mad! He brought me here. I'm going to be put to sleep too. And you, what about you?'

"'Well me,' said the Ojibwe dog, 'I was sitting on the couch one day just dozing off. I was half asleep and my owner, she likes to vacuum her house in the nude, she was doing her usual housework. She was working on the carpet right in front of me and usually, even though I'm not fixed, I've got a fair amount of self-control. But then she bent over right in front of me and I just lost it. I went right for her.'

"'Sexually?' asked the others.

"'Yeah,' the Ojibwe dog admitted.

"'Gee,' said the other dogs, shaking their heads, 'that's too bad. So she's putting you to sleep too.'

"'Gawiin,' said the Ojibwa dog, modestly. 'You know us

Chippewa dogs, we got the love medicine. Me, I'm getting a shampoo and my nails clipped.'"

"YOU'RE A VERY sick dog," says Klaus.

"You're the blooming picture of health yourself," says the Wiindigoo Dog. "I gotta motivate out of here."

"Listen." Klaus tries to look pitiful. "Go get her, will you? Bring her back to me."

"Get who?"

"You know," says Klaus, very shy, "please. My sweetheart."

"Your sweetheart who doesn't love you. Let her go," says the dog.

I WONDER IF I am going to change now, thinks Richard, as the ambulance rockets through Gakaabikaang. I am not going to die, which is a disappointment. After he left Frank's bakery, he walked about a mile, then collapsed on his head. He may have a concussion, but he can't seem to pass out again. Richard pauses in his thoughts to feel the piercing regret. But there is also an odd pulse of pleasure as his life threads strongly through him, stabilized. His ambulance-ride meditation continues.

Why not live as if I did die? Why not live as if nothing matters? All the consequences of being the old Richard will land upon me, but perhaps I can endure. After all, I am the last of a family who mostly perished underneath a grand piano that nobody knew how to play. At my grandmother's funeral a young nun tried, but the piano was ruined by the same rain and snow that had weakened their lungs. Yet here I am, a survivor. This life is heavy, but also, it is nothing.

The ambulance stops and he is wheeled into a lighted place of shining surfaces. He is obviously an indigent man with no insurance, so he is parked in the hall with no painkillers. When the pain starts, it is fierce. He moans and sobs until a nurse gives him a wonderful shot that erases his disappointment in living.

Don't ever forget, says the morphine, how sweet I am.

The hallway lights dim and a humming hush falls over the actions of the nurses and doctors and trained paramedics and cleaning people and the other patients, too, with their urgent complaints and serious faces. A young girl is wheeled by; she is the age of his daughters. A pale child weeping with fear.

Richard thinks of the young nun who tried to play the piano for his grandparents. Love washes powerfully through his heart.

Oh, pale child, he thinks, pale child of astounding beauty. Don't be afraid. But she continues to wail down the hall until heavy doors shut soundlessly.

RICHARD DRIFTS, SLEEPS, and when he wakes he is stitched up, bandaged, discharged, and walking the street. The morphine leaves his body stealthily, whispering, You want me. And then the pain is outrageous. Richard picks up one foot and then the other until he is at a shelter where they know him. They feed him mashed potatoes, gravy, watery corn, and give him a cot to sleep on. He sinks into a long blackness. But then the ripsaw snore of the man sleeping next to him stabs regularly into his brain, and that night, staring into fuzzy space, Richard understands he can no longer bear the random snores of other winos. In prison, he will be safer from random snores—a roommate, maybe, whose snore he will get used to. He will be warm. He will be fed and there will be lots of other Indians. There will be a television and a routine and maybe he can figure out his next move in life.

I will surrender myself to justice, he says to the snoring man.

THE NEXT DAY, Richard walks to the police station, through the doors that open so easily and shut so completely.

"I surrender," he says to the desk clerk.

The desk clerk takes his information and puts it into a computer.

"Stay here," he says after a moment, and indicates a line of chairs.

"Good-bye, random snores," says Richard, and sits down. He waits for an hour. The officer makes a phone call. Richard waits some more. Finally, a man in a gray suit with no tie walks up to him and hands him a packet of papers. The man walks away. Richard opens the packet. They are divorce papers.

Richard walks back to the desk clerk.

"I surrendered to a different thing," he says. "I disposed of toxic carpet in an ordinary barn. There should be some charges against me sitting in your computer."

The desk clerk politely looks Richard up again, but says that there is nothing pending.

"No warrant? Nothing from the EPA?" Richard can hear desperation in his voice.

"Not at this time," says the clerk.

"This federal administration sucks," says Richard as he walks out the door. "No concern at all for illegal dumping. And my head hurts like hell."

"Wait!" says another officer. "Your name once again?"

"I was in the newspapers," Richard says modestly. From his pocket he takes a wine-blurred clipping.

"So you're the asshole that screwed that nice old Norwegian couple," says the officer. "I'm sure there is a warrant somewhere."

Richard reclaims his chair and sits back, shuts his eyes.

20

The Surprise Party

THE BRUISED PODS of cardamom. Sweet cake flour fine as powder. Scent of vanilla easing up the stairwell. Frank is browning tart crusts. Makes his own lemon curd to fill them. Juices the lemons, shreds the peel, stirs the pudding in a thick-bottomed kettle with the timeless assurance of a man whose beloved wife is just upstairs. They have finally moved in together, so they are, he figures, married in the old-time Indian way. As in the old-time traditions, he will keep fixing up her house forever. But instead of hunting, he'll bake. Rozin is at her desk organizing, studying, taking notes, all with the relieved intensity of a born-again student. She has decided to finish her undergraduate degree and go to law school. She breathes the vanilla wafting up the stairs and feels on her skin the slow increasing tension of the baking crusts below her. Vaguely she anticipates the moment of piercing sweetness, the first bite, the taste he will bring her at noon.

She shuffles her note cards and lets the screen saver—

silver bolts of lightning turning purple, magenta, yellow, silver again—streak and snag across the humming face of her computer. Rozin wants to do something special for Frank's birthday, something memorable, something even a little outrageous so that, in the future, he will remember how much she cared about his birthday. Even if they never get married (she considers this just living together), they will tell each other about it and eventually the birthday narrative will be just as good as, say, a wedding.

Frank is bored by gestures of storybook romance. Flowers and music leave him blank, even fancy wines. Those things are too predictable anyway. She needs something more, something that will reach toward Frank in a way that touches some essence of who he is, and it will be private, and it will be just the two of them, which will surprise him, because Frank has heard her speak wistfully of gathering together the very people he would invite to, say, a wedding. But she will instead create some sexy private moment, some personal ritual that would be known only to them.

To this end, she sets her mind.

In a how-to-get-him magazine article, she once read about a woman who greeted her man at the door wearing only plastic wrap. It is, she considers, a sort of miracle substance to Frank—he uses it all the time when he bakes. She thinks of getting a roll from the kitchen and making of herself the surprise. But then, the stuff itself is so clingy, so staticky, so dry and unwieldy and easily ripped that she doubts it will feel that good to make love dragging in its folds. She thinks of wearing only chocolate, or homemade raspberry jam, or sugar frosting, or peach. She thinks of lemon curd and cheesecake filling. Considers buttering herself and rolling in a bath of cinnamon. Or fluff, she thinks, go cheap maybe. Marshmallow fluff. Marshmallows. A bikini of tiny multicolored marshmallows. Frank can take his time eating them, but then, once she is naked, he will be stuffed full of stale marshmallows. Rozin's mind drifts. Whatever they are. Are they made of marsh? Or mallow? She imagines preparing the cake, the thing itself, the cake from the recipe he has perfected. The blitzkuchen. Theirs. But then what? How will she wear it? How will they eat it? What if she makes a mistake? In her dream she sees them grind the cake to crumbs between them. Yes, and no. She will wear something else, or some lack of something. She comes full circle to the plastic wrap. Thinks obsessively about the way to devise her dress.

FRANK ISN'T CRAZY about his birthday. So he decides he'll ignore it and give Rozin a party instead. She will plan something for him, sure—but he'll do her one better by surprising her.

On a bit of cash register paper he makes a list of gifts and possibilities. Jewelry. Little luxuries. A private, exquisite dinner he can cook. A night of solitude in some remote place or just a camp-out on the kitchen floor. He thinks of her, what she will like, however, and then he thinks of her again, understanding what she really wants. After all, he's heard her mention the party with longing, out loud.

Friends, family, reunited enemies, survivors of the last six months. They'd meet. They'd have a party—where . . . here. Frank looks around him. Here! In the house. Here, where the locust trees shed that fluttering shade, he will string lights. Speakers. He sighs, resigned to it. There will be music. Dancing. Beer. Kool-Aid. Pastries. Cake and barbecue. He'll make the cake of cakes once more, again, from the refined recipe. They'll all be there. It will be generous, big, loud, and best of all, a smile slowly dawns in him, exquisite, he will make it a surprise.

THE WEEK BEFORE, she panics. Thinks of buying him a watch. A name bracelet. Shoes. Something he can look at every day. Neither one of them mentions the birthday, and its avoided bulk grows between them—bigger and bigger like a twice-risen bread, and then a vast wild-yeasted dough. It doubles and redoubles itself—and the tipping load of it grows flimsy and the two grow shy. They can't touch, retreat after work; isolated in their plans, they neglect each other's company and brood. Make secret phone calls. Each cultivates a convincing memory loss. They mention little as the date approaches, then less, then nothing. It is as though they are both secretly adulterous.

The Birthday

The air is dusty and faintly golden, but the morning has been cold so that the scent of the lilacs newly blossoming hangs here and there in pockets of sweetness. All day, Rozin glances at the index card that holds her plan—the twins with Cecille, a supposed dinner out. After the store closes he will come home. She will be setting flowers in vases. Unwrapping candles. Sautéing mushrooms. Changing the sheets on their saggy double-bed mattress. As he nears the predictable end of his routine she'll light the candles upstairs in the bedroom. Doff her clothes. Apply perfume. She will cover, or rather decorate, herself strategically with stick-on bows. Two bright pink ones on her tawny nipples. One below.

That evening, she does all exactly as she has envisioned. Last thing, she peels the waxy paper off the stick-on rectangle and applies the bows. The two pink. Below her navel, she smacks on a frilly expensive bow, white and silver, bought at a Hallmark shop. She pins her hair up and presses another tiny hot pink bow on over her ear, a white one on her shoulder. A tiny spice-brown bow on each earlobe. She wedges her feet into silver high-heeled pumps. Picks up a match, a sparkler, a cupcake. Nothing else. Her heart drums as she smoothes on her lipstick and touches an extra dab of perfume to each temple.

DOWNSTAIRS IN THE HOUSE, sliding through the front door from which Frank has removed the creak, and from the back alley through the wild yard, the wedding party guests come whispering, tiptoeing, sneaking childishly, huddling together. In the big room below, where the staircase from the upstairs gives out into the kitchen, there is a wider step, almost a landing, next to which Frank stands with his hand on the light switch. He has informed them all of the routine. When Rozin comes down the stairs and reaches the landing, placed almost like a small stage at the entrance to the kitchen, when she pauses in the gloom, he'll hit the switch. They'll all yell. . . .

WALKING DOWN THE STAIRCASE through the hush of the evening toward Frank's voice, hollow at the bottom of the steps, Rozin is preoccupied with balance and timing. The heels are higher than she is used to. Naked but for the bows, she shivers. She comes down slowly so as not to stumble. That would ruin it all. She plans that she will stand at the bottom of the stairs, where light will catch the satin in the ribbons of the stick-on bows. In one hand, the cupcake with the sparkler in it. In the other hand, the match she will strike on the rough wood of the door frame . . .

THE SCRAPE OF the match, the flame, and her uncertain voice. Frank flips on the lights. The packed crowd shouts on cue. Surprise!

And everybody is surprised.

Rozin blinks. She stands, heels together, mouth open. She is naked, but for the trembling bows. The sparkler sparks on the cupcake she holds. For an endless moment, the party of friends and family stand paralyzed, gaping. Then Rozin stumbles backward, gasping, as Frank with extraordinary presence of mind whips a starched white apron off the hook behind him and drapes it over her. He bends close to her in concern. Face working, she waves him off. Tears sting his eyes. Nobody has the presence of mind to speak. The silence holds until it is broken by one solitary hiccup from Rozin. Huddled over the apron, the cupcake smoldering and smashed at the silver tip of her shoe, she hiccups again.

The party waits. The hiccups sound like the prelude to a bout of hysteria. Though she is no weeper, Frank nonetheless expects her to cry. Her shoulders shake. Her forehead is red in her hands. But when she lifts her face, her small laugh lights a string of firecracker laughs through the kitchen so that Frank's own scratchy, hoarse, unfamiliar laughing croak is part of the general roar.

21

Northwest Trader Blue

GRANDMAS GIIZIS AND NOODIN enter the early morning kitchen stealthily, hungry for leftover birthday cake. Knowing their habit, their love of sweets, the girls have risen to entrap them. Cally is already pouring coffee. Deanna is already cutting the remains of the twelve-layer chocolate raspberry cake that Frank nearly pulled off his ponytail in frustration to get right.

The grandmas accept the thick, uneven slices of cake and look at Cally and Deanna quizzically, with a slow and doggy quiet regard. Giizis takes a burning sip of hot coffee.

"You girls are up early," she observes. "What do you want?"

Cally and Deanna shoot a look at each other, bite their lips. Each takes a huge deep breath. Cally elbows Deanna. She elbows her sister back.

"Nookoo?" says Deanna.

"Grandma?" says Cally.

"Eya'?" says Giizis.

"Eya'?" says Noodin.

"We want to know something."

Giizis and Noodin shoot a look at each other, bite their lips, and each takes her own huge deep breath. They hope it will not be about those things that their mother should talk about. They hope they will not have to plan a menstrual moon-lodge ceremony or a berry feast or talk about the old ways and the new, regarding woman matters, not yet!

"About our names. We want to know."

The grandmothers' crooked, hungry smiles grow softly indulgent and even delighted. Here their granddaughters are asking for the names that have frightened their mother off. The names that came so powerfully in dreams. History scared Rozin, but history is what her daughters want. The right ones are asking for their names here, the young ones, and their mother can just go whistle up a tree trunk.

"How do we get them? What do we do? Do you know them? Mama said you dreamed them once. We tried to get her to tell us. She wouldn't tell us. She said there had to be a ceremony. What ceremony. How does it go? Do we have to get married? We hate boys. They are so gross. Dogs are better. But Sweetheart Calico took her dog. And how do we get our names?"

The grandmas take big bites of unhealthy chocolate raspberry sugar cake, chew it, and enjoy the taste. Their smiles appear. A sunny moment of startling peace. In walks Rozin wearing her fuzzy pink bathrobe, yawning.

"Cake!" She frowns at the grandmas and is about to scold them about their blood sugar when the girls grab her arms. Before she even pours herself a coffee, they tell her that they have asked their grandmas to give them names. The names she would not tell them. They are gloating. Rozin turns her back and chooses a tribal college ceramic cup in despair. It is chipped. She thinks of smashing it in the sink.

"I was afraid this would happen. I never should have said anything."

"Don't be afraid," says Cally.

"It will be all right, Mom," says Deanna, and brings her the carton of half-and-half from the refrigerator.

"Thanks," says Rozin. It is odd how girls know everything about your habits. They have been watching and learning all about you. They know that you cannot take your first sip of coffee without cream-milk in the cup. They know that after your first sip of black medicine water you are a better person.

"Yes," says Rozin, after the first taste. "Yes, I guess it is time."

The Names

There will be a feast and a ceremony later. But at this moment, the grandmas feel they should proceed. Before Rozin drinks enough coffee to change her mind. First, the grandmas fill two cups for Rozin and make her promise not to open her mouth until they are done talking. Then Giizis settles herself, pulling at her big soft T-shirt. Frowning into her coffee cup, she speaks.

FIRST OF ALL the old woman came to me. Our ancestor who was killed by the bluecoat soldier. "During my time I made such beautiful things," she said. "I wanted my children and grandchildren to know they were loved. Other people see those special dresses, moccasins, leggings, or a baby's first dikinaagan, and know that child is cared for. I made that cradle board real special. I copied into velvet the flowers we love, the wild prairie roses. You can eat them if you are hungry. Those sweet petals keep you going. But we didn't need them, for here we had killed a lot of buffalo, and we had dried the meat before we were attacked.

"I saw the soldier shoot at children and I ran at him with a stone. But he killed me on the end of his gun. Not so easy, however, because I stared at him in his eyes. I stared him back in time, to when he was defenseless, before his birth. And then I put my spirit into him as best I could.

"That long moment passed. I looked at the distance. Over his shoulder, I saw the dog running off with my baby granddaughter, the dikinaagan strapped on its back. Oh, I was happy. They were getting away. I was filled with joy and nothing hurt me. I had given that child my own name, a very old name that goes back for many generations, and would be carried forward now. I cried out that name, and fell away and held the earth, and melted into the earth, and am part of everything now. My spirit guided the other spirits who died with me on that day, for I was named after the band of radiant light we travel.

"Why is it given to us to see the colors and the power and the imperishable message? We are so limited, so small. Gaagigenagweyaabiikwe, I cried, and put the name into the soldier's mind so he repeated it and repeated it. He scratched it into the sand the first time he sat down—whiteman's letters, a name never written down—and eventually he carved it into his arm. My name killed him eventually, though he died by his own knife, it is true. But our people had pity on his spirit. We helped him to depart this earth. As he walked the road to the next life, the letters never melted from his arm, they guided him. And now they are part of everything, too. They are the name I give you. Everlasting Rainbow. The footbridge that connects us with the other world."

"OF COURSE," SAYS Giizis, sipping her coffee, "it is very difficult to translate a real Ojibwe name into the whiteman's language. So often, our names include movement, the stirring of leaves, the glint of light on water, the trembling of color. English is so limited."

"We do our best," says Noodin with a critical sigh.

"Ombe omaa," says Giizis to Deanna, and she places her hands on her grandniece's head and says the name four times. She makes Deanna repeat it. Then Cally and Rozin. She writes it down.

"Not gonna carve it in my arm. Now you memorize this."

She gives the paper to Deanna and then nods at Noodin. "Mi'iw minik, my sister, ginitam."

"THERE ARE THESE beads I love," says Noodin. "Deep ones, made of special glass. Hungarian beads called northwest trader blue. In them, you see the depth of the spirit life. See sky as through a hole in your body. Water. Life. See into the skin of the coming world."

Cally nods, lets a long breath out, impatient to see how this bead talk connects with her name.

"Just a second," Noodin says, "I'm getting it all fixed in my mind. My brain is soaking up the sugar. I have to let the cells energize before I go on telling you."

Noodin draws a deep breath and continues.

"When I was a child," says Noodin, "I wanted beads of that northwest trader blue, and I would do anything to get them. I first glimpsed this blue on the breast of a Pembina woman passing swiftly. I saw her hand rise to the beads and then touch the blue reflection on her throat. Ever after, I knew I must have that certain blueness which was like no other blue. I scored my fingers making quill baskets and when they were finished I went to the trader and sold them. I looked behind his glass and wood counter at the hanks of beads hanging there on nails—beads the ripe silk of prairie roses. Silver beads, black, cut-glass white. Beads the tan of pony hide and green, every green there is on earth. There were blues there, sky blue, water blue, the blue of the eyes of those people who took our trees. The blue of old pants and the blue of mean thoughts. I searched for the blue of those beads I had seen on the Pembina woman, but that blue was different from all the other blues on earth. Disappointed at the trader's cache, I spent my money on sweet candy. There would come a time I would see the beads I needed, but I already knew they could not be bought."

Grandma Noodin stares at Cally, looking through her, figuring.

"During my motherhood, when I was rocking or nursing my baby," she went on, softly, "I had a lot of time to think about this blueness. I could see it before me, how it appeared and disappeared, the blue at the base of a flame, the blue in a fading line when I shut my eyes, the blue in one moment at the edge of the sky at dusk. There. Gone. That blue of those beads, I understood, was the blueness of time. Perhaps you don't know that time has a color. You've seen that color but you were not watching, you were not aware. Time is blue. Or time is the blue in things. I came to understand that my search for the blueness called northwest trader blue was the search to hold time.

"Only twice in my life did I see that blue clear. I saw that blue when my daughter was born—as her life emerged from my life, that color flooded my mind. The other time, my girl, was the day I found your name. Or dreamed it. Or gambled for it. Here's how it happened."

Other Side of the Earth

I was a new mother-to-be, pregnant. Picking berries, I felt sleepy and lay on the ground. It was so soft underneath the tree, the grass long and fine as hair. I put down my bucket to rest and curled in the comfort. While sleeping, I saw the Pembina again—she came to me. I saw her as a tiny speck first, then bigger and bigger until she was down the road and standing right in front of me. Had those beads on. Still hanging from around her neck. They were made of that same blue I have described to you and I still wanted them with all my heart.

"Will you gamble for them?" the Pembina asked me, gently.

I told her that I wanted those beads but had nothing I could use to put down. No money. No jewelry. Just berries. She took marked plum pits out of her pocket, smiled, and right there we sat down together to gamble.

"You have your life," she said gently, "and the ones inside of you as well. Would you bet me two lives in return for my blue beads?"

"YOU GAMBLED," SAYS Rozin. "I believe it! That was me inside, you know!"

"Shut up, my girl," says Noodin.

"You promised," says Giizis.

I DIDN'T EVEN think twice but answered her yes. We started playing the game, throwing down the plum stones and gathering them up, taking turn after turn until the sweat broke out on my forehead. I beat her the first of three games. She took the second. I took the third and gestured at her beads. Slow, careful, she lifted the strand over her neck and then she handed them over.

"Now," she said, "you have the only possession important to me. Now you have my beads called northwest trader blue. The only other thing I own of value are my names, Other Side of the Earth, Blue Prairie Woman before that. You have put your life up. I'll put my names. Let us gamble again to see who keeps the beads."

"No," I said. "I've waited too long for these. Now that I've got them, why risk them?"

She gazed at me with her still, sad eyes, touched her quiet fingers to the back of my hand, and carefully explained.

"Our spirit names, they are like hand-me-downs which have once fit other owners. They still bear the marks and puckers. The shape of the other life."

"Why should I take the chance?" I asked, stubborn. "So what?"

"The name goes with the beads, you see," she said, "because without the name those beads will kill you."

"Of what?"

"Longing."

Which did not frighten me.

Still, I played her another game and yet another. That is how I won her names from her. My girl, that was my naming dream. Long version. Your name is a stubborn and eraseless long-lasting name. One that won't disappear.

CALLY WANTS HER to say it, the old name, the original.

"Ozhaawashkmashkodikwe, Blue Prairie Woman." She hears, but she isn't satisfied.

"And the beads?"

Cally is surprised to hear the sharpness in her voice. She hasn't even thanked her grandma, yet already the need is on her. She has got to know what the necklace of beads looks like, that blue. She can imagine it at the edge of her vision. A blueness that is a hook of feeling in the heart.

"The beads." Noodin's whole face wrinkles, her thin lips slowly spread in an innocent smile. "Already, you want them, I know. But you will have to trade for them with their owner, Sweetheart Calico."

Who stands behind them suddenly, her gaze on Cally's back like a cape of quills.

The Blue Beads

The twins have become been afraid of her. She is not just any woman. She is something created out there where the distances turn words to air and thoughts to colors. She wiggles the first bead from the broken place in her smile. Then she pulls bead after strung bead from her dark mouth out. That's where she was keeping them all of this time, they understand. Beneath her tongue. No wonder she was silent. And sure enough, as she holds them forward to barter, now, she speaks. Her voice is lilting and flutelike on the vowels and sibilant between the jagged ends of her tooth.

"Make that damn Klaus let me go!"

"Okay," says Cally. "First give me the beads."

22

Wiindigoo Dog

So there was this big canine rabies outbreak in the state of Minnesota. Here's what happened. The state sent three dog-catchers to work day and night rounding up the dogs. The first dogcatcher was from a crack Norwegian dog-catching school, the second was Swedish, the third was an Indian dogcatcher. Each had a truck. They traveled together in a squad. They worked hard all morning and by noon each of the dogcatchers had a pretty-fair-sized truck full of dogs. About then, they were getting hungry, so they chained up the back of the trucks. But they forgot to lock the doors themselves, see, so by pushing and wiggling the dogs could open the doors behind the loose chain just enough to squeeze out, carefully, one at a time.

When the dogcatchers came back from lunch, then, first thing they looked into the back of their trucks. The crack Norwegian dogcatcher's truck was totally empty and so was the Swede's truck. But the Ojibwe dogcatcher's truck, though unlatched the same and only chained, was still full of dogs.

"This is something, though," said the Swede and the

Norwegian to the Ojibwe. "How do you account for the fact all our dogs are gone and yours are still there?"

"Oh," said the Ojibwa, "mine are Indian dogs. Wherever they are, that's their rez. Every time one of them tries to sneak off, the others pull him back."

"I DON'T LIKE that joke," says Klaus. "My rez is very special to me. It is my place of authority."

"Geget, you filthy piece of guts," says the Wiindigoo Dog. "I like it there, too. Don't get spiritual on me."

"Why do you like it?" asks Klaus. "You have no spirituality whatsoever. What's there for you?"

"On the rez," says the Wiindigoo, "the ladies, they roam. Bye now. Gotta maaj."

"Good riddance." Klaus turns over and sleeps.

WHILE SLEEPING he remembers that he is really someone else with a life and a toothbrush and a paycheck. He lives a normal day in his sleep, rising in the morning to do a hundred crunches and fifty push-ups, then pours himself a bowl of cereal before he showers. That feels good! Next, he is shaving, just those few whiskers on the blunt end of his chin. He is walking away from his actual house. Locking his door. Getting into his car.

Car! Once upon a time far away and long ago. These things were his. He earned them with work and money. His mouth waters. Coins and bills. He remembers the solid pack of his wallet in his left jeans pocket. He is left-handed, a lefty. What does that matter now? He is totally ambidextrous with the bottle.

KLAUS IS SLEEPING with his head sticking out of the bushes in the park, and he is wearing a green baseball cap. A young man wearing thick earphones and chewing a piece of bread-tie plastic whips around the bushes, expertly mowing grass for the city park system. He rides the mower with sloppy assurance—the big red machine itself encourages reckless driving with its fat cushy seat and wide cramping whine of protest. That's what his lawn mower is—one long scream of protest. The world of grass was never meant to be shortened to a carpet so that the outdoors is like one big wall-to-wall room. The young man rounds the corner and runs over Klaus's head.

There is no warning, of course. No chance for Klaus to prepare himself in his dream for getting his head run over by a lawn mower. Only the jagged earsplitting raucous blade shrieks, only the helmet of metallic motor sound, only the fact, lucky Klaus, that a powerful stray dog bolts toward the machine and gets hit, slams into the air. Bounces off a tree and vanishes. The impact jars the machine to a giant skip so that the accident leaves no more than a neat bloody crease down the exact middle of Klaus's face.

KLAUS DREAMS HE is a drum struck violently and rapidly. His drum face wears the sacred center stripe. Klaus blinks up into the sky. Sun shot and pearly. Leaves gleaming and tossing. His ears are suddenly unpacked of cotton and his thoughts run pure between his temples, open and sparkling. In the extraordinary light Klaus makes a thousand decisions. Two of them matter. Number one, he will finally stop. Just stop. And he knows, the way he has known so many times before, right down to his aching big toe, center of his soul, that he is done drinking. He can do that. The other of his important decisions is not so consciously settled. It is just that he knows, in vague detail but with overriding certainty, the next thing to do.

Bring her back. Bring her back to us, you fool.

Getting sober. Letting her go. The idea of it hurts so bad he momentarily wishes that the lawn mower had struck him full on, taken off his head, his thoughts.

THERE IS A little bench down the street in a dogshit triangle of lawn. Some strangled dark red ambrosia-colored snapdragons are planted there by who knows who? *Better go there,* says a voice. Her dog, Wiindigoo. *Get out. Don't look back.* Now, right now, attend to yourself and focus on the next fifteen minutes of your life. For you were never able to do it a day at a time, not you. An hour. Two hours. Half a day at a time. Or not.

Klaus goes looking for her. Now and again they'll ask him, what was so fucking great about her? What did she do, in bed for instance, or what did she cook? Was it something she did with her hands, her face, some way she had, perhaps? A love way. A food. Not one thing in particular, he says. She never cooked anything from a recipe. Potatoes, mac and cheese, that kind of stuff. It wasn't that. They'll ask did she have his children. No, he'll say. No kids. Was she related to you? Was she from your own clan?

Sometimes he thinks she was. Yes.

In his worst down and outs, he gets comfort from the thought that she was just a fragment of his imagination, his pretty antelope woman. But he knows she is actual in every way. What scares him worst is this: The simple knowledge that his Sweetheart Calico is a whole other person. Lives in another body, walks in a different skin. Thinks different thoughts he can't know about. Wants a freedom he can't give.

She dragged me in, he says greedily, can't she handle it now?

Yet he knows with bleak shame he is excusing his trapper's appetite. He's tangled in a net of holes. He doesn't know how to stop wanting her in him, with him, part of him, existing in his food and water and booze. He doesn't know how to stop the circle of his thoughts.

In the old days, they used to paint the red stripe of the drum down the middle of their faces. Right now, sitting on the carved bench in the hopeful little ugly park he closes his eyes. His face bears the blood-painted stripe. He tries to divide himself up equally—two parts. *Send half of yourself to each direction.* West, east. Let her go with the western half, free. But the part of Klaus that goes to the west reaches out and clings to his love like a baby, following her into sky-hung space.

Giiwebatoon

Klaus folds and unfolds the strip of cloth that he uses as his headband, traces the small buds and sprigs of pink unbudding roses and white roses, the sweetheart calico. Sweat and dirt, drunken sleeps, railroad bed, underpass and overpass dust, volleyball-court gravel, frozen snirt, river water, and many tears are all pressed into the piece of cloth. It holds the story of his wretched love. Though grit scored, dirt changed, and sun faded, it isn't frayed. It is woven of the same toughness as his longing. He wraps the strip of calico around his wrist like a bandage and he waits. He becomes part of the scenery, a tree, or anyway a stump. He is waiting for her to appear.

Red flash. A curtain drops away. She walks across the downtown concrete. His wife, his Niinimoshenh, his Blue Fairy, his torture, his merwoman, mercy and love. She is walking along very slow and hesitant, waiting for lights to change before she crosses, reaching for her own hand. Her dark fall of hair hangs tatty and lifeless. She breathes in clear air and blows smoke out her nose. Looking over her shoulder at him, sensing his presence, her eyes are no longer living agates. Her eyes have turned the dead gray of sidewalk.

Klaus steps toward her and flaps his hands.

"Run! Run home. You can go now!"

She starts nervously, but then shrugs, lights a cigarette from off the one she was smoking already, and doesn't run away. She looks at him, through and through, weary. His dear love's face is thin, the bones showing pure and stark, pressing just the right places under her skin. How he used to trace them is still locked in his hands. His fingers begin to move across the rips in his T-shirt.

She steps closer. He reaches out and holds her long-fingered delicate hand. Then, pulling the cloth around their wrists, he ties her hand to his hand gently with the sweetheart calico. He has no plan to do this either. No plan for what happens next, but it is simple. They start out. Start walking.

North and west, along the river until the herringbone brick path with decorative plantings becomes a common sidewalk. Eventually it turns to tar black as licorice at first and then lighter, lighter, showing stones in the aggregate, thinning, rubbing out, erasing, absorbed back slowly into the earth. Then earth itself is under their feet, a worn path for joggers and for bicyclists. It is clear at first and then grassier, fainter, grown over, traversing backyards or parkland. Back lots of tire stores, warehouses, malls, developments, wild mustard, polleny green-gold, a farm, then another one, all of a sudden undergrowth so thick along the banks they cannot enter.

They turn from the water flowing off the edge of the world and start walking due west.

They walk all evening, rest. Fall asleep in a grassy old yard just beside an abandoned shed that still shelters a hulk of metal that once was a car. Against the shed, still chained to the door, there is a cracked leather collar. Strung through it bones of a dog vertebrae. Scattered beside more bones and baked hide.

That dead dog comes alive and is her dog. Coyote gray, grinning and slobbering, it trots just behind them.

They keep walking. Next morning, too. They drink from a clean pothole lake and walk on until, over a slight rise, the sky immensely opens up before them in a blast of space.

"Niinimoshenh," he says softly. "Run home. Giiwebatoon."

He feels her start, tense, breathe the air in deeper gulps.

A flowing fawn material, her grace comes over her. If he looks at her he won't be able to do it. So he does not look at her face. Slowly, fighting his own need, dizzy, Klaus pulls at the loop of dirty gray sweetheart calico. He undoes the knot that binds her to him. At first, she doesn't seem to know what her freedom means. She gazes at the distance until it fills her eyes. Then she shakes her hand and sees that she is no longer bound to Klaus. She stretches her arm out before her, turns her fingers over curiously, examines her blank brown palms.

"You let me go," she says to him. He's shocked to hear her soft, raspy voice.

"Yes," he whispers. He sits down suddenly like a baby dropping to its seat. Sprawled in the grass, addled, his tears slowly pump. He throws down the strip of cloth that tied her to him and tied him to the bottle.

When he does that, he imagines that she will bound forward in the lyric of motion that only her people have. But she does not spring from his shadow, only walks forward a weary step. Confused, broken inside, shaking her head, she stumbles over the uneven ground. The dog stays right at her heels. As she walks west, she begins to sing. Klaus watches her. The land is so flat. She is perfectly in focus. He can see her slender back, quick legs, once or twice a staggering leap, a fall, an attempt to run. Klaus thinks that she might turn around but she keeps moving until she is a white needle, quivering, then a dark fleck on the western band.

Nimiigwechiwi-aanaanig: Awanigaabaw (Dr. Brendan Fairbanks), also Netaa-niimid Aamoo-ikwe, Biidaanamad, Migizi, and Nenaa'ikiizhikok, my daughters.

Thank you: Trent Duffy, my indefatigable copy editor, and Terry Karten, my editor at HarperCollins. Brendan Fairbanks was my consultant for most of the Ojibwe language in this book; any mistakes are mine. Thank you also to my sister, Heid E. Erdrich, who over the years helped me think about this book.

LOUISE ERDRICH grew up in North Dakota and is a member of the Turtle Mountain Band of Chippewa. Her most recent novels include *The Plague of Doves,* a finalist for the Pulitzer Prize, and *Shadow Tag,* a national bestseller. She lives in Minnesota and owns a small independent bookstore, Birchbark Books (www.birchbarkbooks.com).

Insights,
Interviews
& More . . .

About the author

About the book

Read on

About the author

Louise Erdrich, The Art of Fiction

Only one passenger train per day makes the Empire Builder journey from Chicago to Seattle, and when it stops in Fargo, North Dakota, at 3:35 in the morning, one senses how, as Louise Erdrich has written, the "earth and sky touch everywhere and nowhere, like sex between two strangers." Erdrich lives in Minneapolis, but we met in the Fargo Econo Lodge parking lot. From there, with Erdrich's eight-year-old daughter, Kiizh (Sky in Ojibwe), we drove five hours up to the Turtle Mountain Chippewa reservation, on the Manitoba border. Every August, when tick season has subsided, Erdrich and her sister Heid spend a week in a former monastery here to attend the Little Shell Powwow and to conduct a writing workshop at the Turtle Mountain Community College. One afternoon, participants took turns reciting poetry under a basswood tree

Peter Tagiuri

Moving east with my mattress and writing table.

beside the single-room house where Erdrich's mother grew up. The workshop is mainly attended by Ojibwe or other Native people from neighboring reservations, and is in its eighth year.

Karen Louise Erdrich, born June 7, 1954, in Little Falls, Minnesota, was the first of seven children raised in Wahpeton, North Dakota, by a German American father and a mother who is half "a mixture of other tribes plus French" and half Ojibwe—Ojibwe, also known as Chippewa, being one of numerous Native American tribes comprised by the Anishinaabe ("Original People"). Both of Erdrich's parents taught at a Bureau of Indian Affairs boarding school. For many years, her grandfather Patrick Gourneau, Aunishinaubay, was the Turtle Mountain Chippewa tribal chair.

Erdrich graduated from Dartmouth College in 1976, and returned in June 2009 to receive an honorary doctorate of letters and deliver the main commencement address; the same year, her novel *The Plague of Doves*, which centers on the lynching of four Indians wrongly accused of murdering a white family (and which Philip Roth has called "her dazzling masterpiece"), was named a finalist for the Pulitzer Prize. After invariably classifying Erdrich as a Native American writer, many reviewers proceed to compare her work to that of William Faulkner or Gabriel García Márquez: Faulkner for her tangled family trees, her ventriloquist skill, and her expansive use of a fictional province no less fully imagined than Yoknapatawpha County; García Márquez for her ▸

flirtations with magical realism. But so strange are Erdrich's narrative rhythms, and so bonded is her language to its subject matter, that it seems just as accurate to call hers a genre of one.

When the workshop was over, Erdrich drove us back to Fargo for walleye cakes at the Hotel Donaldson, and then to visit her parents, who still live in the modest house in Wahpeton where Erdrich grew up. The next day, while Erdrich attended a wedding in Flandreau, South Dakota, her sister took me the remaining two hundred miles to Minneapolis, where, three days later, Erdrich and I reconvened at her bookstore and Native American arts shop, Birchbark Books. Here, Erdrich's eldest daughter, Persia, decides which children's books to stock. Taped to most of the shelves are detailed recommendations handwritten by Erdrich herself. An upside-down canoe hangs from the ceiling, suspended between a birchbark reading loft and a Roman Catholic confessional decorated with sweetgrass rosaries. We linger at the store, but not until we make the long walk to Erdrich's house do we finally sit down on the back porch and turn the tape recorder on.

Erdrich was wearing her driving clothes: jeans, sandals, and an untucked button-down shirt. A Belgian shepherd named Maki dozed at our feet, and Erdrich's youngest daughter came out a couple of times—once to ask whether we wanted Play-Doh ice-cream cones, later to report that a Mr. Sparky was on the phone. Then a neighboring buzz saw started up, and we moved inside: up to a small attic room pleasantly cluttered with photographs, artifacts, and many more Catholic and Ojibwe totems, including moccasins, shells, bells, dice, bitterroot, a bone breastplate, an abalone shell for burning sage, a turtle stool, a Huichol mask with a scorpion across its mouth and a double-headed eagle on its brow, and a small army of Virgin statuettes. Crowded into a bookshelf beside a worn armchair in the center of the room are the hardbound spiral notebooks in which, in a deeply slanted longhand, Erdrich still writes most of her books—sitting in the chair with a wooden board laid across its arms as a desk.

INTERVIEWER: ***In*** **The Beet Queen,** ***Dot Adare's first-grade teacher puts Dot into the "naughty box." Was there a naughty box in your own childhood?***

LOUISE ERDRICH: Do I have to talk about this? It is a primal wound. Yes, I was put into the naughty box.

INTERVIEWER: ***What had you done?***

ERDRICH: Nothing. I was a model child. It was the teacher's mistake, I am sure. The box was drawn on the blackboard and the names of misbehaving children were written in it. As I adored my teacher, Miss Smith, I was destroyed to see my name appear. This was just the first of the many humiliations of my youth that I've tried to revenge through my writing. I have never fully exorcised shames that struck me to the heart as a child except through written violence, shadowy caricature, and dark jokes.

INTERVIEWER: ***Was your teacher anything like the one in your story "Sister Godzilla"?***

ERDRICH: No, but I had Franciscan Sisters for teachers later. Some were celestial, others were disturbed. My sixth-grade teacher, Sister Dominica, hit home runs at recess and I loved her, but there was no exact Sister Godzilla. As for Miss Smith, I still have her photograph. She had cat's-eye glasses and a blond bouffant do, and wore a chiffon scarf tied at the tip of her chin. Before Miss Smith, I'd never recognized a presence inside of words. The Ojibwe say that each word has a spirit. Miss Smith drew eyelashes on the o's in *look*, and irises in the middle of the o's, and suddenly *look* contained the act of looking. I had a flash of pure joy, and was a reader from then on.

My father is my biggest literary influence. Recently I've been looking through his letters. He was in the National Guard when I was a child and whenever he left, he would write to me. He wrote letters to me all through college, and we still correspond. His letters, and my mother's, are one of my life's treasures.

INTERVIEWER: ***What are the letters about?***

ERDRICH: Mushroom hunting. Roman Stoics. American Indian Movement politics. Longfellow. Stamp collecting. Apples. He ►

and my mother have an orchard. When I went off to college, he wrote about the family, but in highly inflated terms, so that whatever my sisters and brothers were doing seemed outrageously funny or tragic. If my mother bought something it would be a cumbersome, dramatic addition to the household, but of course unnecessary. If the dog got into the neighbor's garbage it would be a saga of canine effort and exertion—and if the police caught the dog it would be a case of grand injustice.

INTERVIEWER: ***Did your mother speak Ojibwemowin (the Ojibwe language) when you were growing up?***

ERDRICH: My grandfather spoke the Red Lake dialect of the language as his family had originated there, but he also spoke and wrote an exquisite English. My mother learned words here and there, but you have to be immersed in a language as a child to pick it up completely. Learning language is far more difficult later on.

Often when I'm trying to speak Ojibwe my brain freezes. But my daughter is learning to speak it, and that has given me new resolve. Of course, English is a very powerful language, a colonizer's language and a gift to a writer. English has destroyed and sucked up the languages of other cultures—its cruelty is its vitality.

INTERVIEWER: ***Were you raised to be devout?***

ERDRICH: Every Catholic is raised to be devout and love the Gospels, but I was spoiled by the Old Testament. I was very young when I started reading the Bible, and the Old Testament sucked me in. I was at the age of magical thinking and believed sticks could change to serpents, a voice might speak from a burning bush, angels wrestled with people. After I went to school and started catechism I realized that religion was about rules. I remember staring at a neighbor's bridal-wreath bush. It bloomed every year but was voiceless. No angels, no parting of the Red River. It all seemed so dull once I realized that nothing spectacular was going to happen.

I've come to love the traditional Ojibwe ceremonies, and some rituals, but I hate religious rules. They are usually about controlling women. On Sundays when other people go to wood-and-stone churches, I like to take my daughters into the woods. Or at least work in the garden and be outside. Any god we have is out there. I'd hate to be certain that there was nothing. When it comes to God, I cherish doubt.

INTERVIEWER: ***What was it like to leave Wahpeton for Dartmouth?***

ERDRICH: My father, rightly, picked out a paragraph in *The Plague of Doves* as a somewhat autobiographical piece of the book. Evelina leaves for college and at their parting her parents give her a love-filled stare that is devastating and sustaining. It is an emotion they've never before been able to express without great awkwardness and pain. Now that she's leaving, that love beams out in an intense form.

As the eldest child, I often felt that I belonged more to my parents' generation than to my own. In the beginning of the book, Evelina is always scheming to watch television. My parents didn't let us watch much television. Dad had us cover our eyes when the commercials came on. He didn't want us to nurse any unnecessary desires and succumb to capitalism. Shakespeare's history plays and *The Three Stooges* were major influences.

INTERVIEWER: ***When did you start writing?***

ERDRICH: I went back to North Dakota after college and became a visiting poet in a program called Poets in the Schools. It was a marvelous gig. I went all around the state in my Chevy Nova, teaching, until I contracted hepatitis at the old Rudolf Hotel in Valley City. What did I expect for eight dollars a night? I was in my smoking, brooding phase, and I was mostly writing poetry. In time, the poems became more storylike—prose, really—then the stories began to connect. Before the hepatitis I also drank, much more than I do now, so I spent a lot of time in bars and had a number of crazy conversations that went into *Love Medicine*. I also used to go to tent revivals up in the Turtle Mountains—that experience eventually became part of *The Plague of Doves*. ▸

I started writing poems with inner rhymes, but as they became more complex they turned into narrative. I started telling stories in the poems. But the poems I could write jumping up from my desk or lying on the bed. Anywhere. At last, I had this epiphany. I wanted to write prose, and I understood that my real problem with writing was not that I couldn't do it mentally. I couldn't do it physically. I could not sit still. Literally, could not sit still. So I had to solve that. I used some long scarves to tie myself into my chair. I tied myself in with a pack of cigarettes on one side and coffee on the other, and when I instinctively bolted upright after a few minutes, I'd say, Oh, shit. I'm tied down. I've got to keep writing.

INTERVIEWER: ***Where were you when you wrote*** **Love Medicine*****?***

ERDRICH: I had come back to Fargo again and was living downtown. I worked in a little office space with a great arched window on the top floor. It was seventy bucks a month. It was heaven to have my own quiet, beautiful office with a great window, green linoleum floors, and a little desk with a view that carried to the outskirts of Fargo. The apartment I lived in over Frederick's Flowers belonged to my brother and had no windows, only a central air shaft that was gloomy and gray. That apartment also got into the book. It was a peculiar apartment—you couldn't stay in it all day or you'd go nuts. It cost fifty dollars a month, so all I had to pay every month was one hundred and twenty bucks in rent. I had a bicycle. I ate at the Dutch Maid café. I was living well.

INTERVIEWER: ***What happened with what was actually your first novel,*** **Tracks*****?***

ERDRICH: It continued to be rejected. It was rejected all over the place. And thank God for that—it was the kind of first novel where the writer tries to take a high tone while loads of mysterious things happen, and there was way too much Faulkner in there. People would find themselves suddenly in cornfields with desperate, aching anguish over the weight of history. I kept it, though, the way people keep a car on blocks out in the yard—for spare parts.

INTERVIEWER: ***The* Tracks *I've read is a short book.***

ERDRICH: That's because all of the spare parts got used in other vehicles.

INTERVIEWER: ***Why did you decide to add family trees to your books?***

ERDRICH: I resisted for many years, but then at readings people began to come up and show me their painfully drawn out family trees. At long last, I was overcome by guilt.

INTERVIEWER: ***How do your books come into being? Where do they start?***

ERDRICH: I have little pieces of writing that sit around collecting magnetism. They are drawn to other bits of narrative like iron filings. Eventually, by some process I am hardly aware of, the pieces of writing suggest a narrative. One of the pieces might be told in a particular voice—that voice might tell everything. Or an image might throw the piece into third person—or whatever person. I don't have control over whether I get ideas, voices, images. The trick is to maintain control and to shape what I get.

INTERVIEWER: ***Is it true that you have control over the cover designs of your books? Writers aren't always afforded that privilege.***

ERDRICH: That's because the most clichéd Native images used to be suggested for the cover design, so I fought to have some say. On a foreign copy of *Tracks* there was a pair of massive breasts with an amulet hanging between them. Often, a Southwestern landscape appears. Or an Indian princess. A European publisher once sent me a design for *Master Butchers Singing Club* that was all huge loops of phallic sausages. They were of every shape and ▸

all different textures, colors, sizes. I showed it to my daughter and we looked at it in stunned silence, then we said, Yes! This is a great cover! I have twenty copies left of that edition. Sometimes I'll show one to a man and ask what he thinks of it. He'll put it in his lap and stare at it for a while and then an odd expression will cross his face. He'll look sideways at the women in the room, point the biggest sausage out, and say, I think I see myself in that one.

INTERVIEWER: ***Do you revise already-published work?***

ERDRICH: At every opportunity. Usually, I add chapters that I have written too late to include in the original. Or I try to improve the Ojibwe language used in the book. With *The Bluejay's Dancer* I wanted to take out the recipes. Don't try the lemon-meringue pie, it doesn't work. I've received letters. The most thoroughly revised book I've ever republished is *The Antelope Wife*. It is really a completely different novel, but I feel it is the true novel that was hidden in the first version. The beginning is the same, and then the book changes utterly. Sometimes a writer needs fifteen or twenty years to follow the thread laid out by a set of characters and a narrative.

INTERVIEWER: ***Every summer you drive several hours north to visit the Turtle Mountains, sometimes also Lake of the Woods. Why?***

ERDRICH: Actually, I do this all year. These places are home for me. And I like to travel. Driving takes hold of the left brain and then the right brain is freed—that's what some writer friends and I have theorized. But I can't always stop when I get an idea. It depends on the road—North Dakota or Manitoba, light traffic. When I'm driving on a very empty stretch of road I do write with one hand. It's hardly legible, but still, you don't want to have to stop every time. Of course, if you have a child along, then you do have to stop.

INTERVIEWER: ***Does this interrupt your thinking?***

ERDRICH: Sometimes. I will usually pull up into a Culver's or gas station parking lot and say, "if you are very quiet while I write, there will be french fries." That almost always works, but still, there are times the thought vanishes just because I, then, think of french fries. Perhaps by having children, I've both sabotaged and saved myself as a writer. Being a mother and a Native American are important aspects of my work, and even more than being mixed blood or Native, it's difficult to be a mother and a writer.

INTERVIEWER: ***Because of the demands on your time?***

ERDRICH: Not entirely, and it's not altogether because of hormones or pregnancies either. All writers struggle with some obstacle, but being a mother sets up specific problems—for one thing, motherhood is a cliché-ridden state. You're always fighting sentiment. You're fighting sentimentality all of the time because being a mother alerts you in such a primal way. You are alerted to any danger to your child, and by extension you become afraid of anybody getting hurt. This becomes the most powerful thing to you; it's instinctual. Either you end up writing about terrible things happening to children—as if you could ward them off simply by writing about them—or you tie things up in easily opened packages, or you pull your punches as a writer. All deadfalls to watch for.

Having children also makes it difficult to get out of the house. With a child you certainly can't be a Bruce Chatwin or a Hemingway, living the adventurer-writer life. No running with the bulls at Pamplona. There is also one's inclination to be charming to neighbors, teachers, your children's friends, so that they won't be labeled as associated with a freakish mother. One must take care that this ingratiation not leak into the writing. But then, having children has also made me this particular writer. Without my children, I'd have written with less vehemence; I wouldn't understand life in the same way. Also, I have them to fight for, so actually, I don't pull my punches. Without my children I'd write fewer comic scenes, which are the most challenging. I'd probably have become obsessively self-absorbed. Maybe I'd have become an alcoholic. Many of the writers I love ▸

most were alcoholics. I've made my choice, I sometimes think: Wonderful children instead of hard liquor.

INTERVIEWER: ***Were you ever in danger of becoming a drunk?***

ERDRICH: Perhaps, but for the gift of the Rudolf Hotel. I got hepatitis. That saved me.

INTERVIEWER: ***Some people refer to your writing as magical realism. Is that another pigeonhole?***

ERDRICH: I have six brothers and sisters, and nearly all of them work with Ojibwe or Dakota or other Native people. My youngest brother, youngest sister, and brother-in-law have worked with the Indian Health Service for a total of more than forty years. My second-oldest brother works in northern Minnesota sorting out the environmental issues for all of the Ojibwe Nations throughout the entire Midwest. Their experiences make magical realism seem ho-hum. It's too bad I can't use their experiences because everyone would know who they are, but believe me, my writing comes from ordinary life.

INTERVIEWER: ***A man nursing a baby in* The Antelope Wife*?***

ERDRICH: What's strange about that? There are several documented cases of male lactation. It's sometimes uncomfortable for me to read that scene in front of mixed audiences. Men get tense. But I think it's a great idea. It would solve about half of the world's problems.

INTERVIEWER: ***When you're writing and a character or situation starts to approach the supernatural, do you think twice about writing it?***

ERDRICH: I'm not aware of the supernatural in the same way, so I can't tell when it starts to approach. Maybe it goes back to childhood, still spoiled by the Old Testament. Maybe it's Catholic after all, this conviction that there are miracles. The piece in *The*

Plague of Doves where the men are taking what becomes a surreal journey—there's nothing magical in the least about it. "Town Fever" is based on a historical trip that ended up in Wahpeton. There is now a stone that commemorates their near starvation. It fascinated me that they began right down at the river here in what became Minneapolis, where I go every week or so. With their ox-pulled sleighs, they traveled what is now Interstate 94. So I knew the exact route they took, and my description was based on reality. Daniel Johnston, who wrote the account, recorded that the party had bowel troubles and so took "a remedy." Then it only remained for me to look up what remedy there was at the time, and it was laudanum. They were high on opium the whole time.

INTERVIEWER: ***What do you do if you get writer's block?***

ERDRICH: I walk—I usually have a little pen and some note cards with me. But one day I didn't and I was halfway around the lake when the words started to appear, the end of *Shadow Tag*. The words rained into my mind. I looked up and saw my sister Heid's car on the road around the lake, and I ran over to her, flagged down her car, and said, "Give me a pencil and paper! Quick, quick, quick! Please." I still have the piece of paper that she gave me taped into my notebook.

INTERVIEWER: ***If not with a title, how did you begin working on what you're working on now?*** **[*Note: this turned out to be* The Round House.]**

ERDRICH: That began with digging shoots and saplings out of the foundation of my parents' house. I was quite aware that this was the beginning of something. Driving from Wahpeton to Minneapolis, I started writing it in my head and I had to pull over and start writing. I pulled over because I had my youngest child in the car.

I write everything out when I get home. It's a touchstone for me to have everything written down by hand.

INTERVIEWER: ***Do you transfer your writing to the computer yourself?*** ▸

ERDRICH: I don't let anybody touch my writing.

INTERVIEWER: ***And do you revise at that point?***

ERDRICH: I revise as I type, and I write a lot by hand on the printouts so they feel repossessed. I have always kept notebooks—I have an obsessive devotion to them—and I go back to them over and over. They are my compost pile of ideas. Any scrap goes in, and after a number of years I'll get a handful of earth. I am working right now out of a notebook I used when I wrote *The Blue Jay's Dance.*

INTERVIEWER: ***A journalist once asked you what advice you would give someone trying to write a novel. You said, "Don't take the project too seriously." Is that what you would say today?***

ERDRICH: I think I meant that grand ideas kill first efforts. Begin with something in your range. Then write it as a secret. I'd be paralyzed if I thought I had to write a great novel, and no matter how good I think a book is on one day, I know now that a time will come when I will look upon it as a failure. The gratification has to come from the effort itself. I try not to look back. I approach the work as though, in truth, I'm nothing and the words are everything. Then I write to save my life. If you are a writer, that will be true. Writing has saved my life.

INTERVIEWER: ***How?***

ERDRICH: By transforming the madness I have in me.

INTERVIEWER: ***Is writing a lonely life for you?***

ERDRICH: Strangely, I think it is. I am surrounded by an abundance of family and friends, and yet I am alone with the writing. And that is perfect.

About the Revision

THE ORIGINAL *ANTELOPE WIFE* was written in the 1990s; because I rarely read my books after they are published, I didn't return to this one until three years ago. When I did read the original, I was astonished that I'd dropped the powerful characters from the first thirty pages. Having discovered their flawed depth, I wanted them back. Once I started thinking of them and sketching out their lives, a different, overwhelmingly insistent vision of the book took shape. The voices I'd abandoned, new sources of humor, characters I thought I had given up, soon gripped me.

Revising this book was like repairing an old piece of beadwork. I stitched in new connections and added entirely new chapters. I dropped some chaos but kept some of the mistakes. Ojibwe floral beadwork usually employs one sinuous vine with marvelously inventive offshoots. That became my pattern for the book. The Antelope Woman's narrative would be the vine, the chapters the flowers—some true to life, some wildly dreamlike, some a mixture of real and surreal.

It has taken me twenty years to understand where I was going when I first started *The Antelope Wife*. I think this was how the book was supposed to be written all along. Still, I have tenderness for the old version. It seems to me that the characters were patiently waiting for me to return and continue with their stories.

—Louise

Have You Read? More by Louise Erdrich

ROUND HOUSE

The revered author returns to the territory of her bestselling Pulitzer Prize finalist, *The Plague of Doves*, with this riveting, exquisitely told story of a boy on the cusp of manhood who seeks justice and understanding in the wake of a terrible crime that upends and forever transforms his family.

THE PLAGUE OF DOVES

The unsolved murder of a farm family still haunts the white small town of Pluto, North Dakota, generations after the vengeance exacted and the distortions of fact transformed the lives of Ojibwe living on the nearby reservation.

Part Ojibwe, part white, Evelina Harp is an ambitious young girl prone to falling hopelessly in love. Mooshum, Evelina's grandfather, is a repository of family and tribal history with an all too intimate knowledge of the violent past. And Judge Antone Bazil Coutts, who bears witness, understands the weight of historical injustice better than anyone. Through the distinct and winning voices of three unforgettable narrators, the collective stories of two interwoven communities ultimately come together to reveal a final wrenching truth.

SHADOW TAG

When Irene America discovers that her artist husband, Gil, has been reading her diary, she begins a secret Blue Notebook, stashed securely in a safe-deposit box. There she records the truth about her life and marriage, while turning her Red Diary—hidden where Gil will find it—into a manipulative charade. As Irene and Gil fight to keep up appearances for their three children, their home becomes a place of increasing violence and secrecy. And Irene drifts into alcoholism, moving ever closer to the ultimate destruction of a relationship filled with shadowy need and strange ironies.

Alternating between Irene's twin journals and an unflinching third-person narrative, Louise Erdrich's *Shadow Tag* fearlessly explores the complex nature of love, the fluid boundaries of identity, and the anatomy of one family's struggle for survival and redemption.

THE RED CONVERTIBLE

This unique volume brings together, for the first time, three decades of stories by one of the most innovative and exciting writers of our day.

Erdrich is a fearless and inventive writer. In her fictional world, the mystical can emerge from the everyday, the comic turn suddenly tragic, and violence and beauty inhabit a single emotional landscape. Each character in these stories is full of surprises, and the twists and leaps of Erdrich's imagination are made all the more meaningful by the deeper truth of human feeling that underlies them.

In "Saint Marie," the ardent longing that propels a fourteen-year-old Indian girl up the hill to the Sacred Heart Convent and into a life-and-death struggle with the diabolical Sister Leopolda fuels a story of breathtaking power and originality. "Knives" features a homely butcher's assistant, a devoted reader of love stories, who falls for a good-looking predator, a traveling salesman, with devastating consequences for each of them. "Le Mooz" evokes the stinging flames of passion in old age—"Margaret had exhausted three husbands, and Nanapush had outlived his six wives"—with unexpected humor that turns suddenly bittersweet at the story's close. A passion for music in "Naked Woman Playing Chopin" proves more powerful than any experience of carnal or spiritual love; indeed, when Agnes DeWitt removes her clothing to enter the music of a particular composer, she sweeps all before her and transcends mortality and time itself.

In *The Red Convertible*, readers can follow the evolution of narrative styles, the shifts and metamorphoses in Erdrich's fiction, over the past thirty years. These stories, spellbinding in their boldness and beauty, are a stunning literary achievement.

"A wondrous short story writer . . . creating a keepsake of the American experience. . . . A master tuner of the taut emotions that keen between parent and child, man and woman, brother and sister, and man and beast."

—Liesl Schillinger, *New York Times Book Review*

THE PAINTED DRUM

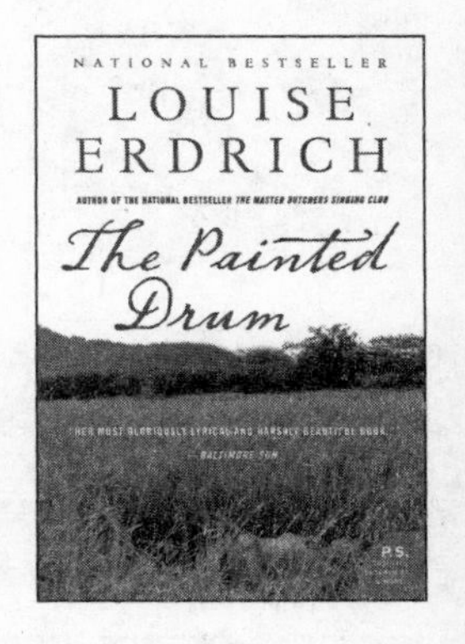

While appraising the estate of a New Hampshire family descended from a North Dakota Indian agent, Faye Travers is startled to discover a rare moose skin and cedar drum fashioned long ago by an Ojibwe artisan. And so begins an illuminating journey both backward and forward in time, following the strange passage of a powerful yet delicate instrument, and revealing the extraordinary lives it has touched and defined.

Louise Erdrich's *Painted Drum* explores the often fraught relationship between mothers and daughters, the strength of family, and the intricate rhythms of grief with all the grace, wit, and startling beauty that characterizes this acclaimed author's finest work.

"With fearlessness and humility, in a narrative that flows more artfully than ever between destruction and rebirth, Erdrich has opened herself to possibilities beyond what we merely see—to the dead alive and busy, to the breath of trees and the souls of wolves—and inspires readers to open their hearts to these mysteries as well."

—*Washington Post Book World*

Have You Read? *(continued)*

FOUR SOULS

Fleur Pillager takes her mother's name, Four Souls, for strength and walks from her Ojibwe reservation to the cities of Minneapolis and Saint Paul. There she seeks restitution from and revenge on the lumber baron who has stripped her reservation. But revenge is never simple; her intentions are complicated by her dangerous compassion for the man who wronged her.

"Full of satisfying yet unexpected twists. . . . *Four Souls* begins with clean, spare prose but finishes in gorgeous incantations and poetry."

—*New York Times Book Review*

THE MASTER BUTCHERS SINGING CLUB

Fidelis Waldvogel leaves behind his small German village in the quiet aftermath of World War I; he sets out for America with his new wife, Eva—the widow of his best friend, killed in action. Finally settling in North Dakota, Fidelis works hard to build a business, a home for his family, and a singing club consisting of the best voices in town. But his adventures in the New World truly begin when he encounters Delphine Watzka, a local woman whose origins are a mystery, even to herself. Delphine meets Eva and is enchanted; she meets Fidelis and the ground trembles. . . .

"An enrapturing plunge into the depths of the human heart."
—*Washington Post Book World*

"[A] masterpiece. . . . Erdrich never hits a false note." —*Pittsburgh Post-Gazette*

ORIGINAL FIRE: SELECTED AND NEW POEMS

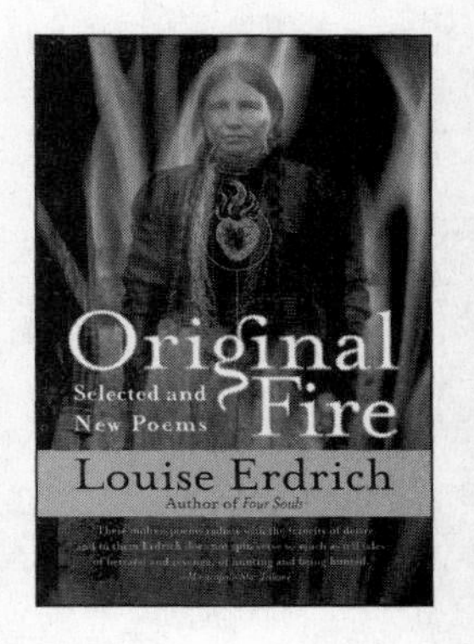

In this important new collection, her first in fourteen years, Louise Erdrich has selected poems from her two previous books of poetry (*Jacklight* and *Baptism of Desire*) and added new poems to create *Original Fire.*

This profound and accessible collection anticipates and enlarges upon many of the themes, and even the characters, of Erdrich's prose. A sequence of story poems called "The Potchikoo Stories" recounts the life and afterlife of the questing trickster Potchikoo; here, Erdrich echoes the wit and humanity of the inimitable Nanapush, who appears in several of her novels. Similarly, the group of poems called "The Butcher's Wife" contains the germ of Erdrich's novel *The Master Butchers Singing Club.*

Have You Read? ***(continued)***

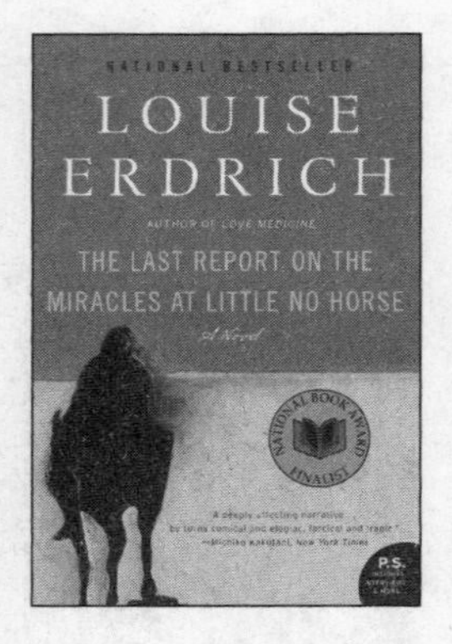

THE LAST REPORT ON THE MIRACLES AT LITTLE NO HORSE

A finalist for the National Book Award, *The Last Report on the Miracles at Little No Horse* tells the story of Father Damien Modeste, who for more than half a century has served his beloved people, the Ojibwe, on the remote reservation of Little No Horse. Now, nearing the end of his life, he dreads the discovery of his physical identity, for he is a woman who has lived as a man. To complicate his fears, Father Damien's quiet life changes when a troubled colleague comes to the reservation to investigate the life of a perplexing, difficult, possibly false saint, Sister Leopolda. Father Damien alone knows the strange truth of Sister Leopolda's piety and is faced with the most difficult decision of his life: Should he reveal all that he knows and risk everything? Or should he manufacture a protective history though he believes Leopolda's wonder-working is motivated by evil?

"A deeply affecting narrative. . . . Ms. Erdrich uses her remarkable storytelling gifts to endow it with both emotional immediacy and the timeless power of fable. . . . By turns comical and tragic, the stories span the history of this Ojibwe tribe and its members' wrestlings with time and change and loss."

—Michiko Kakutani, *New York Times*

THE ANTELOPE WIFE

When a powwow trader kidnaps a strange and silent young woman from a Native American camp and brings her back to live with him as his wife, connections to the past rear up to confront an urban community. Soon the patterns of people's ancestors begin to repeat themselves with consequences both tragic and ridiculous.

"Spiritual yet pragmatic, Erdrich's deft lyricism affirms while it defies the usual lines separating the mythical from the daily. Erdrich leads every event in her book to its outer limits, so no detail is mundane. And each scene contains bits of hilarity, extravagance, and horror."

—*Boston Globe Sunday Magazine*

TALES OF BURNING LOVE

Jack Mauser has women problems; he's been married five times and none of his wives really know him. This becomes strikingly apparent when all his wives, marooned in the same snowbound car, start to tell stories about their onetime husband. He's a man with a talent for reinvention and a less than circumspect regard for the truth. But as the women talk, their stories begin to revive them; they start thinking about Jack in a whole new light.

"Erdrich's finest novel in years. . . . Shockingly beautiful prose."

—*San Francisco Chronicle*

Have You Read? *(continued)*

THE BLUE JAY'S DANCE: A BIRTH YEAR (nonfiction)

The Blue Jay's Dance is a poetic meditation on what it means to be a mother. Describing her pregnancy and the birth of her child, Erdrich charts the weather outside her window and the moods inside her heart. It is, she says, "a book of conflict, a book of babyhood, a book about luck, cats, a writing life, wild places in the world, and my husband's cooking. It is a book about the vitality between mothers and infants, that passionate and artful bond into which we pour the direct expression of our being."

"The language in this book is stunning, elastic, often full of silence. . . . Erdrich is forthright and tough-minded in her intentions, generous in her speculations, and courageous in her vulnerability before her readers. *The Blue Jay's Dance* is a book that breaks ground."

—*Boston Globe*

THE BINGO PALACE

Seeking direction and enlightenment, charismatic young drifter Lipsha Morrissey answers his grandmother's summons to return to his birthplace. As he tries to settle into a challenging new job on the reservation, Lipsha falls passionately in love for the first time. But the object of his affection, the beautiful Shawnee Ray, is in the midst of deciding whether to marry Lipsha's boss, Lyman Lamartine. Matters are further complicated when Lipsha discovers that Lyman, in league with an influential group of aggressive businessmen, has chosen to open a gambling complex on reservation land—a development that threatens to destroy the community's fundamental links with the past.

"Beautiful. . . . *The Bingo Palace* shows us a place where love, fate, and chance are woven together like a braid, a world where daily life is enriched by a powerful spiritual presence." —*New York Times*

Have You Read? ***(continued)***

THE CROWN OF COLUMBUS
(cowritten with Michael Dorris)

A gripping novel of history, suspense, recovery, and new beginnings, *The Crown of Columbus* chronicles the adventures of a pair of mismatched lovers—Vivian Twostar, a divorced, pregnant anthropologist, and Roger Williams, a consummate academic, epic poet, and bewildered father of Vivian's baby—on their quest for the truth about Christopher Columbus and themselves. When Vivian uncovers what is presumed to be the lost diary of Christopher Columbus, she and Roger are drawn into a journey from icy New Hampshire to the idyllic Caribbean in search of "the greatest treasure of Europe." Lured by the wild promise of redeeming the past, they are plunged into a harrowing race against time and death that threatens—and finally changes—their lives. A rollicking tale of adventure, *The Crown of Columbus* is also a contemporary love story and a tender examination of parenthood and passion.

"The rare novel that is both literature and good fun." —*Barbara Kingsolver*

TRACKS

"We started dying before the snow, and like the snow, we continued to fall." So begins Nanapush as he recalls the winter of 1912, when consumption wiped out whole families of Ojibwe. But the magnificent Fleur Pillager refuses to be done away with; she drowns twice in Lake Matchimanito but returns to life to bedevil her enemies using the strength of the black underwaters. This is a book about love, loss, endurance, and survival.

"Erdrich captures the passions, fears, myths, and doom of a living people, and she does so with ease that leaves the reader breathless." —*The New Yorker*

THE BEET QUEEN

Two children, Karl and Mary Adare, leap from a boxcar one chilly spring morning in 1932. Karl and Mary have been orphaned in a most peculiar way. The children have come to Argus, in the heart of rural North Dakota, to seek refuge with their aunt, who runs a butcher shop. So begins this enthralling tale, spanning some forty years and brimming with unforgettable characters: ordinary Mary, who causes a miracle; seductive, restless Karl, who lacks his sister's gift for survival; Sita, their lovely, ambitious, disturbed cousin; Celestine James, Mary's lifelong friend; and

Have You Read? ***(continued)***

Celestine's fearless, wild daughter Dot—the Beet Queen.

"[Erdrich] is a luminous writer and has produced a novel rich in movement, beauty, event. Her prose spins and sparkles." —*Los Angeles Times*

LOVE MEDICINE

Winner of a 1984 National Book Critics Circle Award, Louise Erdrich's beloved first novel is now newly revised by the author—the Definitive Edition of the book that introduced one of contemporary literature's most innovative voices. Set on and around a North Dakota reservation over fifty years, *Love Medicine* tells of the intertwined fates of two families, the Lamartines and the Kashpaws. Their world is harsh and hazardous, full of old grievances and bad decisions, but it is illuminated by the kind of love that can leave a person crazily empty or full to overflowing with its spellbinding magic.

"The beauty of *Love Medicine* saves us from being completely devastated by its power." —Toni Morrison

"A dazzling series of family portraits. . . . This novel is simply about the power of love." —*Chicago Tribune*

The Birchbark House Books (for children)

THE BIRCHBARK HOUSE

Her name is Omakayas, or Little Frog, because her first step was a hop and she lives on an island in Lake Superior. Louise Erdrich's first book for children, a National Book Award Finalist, introduces readers to this wise and passionate seven-year-old and her family: Tallow, the woman who adopted Omakayas when she was just a baby, the only survivor of a smallpox epidemic, and siblings Pinch, Neewo, and Angeline. As the family harvests the year's food, weathers the harsh winter, and tell stories handed down for generations, Erdrich vividly captures the language and culture of the Ojibwe in the nineteenth century. But the satisfying rhythms of their life are shattered when a visitor comes to their lodge one winter night, bringing with him an invisible enemy that will change things forever—but that will eventually lead Omakayas to discover her calling.

Have You Read? *(continued)*

THE GAME OF SILENCE

On that rich early summer day, anything seemed possible.

It is 1850 and the lives of the Ojibwe have returned to a familiar rhythm: they build their birchbark houses in the summer, go to the ricing camps in the fall to harvest and feast, and move to their cozy cedar log cabins near the town of LaPointe before the first snows.

The satisfying routines of Omakayas's days are interrupted by a surprise visit from a group of desperate and mysterious people. From them, she learns that the *chimookomanag*, or white people, want Omakayas and her people to leave their island and move farther west. That day, Omakayas realizes that something so valuable, so important that she never knew she had it in the first place, could be in danger. Her home. Her way of life.

Winner of the Scott O'Dell Award for Historical Fiction, *The Game of Silence* continues Louise Erdrich's celebrated series, which began with *The Birchbark House*, a National Book Award nominee.

THE PORCUPINE YEAR

Here follows the story of a most extraordinary year in the life of an Ojibwe family and of a girl named "Omakayas," or Little Frog, who lived a year of flight and adventure, pain and joy, in 1852.

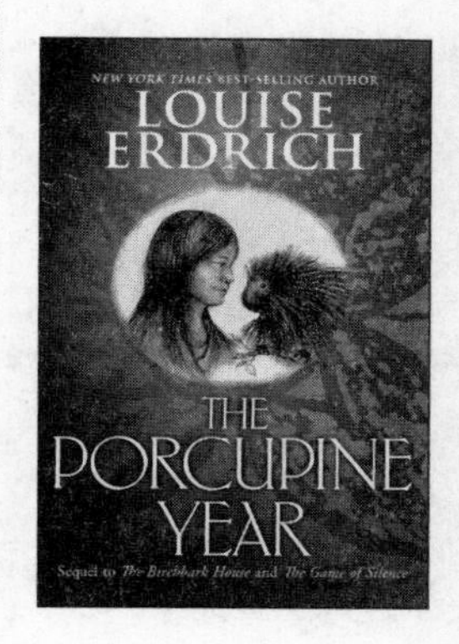

When Omakayas is twelve winters old, she and her family set off on a harrowing journey. In search of a new home, they travel westward from the shores of Lake Superior by canoe, along the rivers of northern Minnesota. While the family has prepared well, unexpected danger, enemies, and hardships will push them to the brink of survival. Omakayas continues to learn from the land and the spirits around her, and she discovers that no matter where she is, or how she is living, there is only one thing she needs to carry her through.

Richly imagined, full of laughter and sorrow, *The Porcupine Year*, an ALA Notable Book, continues Louise Erdrich's celebrated series, which began with *The Birchbark House*, a National Book Award Nominee, and continued with *The Game of Silence*, winner of the Scott O'Dell Award for Historical Fiction.

Have You Read? ***(continued)***

Praise for Louise Erdrich's Birchbark House Books

"Erdrich is a talented storyteller. She has created a world, fictional but real: absorbing, funny, serious, and convincingly human."
—*New York Times Book Review*

"Readers will welcome the return of richly drawn characters."
—*Booklist* (starred review)

"Readers who loved Omakayas and her family in *The Birchbark House* have ample reason to rejoice in this beautifully constructed sequel. . . . Hard not to hope for what comes next for this radiant nine-year-old."
—*Kirkus Reviews* (starred review)

"This meticulously researched novel offers an even balance of joyful and sorrowful moments while conveying a perspective of America's past that is rarely found in history books."
—*Publishers Weekly*